REMNANTS OF EVIL

McAllister Justice Series
Book Six

by
REILY GARRETT

Copyright

A Note from the author

This book is dedicated to Darius, Leyna, and Raptor, my incredible trio of furballs, loyal, kind, and energetic. Three incredible beings who have never understood the words "give up." To Faith, whose love and compassion changed my life.

To my friends and beta readers, this is becoming quite an interesting journey, and I have you all to thank in helping me along the way. Your lives are very busy, yet you take the time to read and make suggestions about my work. Time is the greatest gift of all.

To Thomas Knox, Esq. Thank you for the insights into your world. Though it is a diverse realm, the details are very specific. And always remember, the pen is blue.

To Dr. Chris Terrell and Jean Coldwell, your insights into character development and plot points helped the story run smoothly. I appreciate your time and effort.

To Laurie Sickles for also helping to shape my characters and pointing out things I haven't seen, thank you.

To Siobhan Caughey, for reading through my rough drafts and not laughing. Your perceptions are spot on and always appreciated in delving into a character's mind.

To my readers, each one of you who selects and reads one of my books, thank you for the opportunity to share my work. Thank you for picking up your copy of this book. If you've enjoyed it, please consider leaving a review. They are the best way to help your author spread the word.

In every book, I try to incorporate something new, outside of my experience and comfort zone, which requires a certain amount of research. The following story includes information from various sources.

To Ella Cafatsakis from Zorb.com, located in Rotorua, New Zealand.

Thank you for an inside look into the world of zorbing. Videos of rolling downhill inside a clear plastic ball at a good clip should make every adventurer's to-do list. Kudos for having a beautiful facility and countryside to share such escapades.

To Aaron at OhioCaverns.com

Thank you for responding to endless questions concerning details of the world underground. The sheer beauty of the unique formations coupled with a guided tour makes it an incredible attraction for all ages.

Chapter One

Rotorua, New Zealand

"Tell me again why we're doing this, Abs." Royden squinted against the glare reflecting off the turbulent sea. He liked his adrenaline served fresh and strong as well as the next guy, yet bouncing around inside a giant plastic ball floating on rough seawater missed the mark.

Nothing could diminish the perpetual grin inspired by Abby's presence.

"Because we're both closeted, adventurous daredevils needing a new high, and water walking balls nail it on the head. Haven't you ever wondered what a hamster felt like on a spinning wheel? Throw in this variable wind and you have a recipe few people will ever experience." Abby winked at the boat's captain before sliding through the reinforced entrance of the clear globe. He merely shrugged before nudging the sphere off the boat's loading ramp.

When Abby first asked to go zorbing, Royden tried appealing to her wide OCD streak and reinforced the certainty she'd have no control over the seawater tossing her around. She'd mimed taking off his shrink hat and promptly made the reservations.

Royden pictured her five minutes in the future, puking her guts out and laughing at the same time. Her determination to have fun on vacation rivaled her recent attraction to risk-taking activities.

Since her kidnapping, she'd scoured every corner of her mind for weakness and devised a way to conquer each. The current exercise would remove her positional control as wind and waves tossed them among the ocean's white caps.

"And I thought you wanted to see me walk on water." Royden scanned the coastline better than a hundred yards away.

The gleaming behemoth of glass and concrete in which they stayed offered all the amenities one could desire. Each floor of the hotel had a balcony where guests could enjoy spectacular sunsets—and the two fools challenging fate in gusty winds. Occupants of several rooms leaned against their railings while sipping a morning drink and observing the nuts attempting to defy nature.

His cop instincts warned of the difference between observing and *watching with intent*. That twitchy feeling between his shoulder blades had urged him to travel halfway around the world to relax.

Along the shoreline, beachcombers searched for small treasures, pausing to watch the tourists' antics while seagulls plied the air currents and skimmed near the water line using ground effect to reduce energy expenditure. A small flock huddled yards from a family gathered for a picnic.

Farther back, tall grasses continued the beauty of the idyllic landscape. It also offered an ideal setup for a sniper.

A throb in his temple and sour wad in his gut warned of danger approaching. His instincts were sharp but failed to point toward anything specific. Police training had taught him to notice small nuances in behavior and environment, magnified by his education as a psychologist. Yet his mind couldn't narrow down the looming threat. Animals in the wild survived because they obeyed those instincts instead of rationalizing them.

Understanding Abby's relentless thrill-seeking drive engendered a certain amount of anxiety. Despite repeated attempts to curb the adrenaline junkie persona, he'd failed. As the other half of her soul, he remained one part exasperated with each tempt of fate and one part excited at watching her spread her wings. When the dust settled, it would either tear them apart or solidify their souls for eternity.

After the captain nudged her giant orb bounced out onto the water, he turned to Royden and repeated the process.

The twitchy feeling morphed into a definite itch.

Before attempting to stand, he sat in the few liters of water to get accustomed to the ebb and flow of the sea. The liquid buffer inside helped him remain upright instead of tumbling as the ball rolled.

Abby tried to stand again. After falling the second time, she sat, pulled her knees to chest, and studied the situation. The liquid in her ball should've turned to steam.

The ocean's surface glittered like diamonds, deceptive with its invitation to explore the beautiful, if deadly, secrets below. He wasn't a fan of playing in the ocean when sensing an unidentifiable threat, yet they'd traveled halfway around the globe for the chance to unwind.

Construction of the dual layer sphere ensured the slight water intake wouldn't alter their buoyancy, yet other dangers existed that he didn't want Abby to face.

A pod of dolphins cavorting nearby added a thin film of normalcy to the day's diversion. All in all, he preferred bright sun and a warm beach to exploring the wonders of staying in an ice hotel. Norway was her next planned adventure. He intended to show her the aurora borealis on a conventional tour.

"I've always wondered what a hamster felt like. Now, I know." A muffled voice and chuckle didn't dull her enthusiasm in trying to stand again. She smiled as her arms went wide and she landed on her butt then to her side as the ball rotated.

Royden moved to his hands and knees, getting a feel for the forces at work and forming a strategy for maintaining his stance. When he achieved a semi-upright position, he glanced over to see how Abby fared.

With her arms and legs spread wide, she couldn't reach the edges, but she stood, swaying with the water's movement. It was moments like this with her fears cast aside that her expression revealed the spirit he loved.

His thumbs up received like in kind but altered her balance.

A small gust of wind turned her sphere sideways just as her ball exploded. Crimson flecks sprayed the clear plastic as it detonated, folding in on itself and slowly smothering its occupant.

He hadn't heard the first shot, nor the following three that jettisoned through the water. No glint from the rifle on the shoreline's low bluff or balcony had given warning.

Her shriek filled his mind. Images of a prior crime scene where a deviant smothered his child with plastic wrap flashed through his thoughts.

He couldn't move fast enough.

Not only did the plastic mold to her body, but the weight of it dragged her beneath the water line. A splash behind him alerted him to the ship's mate diving in to help.

Precious seconds passed before he could maneuver himself out of the sphere and into the cold saltwater. He had moments to find, retrieve, and remove her from the death trap.

White foam swells crashed over his head while visions of sharks scenting the blood heading their way filled his thoughts. Attacks were rare, but bloody swimmers didn't normally take to the open sea. Not far away, Australia had the highest rate of fatal and unprovoked shark attacks in the world.

Cold seeping into his bones couldn't compare to the panic sweeping through his chest. Time slowed and stretched out each fraction of movement, catalogued for future nightmares.

He waited for the bite of a bullet to end his struggle.

Feet from where he estimated her sinking, he angled his body down to intercept. Visibility turned poor with his first few strokes. Like a heat-seeking missile, he swam down, praying fate hadn't swept her away. When his fingers touched plastic, he yanked upward at the same time someone else tugged. Together they hauled her toward the surface.

Resistance increased when he tried to raise her head above the water line to find an edge of plastic to peel back. Abby's feeble struggles indicated her strength nearing an end. Her eyes pleaded for him to hurry, to keep her safe.

He needed a knife to cut her free.

"Back to the boat." The ship's hand yelled then swallowed water as a wave covered his head.

The deflated ball had taken on enough water to multiply its weight exponentially. If not for help, Royden wouldn't have reached the boat at all. Powerful strokes cut through the water while Abby remained sealed inside her airless, watery coffin.

Flashbacks of the shot indicated she sustained a hit on her upper arm or shoulder. If not for the unstable base manipulating her position, the gunman could've killed her.

With the help of the captain who held one side of the flexible coffin, they maneuvered her to the landing, protected in part by the cabin. Royden's mind inventoried potential suspects as they finagled her onto the solid surface.

Pockets of bloody water drained to leave the inflexible material clinging to her skin while relief from water pressure allowed the wound to bleed freely. Crimson pooled in the valley between her shoulder and upper breast but didn't define the exact location of the injury.

She'd ceased struggling, eyes closed and chest unmoving. On a silent prayer, he briefly closed his eyes.

Once aboard, Royden yanked at the heavy material, unable to find an opening or edge.

"Wait. I'll cut through it." Captain Tanner took the knife offered by his ship's mate and made several slices.

The utter stillness of her form cut a black swath through Royden's soul. They'd traveled so far to get away from anything resembling danger, yet it found her anyway.

In denial of the sight presented, his analytical mind sought suspects he would hunt down as he scrambled to provide her air.

"Abby." Royden pulled at the pieces covering her face to expose her mouth and nose then bent to feel any breath on his cheek. No air moved against his face.

Sliding two fingers down her throat, he couldn't be certain if the weak throb originated from Abby or his own fingers. Panic blinded him to any future without her in it. "She's not breathing. Either faint or no pulse."

Pinching her nose, he tilted her head back and blew two breaths into her mouth, watching her chest rise in his peripheral vision. The water had been cold but not cold enough to preserve her body without oxygen.

The next instant, choking filled the air. It was the sweetest sound he'd ever heard.

Water spewed from her mouth as the three men turned her on her side where she continued to gasp and choke. With the help of the crewmember, the captain pulled the rest of the cloying plastic away from her body while Royden helped her settle on her back. Doffing his t-shirt, he used it to apply pressure to her wound.

She groaned.

Royden's measured look added weight to his assumption in addressing the captain. "I doubt whoever took the shot hung around, but you'd best stay low while getting us the hell out of here."

The captain nodded then moved forward in a crouch to keep the cabin between himself and the shoreline.

"I thought I was going to die." Tears filled her eyes.

"Not yet, Abs. We're far from done."

"Yeah... I haven't been able to knock you on your ass, yet." Self-defense classes entailed a less risky attempt to maintain control of her life and regain confidence. She challenged mental and physical constraints in every manner possible.

"Looks like you'll have an excuse for that—at least for a few weeks." Cradling her to his chest came as natural as the precious breath she exhaled. "I'm gonna take you below."

Pasty white despite time spent outdoors, her pale skin contrasted her widened eyes, blue as the cloudless sky. Her body continued to tremble long after he got her below deck and wrapped in a blanket.

Soothing murmurs continued to pour from a well deep inside him, a source that raged at her attacker and mourned for her immediate future filled with fear and pain.

In the end, he held himself to blame for failing to heed his instincts. The through-and-through wound could easily have pierced both their hearts.

THE HOSPITAL STAY provided a breather despite her ready-to-leave assurances. The fact she'd stopped breathing necessitated an overnight stay in a private room and armed guard by the door, the latter ensured after numerous calls from concerned stateside brothers.

By late afternoon, her nervous energy converted to an inclination to act. "C'mon Roy. We've been here for hours. All I have is a few stitches. I want to go home." Her gaze roamed over the hospital room, from the door to the window overlooking the busy street below.

After speaking with the sergeant in CIB, Royden needed to see for himself the nest where the shooter had lain in wait. The flip side equaled leaving Abby's side and praying she'd stay put.

"Yes, your injury should heal without problems, but you were breathless, if only for a short time, and since the doctor wanted you to stay until morning, we stay. That was saltwater you inhaled, *and* you stopped breathing."

Murmured words spoken by the officer in the hallway drifted in the cool night. All remained quiet outside.

"I know, but only for a few seconds. It's just that this place, well, it reminds me of..."

"I know it does, Abs, but this is for your safety. As soon as the doctor makes his rounds in the morning, we'll leave. I promise." He sat beside her bed, holding her hand, knowing he'd have to soon let go.

If he could calm her enough to make her see reason, it would buy him an hour to get an update on the investigation and examine any evidence found.

Stalling her brothers took Herculean effort. Their intent to arrive en masse on New Zealand's shores would've further unsettled Abby. As it was, the local detective in charge called Royden with each telephone interrogation from the eldest sibling.

The last conversation apparently held a bit of an edge. Familiar with McAllister tactics, Royden assured the locals he and Abby would return stateside within twenty-four hours.

Uncharacteristic vulnerability blanketed her spirit since first opening her eyes and vomiting seawater. Mentally, she'd taken a step back to the night of escaping an underground prison.

He covered her hands to keep her from picking at her nails, something she'd never before done. His heart wept for the regression transpiring before his eyes.

"Talk to me, sweetheart."

"I died, Roy. For a few seconds, I actually died. I know it... There are things I still want to do, to experience."

"And?" He would've moved Heaven and Earth to bring her back. She didn't understand it yet, but she wasn't going anywhere without him.

Various emotions strafed her expression, none settling for more than a heartbeat. It was clear she wanted to yield to the pressure building up inside, but an unknown entity held back the words and tears glistening in her gaze.

Be patient. It takes time to regain equilibrium. She wasn't ready to hear the declaration clawing the inside of his chest to get out. She belonged by his side, forever, but had to heal both physically and emotionally. The ring in his pocket would come to form a prison if she wasn't strong enough to stand on her own.

Tears gathered but failed to yield gravity's pull. "I want children, someday. I want..."

"Yes? What do you want most of all?"

An angry swipe across her face restored her determination to not surrender to anything resembling weakness. "I want lots of things. And no dirtball with a rifle is going to take them away."

She locked gazes with the fierceness of a warrior. "Do the police have any suspects?"

"They found an impression in the sand on the bluff where they think the shooter positioned himself. Since he policed his brass, we have no leads."

"But you want to go see for yourself." A half smile kicked up one corner of her mouth.

"I'd like to. There's an armed guard on your door—there until we leave."

"Answer a few questions and you can go. His footwear?"

"Generic, men's size ten they think.

"They think?"

"Sand doesn't exactly hold impressions well."

"Damn. We have no idea *why*." Her other hand fisted in the bed blanket.

"I can't imagine someone following us from the states. It's possible this was a random act." He watched her brows hike up when he moved to sit on the bedside. Any distance between them felt like too much.

"We've had little interaction with other tourists except for snorkeling and water sports. Damn, I just want to go home and put this behind us."

"From here, we're heading to the airport. Either we go back to Portland, or we can make a stopover in Texas. I haven't seen my family for a while, so if you'd like to go—"

"I've never been there, much less seen where you grew up, but I don't want to meet them under these circumstances."

"That's fine." He hesitated, not liking the choice fate had thrown him. He didn't want to leave, not even for an hour.

She wouldn't show it, but she'd be scared and that was untenable. "Listen, while we have an armed guard, I'm going to slip back to the hotel and get our things after I meet with their investigator at the beach."

A measured look accompanied her admonition, "Be careful, cowboy. He may want you, too."

OFF DUTY SERGEANT MACNEMIRE of the Criminal Investigation Branch leaned against his vehicle in the hotel's lot with a grim expression. Jeans and rolled-up sleeves indicated the length of his day.

As a psychologist and trained investigator, Royden knew they'd find little from the reports received, but the stakes were too high to leave anything to chance. "Thank you for meeting me here after work. I know this situation is trying at best."

"More like perplexing. For all the years I've been on the force, this is a new one for me. Why someone would make an attempt under those circumstances is a mystery. The better shot would've been while she was onboard or on land."

Gesturing toward the open reedy ground to his side, the officer led Royden through wild grasses and around small dunes to an area marked off with stakes and tape.

"I hadn't noticed it from our balcony's vantage point, but I see why no one's built along here."

"Yes, the ground dips very low in this area. In her statement, Ms. McAllister said you two have kept to yourselves while here."

"Yes. I can't believe a local would want her dead. Back in the states is a different story."

"Her brothers filled me in. All of them, actually." One arched brow spoke volumes.

"Sorry about that. They are a bit much at times."

"It's all right. I'd be the same way if I had a sister. As I said on the phone, there's not much to see except for a couple footprints in the moister sand."

Royden looked back at the hotel, then the surrounding area. "You said there's no video on nearby buildings."

"No. And with this area unsuitable for much other than snakes and lizards, there's not a lot of foot traffic."

Royden pointed to two rounded impressions where broken grass indicated a body had probably lain. "About eighteen inches apart—Bipod?"

"We think so. The spot is nestled between two dunes, protecting the shooter between setup and cleanup."

"If he were skilled, he would've timed it better. I'd estimated the shore better than a hundred yards at the time."

"But he knew enough to pick a secluded spot. If he carried his gear in a backpack and dressed appropriately, he wouldn't arouse suspicion walking along the beach."

"These footprints look about a size—" He'd expected a dead end, but the reality of it set his mind to whirling with possibilities of what came next.

"Men's size ten or eleven. We'll know more soon, but initial estimates are that the tread pattern is common. I doubt we can track them to a specific shop even if they were purchased on the island."

"So, we're probably looking for a man, a little shorter than my height. Looks like he put more weight on this foot." Royden pointed to the heel of one print. "He might be nursing an injury to his knee or foot."

"Which could be temporary."

"I'm going to grab our bags before going back to the hospital. But thank you for the professional courtesy." Royden shook the offered hand.

"I'm sorry your first visit to our country has ended in tragedy."

Royden nodded. "Intuition says trouble is going to follow us home."

Chapter Two

The saltwater breeze sifting through her hair taunted Abby with memories of suffocation and swallowing water. Panic continued to swell within her chest with flashbacks of confusion, dizziness, and pain.

A deep shudder shifted her spine. Royden had spent the night at her bedside, keeping her mind occupied after nightmares jerked her awake with sweat sheathing her face and nausea swelling in her belly. The plastic smile she'd fastened in place hadn't fooled him, but that and verbal reassurances did keep him from prodding her with leading questions.

He'd held his tongue, waiting for her to break, not realizing she maintained equal determination to hold strong. Growing up with five brothers ensured her many layers of virtual armor remained impervious.

The cost to his mental faculties manifested in hair bearing evidence of repeated finger combing, a gesture of frustration. An air of quiet strength surrounded him, along with that aura of danger backed by a solidly built frame and iron self-control. He was her rock in any storm.

Now, he kept her tucked against his side as they made their way to the parking garage and their vehicle.

Plans for their stateside arrival had changed as the night waned. Instead of going home, she agreed to spend several days with Royden, ostensibly to recover.

A deep inhalation reaffirmed her victory over death, despite its remnants lingering in the back of her thoughts. She wondered if the dark shadow of tragedy would dissipate or instead, mold itself to her form like a second skin.

"You cold?" Royden removed his jacket and set it gently around her shoulders.

It wasn't the Kevlar bubble he'd obviously prefer, but it felt good to have him surround her in any fashion. Once in the shade of the garage, he urged her forward, increasing their pace. Too many shadows held sway, too many potential threats among the rows and rows of vehicles.

"No, it's just..."

"Salty air is a reminder?"

"Yeah. I thought after two months of nightmares and flashbacks, the change of scenery would alter my outlook. Instead—I got more of the same with a different backdrop."

"We'll see this through, Abby, whatever it is." Beside their rental car, Royden nodded to the officer escorting them and pulled Abby up short. "Hold on a sec. There's something on our windshield."

Awareness clicked in her mind with the urge to take a deep breath. If an assassin lay in wait, it seemed unlikely he'd leave a message first.

"What is it?" Abby reached for the folded flap of paper but stepped back with Royden's gentle nudge. Having a police presence accompany them to the airport initially lent a layer of comfort. Now, she just wanted to be thirty thousand feet in the air.

"I'll see to it." Unlike the thin paper of most handbills, the thickness of the folded missive distinguished it from the expected sale flyer.

In looking around, she saw no other cars boasting a similar leaflet. Acid boiled up her throat when he opened it. Maybe her instincts were rusty. She hadn't experienced that latent awareness warning of danger.

Her fingers shook until she crossed her arms in front of her chest and rubbed her shoulders. A light sheen of sweat broke out on her brow.

"It's a picture of you, taken at your apartment."

"Jesus. The bloody bugger." The officer continued to swear under his breath. With an apologetic nod to Royden, he added, "Sorry, mate."

Abby crowded closer to see the eight-by-ten glossy. Her gasp ended in a choking sob. "Ohmygod. Someone took that from the back of my apartment complex." If she turned the picture on its side, she'd assumed a pose when standing on her balcony enjoying an early morning coffee. In the picture, she was lying on a slab, her gaze cast downward. "I didn't bring those pajamas on this trip." The fact she'd brought a token nightgown had outlined her intentions.

"You can see someone doctored it." Royden refolded the photo being careful to handle it as little as possible. The dungeon-type setting and heavy chains binding sobered her thoughts. The swing of a pendulum forecasted a classic but painful demise by evisceration.

"We're taking this back to the states with us since it appears our stalker originated from there." Royden nodded to the officer, not needing to add, *The prick is going to be waiting for us.*

Receiving a nod in return, Royden focused his attention back to Abby. "What is it, Abs?"

"The setting. I don't think it's a reference to the short story." Her attempt to lighten the mood failed. She placed a hand on his chest, noting the slight growl rumbling inside.

Royden clenched his fist then relaxed it when she smoothed her hand down his shirt. Always so calm and self-controlled, he could house an entire volcano of emotion and the only outward sign might be a grimace. His explosion could reshape the face of the world. Her world. No doubt he intended to kill as opposed to arrest the piece of shit when the time came, which would destroy a vital piece of his soul.

He nudged her to his chest and brushed his hands down her back. "Dammit. Just... dammit."

Not an eruption but a trickle of lava.

"I'm not trying to write this off, Roy. I'm trying to regain emotional balance."

"I know, sweetheart. I know. I just wish the coward would face me. Head-on."

"It's not the way he's approaching us. From what I've learned from you, I doubt that's going to change. Do you think he's indicating knowledge of my kidnapping?"

"Yeah, I do. It's a scare tactic. He's gloating." Royden opened the car door and saw her seated before nodding to the officer. "Thanks. I appreciate the backup and escort." Rounding the hood and dropping into the driver's seat, he searched for a glint of metal or danger, just as their armed officer continued to do before sliding into the driver's seat of his cruiser.

"It's working. I'm scared. Do you think he's showing us his plan?"

"No. Absolutely not. Abby, you will survive this. You hear me?"

The fierceness of his words gritted through his clenched jaw. She had no doubt he'd put his life before hers. That wasn't what she wanted. "Roy, I—"

"Don't go there. I know what you're thinking. As a matter of fact. When we get back, we're moving *all* of your things into my house."

"But—"

"No buts. If you want to leave after we've caught the prick, fine. I'll deal with that. But until then, you're staying with me."

Arguing with Royden equated to moving a mountain with a spork. She simply nodded.

Nervous apprehension filled the atmosphere during their ride to the airport. Watching Royden's methodical mind at work normally produced awe and fascination. Now she prayed it was enough to keep them safe. He'd waited until the last possible moment to book flights, thereby hindering the stalker's ability to catch the same ride.

At the terminal, every slamming door posed a potential threat. Every car's backfire became the crack of a rifle. If she didn't relax soon, she'd dissolve into goo.

Royden took her trembling hand and squeezed gently as they strode past ticket counters and baggage claim checkpoints. He always knew and understood the dark thoughts flitting through her mind.

"How about a drink when we get on board. It's going to be a long flight. We can discuss the workload facing you Monday morning."

"You're damn good at distracting me, though I prefer the physical methods." She watched his eyes darken to a warm caramel, knowing what he pictured in his mind.

Again, the assigned officer matched their stride past the small cafes and gift shops, right up to the boarding gate.

Once seated on the window side of the plane, Abby relaxed and took a deep breath, her hand hesitating on the window shade. Heights remained another terror.

"I know you're determined to face every fear, but why not close the curtain? Give yourself a break." Royden leaned over and snugged her seat belt as the plane began taxiing toward the runway.

"I hate that our vacation got cut short."

"Two days we can spend getting you settled in my home, our home."

Abby firmed her lips in a straight line as pressure forced her back against the seat and the engine noise increased in volume. Even the thrill-seeker inside wouldn't venture into aviation.

Deep breaths, closed eyes, and extreme focus kept her thoughts directed toward her goal to make it home alive and sane.

She squeezed Royden's hand until he used his other to rub along her knuckles. Minutes passed while he provided tactile comfort, assuring her of his presence.

"Sorry. Didn't mean to dig in with my nails."

"S'all good. I've been thinking, why don't we have a small garden this spring, maybe some herbs to start. We both want to learn to cook better."

"We could always invite Larrick over to teach us the secrets of barbequed roadkill." The attempted diversion wouldn't work, yet the noise lessened as the plane leveled off and she unclenched her hand. It was time they narrowed the list of possible suspects. "Other than Carrigan's brother, I have no idea who'd have motive to kill me.

"I talked with Ethan. Lexi said Zachery hasn't left the states."

"She couldn't know that unless she hacked all sorts of records, bank, credit card, airlines, etc." Abby knew her good friend had her best interests at heart. When it came to family's safety, she had no reservations about cutting through any digital barrier.

"Hmm, I'm with you on that front. Though I don't share your OCD approach to the law, I do draw a line where my comfort level ends."

"Which is why they don't keep us up on current events."

"What about your latest pro bono? The rape victim who's filing charges against the storekeeper. The ex is a lieutenant in a street gang." Censure in his tone revived the old argument about her taking on high-risk clients.

"She deserves justice, too. And before you ask, she refuses to speak to a male attorney. 'Sides, can you see my associate, Johen, talking to her? He has the moral compass of an ass and would ask her for a date under the guise of proving not all men are bastards."

"Any new high-profile work?"

"One. I've got a woman who's divorcing her husband, a big-shot CEO. No prenup agreement. He's going to lose half the company, and there's not much he can do about it."

Air turbulence had her squeezing his hand and latching onto the other armrest. "Jeez, I hate flying." It was the closest she'd come to voicing fear.

"I guess you'll insist on going to work on Monday then?"

"Aren't you?" Nothing sounded better than an extra day snuggled under the covers with all that incredible male athleticism but hiding wasn't her style.

"I'm not going to work if you'll stay home—which I can't imagine happening."

She leaned in to smooth her palm over the stubble of his jaw, so strong like the rest of him. "As anxious as I am, I refuse to cower. I promised myself I'd never be that weak again."

His eyes widened as he enveloped her hand in his own. The invitation to initiate a conversation she'd avoided for two months weighed her shoulders down. *And by the look in his eyes, he's ready to jump.*

"No, Roy."

"Sweetheart, it's time."

The sadness in his voice melted her heart. As a trained professional, he knew how to help—and had helped her deal with toxic baggage in the past. Yet the magnitude of the stress related to her kidnapping would overwhelm them both, a bottle of nature's whoop-ass neither would survive.

All her brothers, either cops or investigators, had deferred to his warning to not prod. He'd waited for the opening she'd just given.

"Abby. Let me help."

With a heavy sigh and tears brimming her eyes, she looked around. The seat beside him was empty, and other passengers remained occupied with whatever music pumped through their headphones. The couple behind her appeared to be sleeping.

"You've wanted this conversation since I escaped the dungeon. Okay. You win. No time like the present." She closed her eyes and prayed he could prevent the shattered pieces of her mind scattering at high altitude.

Thoughts of her kidnapping months prior formed a bilious mass in her chest. In ripping off the bandage with one swipe, she spewed the toxic contents. "I'm scared. I'm afraid to open my eyes in the morning to see nothing but dirt and darkness. I'm afraid when I step out of the courthouse that there'll be some prick with a drugged cloth waiting to take me back to hell. But most of all, I'm terrified of being alone."

He opened his mouth but held back words that would push her too far. He always let her go at her own pace.

Fear of voicing her weaknesses bloomed in her chest and closed off her airway. A frantic grasp at her throat didn't help her breathe. It felt like an elephant sat on her torso. She heard the small croaking noises coming from her throat yet couldn't manipulate them into sensible words.

He unbuckled her seat belt and nudged her closer to his side. "You're not there anymore, Abs. You're safe. You're with me. Feel my arms around you, my breath on your cheek."

To anyone nearby, it might appear they shared an intimate moment with him whispering in her ear. She let the steady rhythm of his breathing and the radiated heat lure her into a state of peace. It was the same approach he followed when nightmares invaded her subconscious and she screamed from the depth of sleep. The warmth of his hand rubbing up and down her spine soothed as much as his soft words.

"You knew I was going to lose it. You always seem to know what's going on inside me. Is that a shrink thing?"

"Partly, shrinks are MDs, I'm a PhD."

"I still don't understand why you'd become a cop. You're so good with people."

She knew his history, that as a teenager, his older brother had stepped into crossfire between rival gangs. From that point on, Royden had wanted to be a cop with the knowledge to catch the dregs of the earth. The extensive education equaled a concession to his parents and a fallback plan.

"Abby..."

"All right. All right. It was an underground cell, cement block, dirt, dirt, and more dirt. I thought I'd die there and never see you, my parents, or my brothers again. I knew the bastard had drugged my food or water and I was afraid to eat or drink. On the other hand, I didn't want to starve either." Royden knew those things, the basics that terrorized her every waking moment for weeks after her escape.

In her mind's eye, she cowered on that gravelly floor with her ripped clothes and shattered dreams. "When I finally escaped, I ran all night, cussing the woods because there didn't seem to be an end to the trees. Briars kept ripping my skin, and I kept stumbling in the dark. It rained for hours, and I kept slipping. Each time, I thought I'd feel his hand on the back of my head, shoving my face in the mud and smothering me.

"I had no idea where I was or how long he'd held me prisoner. I decided then that I'd die before returning to that hellhole."

"But you did get out of the woods. You even recognized the first road you came across."

"Only because I'd been running for so long. What if I hadn't?"

"No. And think on this. If you hadn't kept your wits about you *while* you were down there, you wouldn't have succeeded in escaping, knowing that he was drugging your food."

"What if—"

"No. There's not going to be a *next* time. Stay in the present. It's good to be cognizant of what's happening around you and prepared for the future but stay in the moment."

Royden soothed her fears while bringing out further details concerning the horrific event. Nothing would erase the fact she hadn't paid attention to her surroundings and could've prevented her abduction. For all her years of listening to her brothers' detective stories, she still had a mile-wide impulsive streak when it came to her clients or anyone in trouble.

In reliving the ordeal and delving through details, she bolstered her confidence with each point where she'd made accurate deductions and a plan to move forward. Royden's subtle, leading questions drew out specifics she hadn't remembered when giving her statement. The fact they'd caught the bastard spared her further extensive interviews from investigators. "He didn't rape me, Royden."

"I know. We wouldn't have been intimate yet if he had."

"I'll be strong enough to testify once the trial rolls around."

"You already are, sweetheart. You're already there. You just haven't wanted to face it."

And yet, before one disaster concluded, another asswipe wanted a piece of her. *They're not going to get it.*

Since waking up in the hospital, she'd wanted, needed to hold him close, skin to skin, an affirmation of life. The inappropriate timing of her libido would have to wait. Yet every time their gazes locked, she felt his need deep down, like an integral part of her soul.

"If Katt or Lexi were here, they'd start spouting inane facts to lighten the mood." Abby smiled at the thought of Kathryn annoying the hell out of her oldest brother with embarrassing tidbits of information. "Like—twenty-five percent of all your bones are located in your feet."

"How about—in space, astronauts can't cry because there's no gravity and tears can't flow."

"Leonardo Da Vinci invented scissors." She tapped his chest for emphasis, thinking she'd bested him for the most useless fact.

"Catsup leaves a squeeze bottle at about twenty-five miles per hour."

"San Francisco cable cars are the only National Monuments that move." He arched a brow, waiting.

"Some alligators can grow up to fifteen feet."

"Hmm, and I thought they only had four." Royden feigned hurt when she slapped him on the shoulder.

"Ten percent of the world's population are southpaws." She wondered if her stalker was left-handed.

Chapter Three

As expected, the entire McAllister clan met them at PDX. The terminal was crowded, and the hustle and bustle proved unnerving, yet their united presence lent a comfort extending only to family.

After hugging each of her parents, she gently nudged her brothers out of the flow of traffic. Concern lined each sibling's brow. To stem the flow of questions, she held up her hand. "I know you all want to talk, but it can wait until I've had a nap and a decent meal." *And a giant-sized piece of Royden.*

"Then who's cooking?" Katt, the oldest sibling's better half, elbowed past the rest and hugged her tight.

Matt stepped forward and planted himself in front of his brothers. "All right, half-pint. But tonight, we're coming over." A nod at Royden and he continued, "We've already checked out your place. Lexi put your security feeds on our network."

"Of course she did." Royden smiled, accustomed to the hacker's methods of operation when it came to family.

Abby expected the family meeting yet was glad for the small reprieve. Her body still shook from the memory of escaping the watery grave. "Fine, then you all bring the food. I'm not up to shopping today."

"Taken care of." Lexi smiled and wrapped her arm around Ethan's waist.

Royden nodded toward her brothers. "I'll call when she's awake."

As Royden led her away, Abby wondered if he realized what had been and was still on her mind since waking up in the hospital. She continued to squirm the entire ride to his home.

Tension coiled tight as she strode through his garage and to the back door. She shoved her hands in her jacket pocket to keep from reaching for him.

The minute he closed the kitchen door and deposited their bags, she grabbed his jacket lapels and pushed him against the adjoining wall.

"Abs? Are you sure?"

Anticipating her need, he lifted her up, wrapping her jean-clad legs around his waist and adjusting position to lean her against the wall. They rode the same wavelength, hot, burning, and explosive.

"Now." She couldn't think past the carnal urgency when his lips created a fiery trail of need along her neck.

He pulled back briefly, their gazes colliding before his mouth crashed down on hers and his groan filled her mind.

Her body came to life under his insistent and commanding touch. Buttons ripped and plinked on the ceramic tile, scattering like her thoughts. Nothing mattered more than the next kiss, his tongue twining with hers, and the feel of his heat pressing between her thighs. Her jeans should've melted.

His arms were thick and strong wrapped around her while his weight pinned her against the wall. He tasted sharp, of lust, male, and hunger. She'd never felt him so unhinged.

She was breathless, not just from his overwhelming passion that mingled with her own to spiral her body to new heights, but from the desperation fueling them both. It would never be enough, *could* never be enough.

His hands moved over her skin then urged her legs down. In a flurry of movement, both their jeans lay on the floor before she could focus on the intoxication of him pressing his weight against her and the heat flooding her lower belly.

"Jesus, I want you now." His voice equaled an aphrodisiac that called to her on the most basic level.

She pulled his head down to kiss him, wrapping one leg around his thighs. He smiled, a fierce savageness that consumed as well as provoked. It took an eternity to retrieve the foil and cover his impressive length.

The feel of his palms brushing over her lower back forced a shudder. He appeared every inch the warrior who took what he wanted, his entire focus directed at her. Again, he lifted her up. "Can you wrap your legs around me and hold on without hurting your shoulder?"

"What shoulder?"

The force of his first thrust knocked a small picture off the wall. His hands gripping her thighs held her in place for his invasion as her heels locked behind his back urged him faster, harder, needing everything he could give, everything he was.

Mindless with need and drunk on his power, she bit his neck, affirming her claim and marking him, superficial in the short run, to the depths of his soul for eternity.

He pulled back as if suddenly aware of their surroundings. "Abs?" The black of his pupils eclipsed the caramel just as his need edged out his softer side once again.

"More. I'm fine." She'd have bruises on her back, hips, and thighs, relishing each one as confirmation of their equal but mindless craving. He was strong enough to stand up to her and smart enough to know when to take without asking. Confirmation of life after a near-death experience demanded a merging of souls.

She loved the taste of him, the sight of his losing control, and the knowledge he would always be there to catch her. Her breath came in pants and reflected her body's climbing toward the pinnacle of lovemaking, that quintessential moment where everything stopped, her breath locked in her lungs until she screamed his name.

His own hoarse shout followed as he slammed forward one more time and held her in place. She felt him pulsing inside her, the involuntary movements emptying his seed.

His weight pressing her back comforted and echoed his need to surround and consume her. One heartbeat at a time, their breathing came under control and his softer side emerged.

"Jesus, sweetheart. I'm sorry to be so rough." Remorse tinted his words, muffled against her neck.

"If I were a man, I'd have slammed you through the wallboard." Her chuckle got absorbed in his kiss. "I've heard near-death experiences can bring about explosive sex, but I never imagined it like this. After my kidnapping—"

"I was afraid of traumatizing you. You never know how strong a person is until they've survived the depths of hell and emerged on the other side."

"I need more. Can we call my brothers and hold them off a bit longer?"

"You read my mind."

THE VIEW FROM her office rivaled everything she thought she'd ever want while slogging her way through law school. Long hours of study and hard work had channeled her career path toward success. The partners were thrilled with her progress.

Recent events began weaving a thread of malcontent with her life's choices. Her workaholic boyfriend revealed a side of her she'd never known existed. Together, they were forging a future filled with shared experiences, new dreams, and eventually, a family of her own.

Thinking of family and how they'd all showed up on Royden's doorstep before Royden escorted her to work, she smiled. They all had the best of intentions. Unfortunately, there wasn't much information to share and they left as frustrated as they'd arrived.

In the courtyard below, picnic tables stood ready for those wanting fresh air during lunch breaks. When the weather allowed, she enjoyed the sun and breeze on her face instead of piped air through a vent.

The dream of private practice, one with her office situated by a park or open country kept her working overtime. Most people didn't realize what a cutthroat business it could be. If a student wasn't born with a silver spoon, the first years after graduation entailed tons of student loans. She'd been lucky enough to have a few scholarships.

The front of the moderate-sized firm overlooked the hustle and bustle along the busy city streets and had energized her at one time. Now, it reminded her of the world's chaos and all the potential drawbacks of city life. It was time to make a change, yet outstanding debt and the need for stability held her hostage.

Litigation encompassed a field she'd aspired to dominate while experience opened her eyes to the devious machinations of particular bottom-feeders. Over time, the subtle shift of her work's focus changed to include the underdog fighting corporate money and overwhelming odds.

"Abby? Your nine o'clock called and said she'd be a few minutes late. Her daughter is sick and needed to see the doctor." Mitzie set an insulated cup on the desk. "I ran down and grabbed a latte for you."

"Thanks, Mitzie. I really needed that this morning."

"How's the shoulder?" Her assistant winced as she nodded toward Abby's arm.

"Just a few stitches that'll come out in another week. The bullet missed bone and major arteries. I was lucky."

"I think you need another girl's night out. You could bring your hunky detective." Mitzie's sly grin demonstrated her obvious appreciation of Royden's physique. "I have a friend, Jenna, who took me to a club where the music is great, drinks are cheap, and the men are drool-worthy, not that *you* need the latter. Hell, your entire family is a treasure trove of DNA's sexiest genes." Mitzie fingered the flower-shaped necklace at her neck.

"Let me heal a bit first." Abby leaned forward for a better look at Mitzie's pendant. "That's pretty. Where'd you find it?"

"Oh, I saw it while window shopping with Jenna and Linda. It's a friendship necklace. They each have matching ones."

"Very nice. What kind of flowers are they?"

"A cluster of freesias. All three of us are getting into a gardening club. It's a lot of fun and so soothing." Mitzie held the heavy-looking piece out for Abby to see.

"Hmm. Two of my brothers prefer starting food fights to relieve stress, especially if it's something I've tried to bake. I've never seen the appeal in tossing cake, myself."

"I don't have any siblings, but when I was younger, my friends and I used to have strawberry fights when we were supposed to be picking them. We'd come in covered with red splotches."

"Royden and I talked about having a small garden this spring, maybe grow some green beans and tomatoes. My parents have a huge garden every year, and I used to love helping out. Now that schooling is over and work is settling down, it might be a good idea."

"You and Royden make a great couple. You're very lucky."

"Don't worry. You're young. The time will come when a man sweeps you off your feet."

"Maybe. I thought Bradley might've been the one. As it turned out, he wanted what most men *think* they deserve. What a piece of scum."

Two years at the firm indicated the assistant eager to learn and please, but manipulative and amoral men soon crushed her naivety. "Time and experience will help you navigate away from men like my supervisor. I can picture you with a houseful of kids and the proverbial picket fence after you've put yourself through law school."

"I'm taking my LSATs again this fall. Keep your fingers crossed that I get a higher score this time."

"Won't need to. You work hard and you're smart. You'll make it. Just keep your eye on the prize." Abby smiled. "As far as going out, we'll do it. Soon." Their friendship was the only thing preventing Mitzie from asking Royden to dinner with the expectation of breakfast in the morning. Despite her enjoyment of the opposite sex, her assistant respected boundaries.

Mitzie's infectious attitude usually drew Abby out for a much-needed, carefree release, yet the risk was too great. It was one thing for Royden to jeopardize his life to stay close; he was a cop and connected to her soul, accepting the risk. His determination to protect rivaled her brothers'. She couldn't justify endangering anyone else.

"I'd like that. As soon as it's safe, we'll plan a full weekend of fun. The whole works. What d'ya say?"

"Sure, but I know how you suffer from cabin fever with just a bit of snow. I bet Royden and your brothers are smothering you. You need to get out and get your mind off snipers and kidnappers."

Abby nodded. "Actually, Royden is taking me caving next weekend, but he probably has the National Guard on speed dial." It was difficult to balance Royden's need for security and her need for independence.

"Ooh, are you going to the Sea Lion Caves, maybe Hug Point? I've been to both. When we took the elevator down to the lower levels in the caverns... wow. It was amazing. It's so romantic."

"Actually, we're staying inland." Checking her calendar, she repeated the business name and wondered if it would be as charming as she'd imagined. "Though I have heard about Hug Point. They say you have to go at low tide, so you don't end up stranded, but it has a lot to offer. Back in the old days, the sheer volume of passing stagecoaches carved wheel ruts into the rock when traveling around the headland. Even at low tide, they had to be careful and hug the coast. Hence, the name."

"Hmm, you're a treasure trove of trivia. There's also hiking through nature trails." Mitzie loved outdoor activities.

"Yeah, I love them, too. My family used to do a lot of hiking."

"Be careful down there. You've had enough adventures for a lifetime." A frown bit into the smooth skin of Mitzie's face.

"No kidding. I think I about gave Royden a heart attack in New Zealand."

"Any news on that?"

"No. They really didn't have much to go on. And since we were only visiting, they would've chalked it up to a random act if it hadn't been for the doctored photo someone graciously delivered to our car."

"Ya know—I use to complain that I had a boring life. I've revisited that opinion and changed my mind. I'll take boring any day." Mitzie held her hand up, her thumb and index finger an inch apart. "I can always find a little bit of excitement on my own. However, the offer still stands. When you're ready and it's safe to go, give me a heads up, and we'll paint the town."

"I could use a carefree night with the girls."

"Do they think it was related to your work or someone in your personal life?"

"No way of knowing yet, but they'll get to the bottom of it."

A subtle throat clearing alerted them to someone in the outer office before a child's voice declared the next appointment had arrived.

Abby straightened her shoulders. The client was determined to put distance between herself and her soon-to-be ex, if only for a while. Protecting her child remained the mother's top priority, yet she had no evidence to support her suspicion of the father's intent to harm. Considering the amount of money at stake, no distance would be enough.

The divorce case had landed in her lap by preference of the client, much to the dismay of the supervising attorneys. The firm stood to gain not only a handsome fee from the research needed but also the notoriety of helping one of Oregon's elite—assuming Abby survived long enough to close the case.

Chapter Four

Abby worked hard to maintain a good working relationship with other attorneys. Everyone benefited when opposing counsel could sort areas of disagreement and help their clients move toward a settlement. Sharing agreed upon information saved time and money in reaching stipulations without compromising either side's position.

And then there's always one bad apple.

Combined with the infuriating husband who could've written a book on hiding assets, the opposing attorney sitting on the opposite aisle made a matching pair. Her counterpart smirked, smug in his superiority. The gap in his teeth defined his appearance while his nickname of Horus remained a mystery.

The occasional habit of smoothing the light scruff on his jaw provided insight to areas of uncomfortable questioning. She'd yet to turn her back on him, preferring to keep him in her peripheral sight especially when cross-examining his client.

"Mr. Marchem, isn't it true you're having an affair with Clara Wagil, hired to watch your son?" After benign preliminary inquiries, Abby held a mental picture of the witness' normal mannerisms.

"No." Short, to the point. The husband's succinct answer earned a faint nod from opposing counsel.

"Then can you explain why she visited your office building at least a dozen times last month?" Abby arched a brow as if she knew more than her client realized. She did, but it wasn't time to reveal those facts. During discovery, he'd failed to reveal large sums of income, instead, laundering the funds through his car wash franchise, one of his many holdings.

"The office building is quite large and contains well over four dozen businesses. I have no idea who she visited or why." The witness radiated a dominance in need of a reality check.

Abby frowned, shaking her head as if stymied. "So, you never saw her in your office?"

"Absolutely not."

"I see. Are you aware that Ms. Wagil has a child? I see on her employment application she noted she had none in the remarks section."

"I'm not aware of her family situation. It's none of my business. If she lied, she must have had her reasons, yet it hasn't affected her work, so I really don't care."

"Okay. You have no business dealings with her, other than her providing child care for your two-year-old son?"

"Correct. We've already established that."

"That's all the questions for now." The perfunctory inquiries all met with expected answers. With each response, his tells consisted of a slight squirm, looking at his attorney, and impossibly wide eyes when a question wasn't to his liking.

Abby returned his smirk with a smile as he exited the witness stand.

"Your honor, I'd like to call Clara Wagil, who is sequestered in the jury room."

Again, the men at opposing counsel's table could've been a matched set—of stupidity. To date, she had no proof of the lawyer's involvement in illegal activities. That issue was outside her scope of practice and concern. The judge, however, would investigate.

Shit's about to get real, as Matt would say.

Taking a deep breath, she shed her façade of uncertainty, straightening her spine, and dropping the mask of doubt. The presiding judge was notorious for cracking down on counselors who practiced the dark art of sandbagging, so she had to tread lightly.

Of the few exceptions, impeaching a witness topped the list and bolstered her confidence in proceeding.

A bailiff escorted the next witness to the stand before the court registrar held the bible and swore her in. This was the gold mine.

Abby smiled to put the babysitter at ease. Dressed in conservative blouse and slacks, the young woman's gaze bounced between the attorneys and the husband, the latter frowned as if in warning.

From the documentation obtained the prior day, it wasn't clear if the nanny was complicit in the scheme or not, nor was that Abby's concern. Again, it didn't matter.

Initial questions defined the young woman's role, length of employment, and specific duties. In her early twenties, she remained composed and open, if a little nervous.

"Ms. Wagil, what is the nature of your business in the office building on 314 West Avenue?"

"Banking. I make frequent deposits and withdrawals since I prefer to deal in cash."

"Do you have any children?" Abby's sidelong glance took in Horus' confusion.

"Yes. I have a son."

"How old is he?" Abby grinned when Horus wiped beads of perspiration from his brow.

"Two."

"Does he share your last name?"

"No. He has his father's last name, and I assure you, it's quite legal even though I never married."

"I see. I also see from the expense sheet you provided, that your total income barely covers your expenses. It must be very difficult to raise a child on this salary."

"Objection, Your Honor. Relevance." Her opponent's snide expression morphed into a frown when Abby retrieved a folder from her table.

"One moment, please, and I will show relevance, Your Honor."

"Overruled. You may proceed, but don't waste my time." Traditional black robes concealed the judge's clothing but not her curiosity.

Turning back to her witness, Abby continued, "Are you having an affair with my client's husband?"

"No." Again, simple and direct. Tiny lines bracketed her eyes and mouth, her lips tucked between her teeth.

"Do you make extra money on the side, Ms. Wagil, or have a large sum stashed away on which you can draw?"

The witness laughed. "If I did, I wouldn't be working as a nanny. I'd be home with my own kid."

"Who takes care of your child while you're working?"

"My mother." Clara shrugged, unimpressed but belligerent just the same.

"So, the eight hundred thousand dollars in offshore accounts and foreign companies does *not* belong to you or your child? It appears there've been no taxes paid according to your returns."

"What? I don't have any money in foreign accounts!" The nanny half stood, then sat when the nearest bailiff approached, hand on his gun belt.

Panic and fear overtook her expression. "I swear, judge, I don't have any other money. It's all I can do to keep food on the table for Timmy and me. The only reason I took this job last year was because of the benefits. My boss lumped me in with the rest of his employees, so I'd have health care."

"I object, your honor. Miss Wagil's finances are of no concern to this case."

"Oh, but they are, Your Honor. And I can prove it." Abby tried to smother her grin.

"Approach the bench. Now. I'll speak to both of you." The judge drummed her fingers on her desk.

This was the part where Abby had to tread lightly. She noticed Royden standing in the back, murmuring to another officer. She hadn't seen him arrive. He caught her eye and grinned wide. He knew her tactics.

"Ms. McAllister. Explain yourself now or face sanctions."

Abby cleared her throat. "My investigator discovered documents yesterday that are extremely relevant."

The judge sighed. "Let me see them and I'll decide. If not, this won't go well for you."

Abby handed over the reports, noting the husband's pallor. Once in the judge's hands, the documents would change the entire workings of the case.

A slight gasp preceded the frown. "Okay. I see there's a lot of money involved, but I don't see the witness's name or the husband's name on these. You're still on shaky ground, counsel."

Abby smiled. "I know there's a lot of documents but let me show you." She took the thick sheath of papers and sorted to the one she wanted before handing it back.

"Oh, I do see. I take it this is the child's name?"

"Yes, Your Honor."

The judge narrowed her eyes at opposing counsel. "And are you going to say you had no knowledge of these documents?"

Horus shook his head vigorously as he accepted the papers from the judge. His jaw dropped and he closed his eyes. "No, your honor. I have no knowledge of them. However, I do wonder why I haven't seen them before now."

The judge drummed her fingers on the podium while narrowing her focus on Abby. "Well?"

"They just came to my attention yesterday, Your Honor."

"Ms. McAllister. Do you have other questions for this witness?"

"Yes, I do. Just a couple and I'll be finished."

Abby's smile turned predatory, recognized by the prey sitting in the witness chair and evidenced by the nanny's shrinking back in her seat with a frightened gaze.

Time to nail this case shut. "Ms. Wagil." Abby retrieved the sheath of papers and handed them to the witness. "Please explain these."

Numb and dumbfounded, Clara accepted the offering and glanced over the documents. "I don't know what they are. I'm not a businesswoman."

"Let me explain briefly." Abby sorted through the stack until finding the specific damning evidence. "This," she pointed to a signature on the bottom of a page, "is the owner of the foreign-based companies, to the tune of over eight hundred thousand dollars. Read the name and social security number that is underlined."

Clara squealed and shoved the papers in Abby's direction. "That's my son's name and social, but it's not his money! This is a forgery." Her expression morphed from confused to dawning to angry within sixty seconds.

"Clara. Shut up. I did this for you, for us." The husband's face turned red with panic or rage.

"Screw you! I—"

A loud thud halted any further conversation. The judge set aside her gavel. "Knock it off. Both of you, before I clear this courtroom."

Needless to say, the affair was over.

"I assure you, Ms. Wagil, the documents are real. Do you realize the IRS takes a very dim view of taxpayers hiding money to avoid paying taxes? There are stiff penalties in place. Do you recognize the names of the companies?"

"Yes. William—Mr. Marchem said he owned them, but that his wife couldn't touch any of them. God, this isn't real... Listen." Anger churned in her gaze as she focused on the husband. "Yes, I've been having an affair with your client's husband. It's been going on for over a year. He promised me he was getting a divorce and that we'd move out of the country and live well, but I don't know anything about this. Are you saying this money is mine?"

"Oh, I very much doubt you could get your hands on it no matter how hard you tried. My investigator hasn't finished digging yet, but it's only a matter of time when it all comes to light once the federal agencies get involved."

At the very least, she'd proven adultery. That alone changed the tide of the case. The financial details would take time to sort. Abby took a deep breath and straightened her suit coat before addressing the judge. "I think that will about do it, Your Honor."

"Ms. McAllister, I assume your investigator is here to answer my questions?"

"Yes, ma'am. He's waiting in the hallway."

Turning to Horus, the judge asked, "Would you like to question him, also?"

"No, Your Honor. Ms. McAllister's work ethic is always beyond reproach." Frustration edged the gritted words.

At the back of the courtroom, Royden grinned, his shoulders shaking.

* * * *

"I love watching you in court, though I thought for a minute the judge was going to eat you for dinner." Royden had parked behind Abby's car at the courthouse, wanting to catch the tail end of her case. Watching her in action reminded him of an apex predator at work.

"Sounds painful." In one simple move, she pulled a clip from her hair and let the heavy mass fall in waves down her back. The dichotomy of observing her during proceedings and striding beside him with free-flowing hair, sultry smile, and heels made him harder than a rock.

"Not the way I do it." The feel of drawing her close with his arm around her waist lent a comfort to sustain him, until he could get her alone. He let his fingers drift through the silken locks then reminded himself to pay attention to his surroundings. Everything she did proved distracting.

"Hmm. I could use a glass of wine and a victory bowl of chocolate yogurt."

"Sounds good. I took steaks out this morning."

"What made you think I'd win?"

"Because I know *you.*" Tugging her car door open, he waited until she settled in before starting to close it. "You didn't tell me about this case."

"I didn't know what the husband was hiding. Did you see his face? He had no idea I was onto his game."

Something moved in the back seat of her sedan.

Without preamble, he jerked her out of the vehicle using a maneuver performed on drunken drivers in his earlier days on the force. Her squeal barely registered.

"What the hell, cowboy?" Abby stumbled on her heels before latching onto his arm to right herself.

"Back seat, snake." It was all he could get out before slamming the door and yanking her against his side. Royden visually followed the length to the end where he saw the rattles. The fact it stretched out on the back seat indicated its need to soak up heat concentrated by the car's window.

"Oh, hell. I hate snakes."

Royden was already on the phone and leading her back to the safety of the building. "Sonofabitch." Once in the back door using her keycard, he explained the findings to the sheriff's deputy staffing the metal detector.

His first phone call included epithets laced with threats. A minute later, he took a deep, calming breath. "We'll wait here for a few minutes."

Her hands shook as she snagged her cell.

"Who are you calling, Abs?" Royden held his phone away briefly.

"Katt. She hikes all the time and will know what variety it is. I should've taken a picture of it."

"It's not going anywhere." Royden listened as Abby explained her situation, knowing the combination of court and finding the snake would supply enough adrenaline to keep her up for a week. Her conversation consisted of stutters and hand gestures. He hadn't pointed to the telltale rattles at the time, knowing she needed to vent.

"What kind was it? I don't know, Katt. That's why I'm asking you. Brown. It was a brown snake."

When she hung up, Royden took her in his arms, needing the contact.

"Katt said it probably laid on the back seat for warmth. Sunning itself. Otherwise, I might not have known until after the accident." Tears formed in her eyes yet didn't breach the perimeter.

"We'll find him, sweetheart. We'll find the bastard."

"But he keeps coming at me from different angles. Every time, it's different."

Chapter Five

Late morning sunlight brightened the office, so contrary to Abby's outlook. The rattlesnake in her car may or may not have caused an accident, but it sure as hell scared her witless.

Matters didn't improve when her supervising attorney strode in and plopped down in an empty chair. His assumption that her time was free aligned with his general attitude that women remain subservient. He'd proven himself as frustrating as he was arrogant.

She'd long perfected the fake smile and knew Brad would recognize it as such.

"What's up?" She couldn't help but wonder to what depth he measured her disdain. She hoped one day to see him as opposing counsel. The thought warmed her heart.

He'd foregone using his good looks and position to coerce her on a date or sway her opinion. It remained a good bet he'd been the one that began circulating her nickname, ballbuster McAllister.

Current tactics involved innuendos and veiled concerns over job performance. Her good standing with the partners provided a direct link whenever insecurity bit her in the ass, much to his chagrin.

"I wanted an update on the Rollison case. The partners are a bit nervous with so much on your plate."

"Hmm, not according to the *atta boy* I received after yesterday's trial."

"Lucky draw. Fill me in."

"Phyllis is picking up stakes and moving back east to be near her family. She still wants me to handle her divorce." Abby had long recognized the greed lurking within her supervisor's gaze. It flared whenever her career surged forward.

"We'd like her to stay in the Portland area."

So you can manage her money when the divorce is over. "I can't influence her to remain here. It's not ethical. She and her child need family support. I think it's the best situation for them both."

Months of conversations with Royden helped her pinpoint the small details defining Bradly's deceptions. The penchant to add details to flesh out his claim accompanied the slight shifts in his gaze. The trifecta included covering his mouth as if deceitful words burned his mucous membranes.

"The only reason the father agreed to it is because it puts his wife too far away to meddle with the company. If she'd stayed for a bit longer, we could've convinced her that keeping the child in familiar surroundings would've provided a greater benefit."

No, you wanted to get in her pants and her bank account in one fell swoop. "Well, she has already left. We finalized some details along with her new will this morning."

"I'll take a look at them both, thank you."

Expecting her boss' interference, Abby had requested Mitzie make copies before filing the documents. As added protection, they'd prepared identical wills based on the client's description of her husband's figurative reach.

"Here you go. I thought you'd want to see them." She handed him a folder with copies of her work to date.

"Where's the original. You know I prefer them." A sneer twisted Brad's handsome features.

"At the courthouse."

"The partners are concerned with your caseload in regard to your personal problems arising. You should convince the client that I would be a better fit to, ah, see to her needs."

"My personal and professional lives are and will remain separate. Since my track record ranks as high as any in this firm, I should think that would reassure them. The client trusts *me*. I'll have a chat with Salsman before leaving today to make sure he's okay with it."

Brad switched subjects on a dime. "You spend too much time working. Hell, this was the first vacation you've had, and it turns into a nightmare. Not to mention someone putting reptiles in your car. You need time off."

"How do you know about that?" Abby's gaze drifted to the open door, wondering if Mitzie worked behind her back.

"I have friends in the sheriff's department. It was still the hot topic of the courthouse this morning."

"I'm not taking time off. If you force the issue, I'm pretty sure the *client* will follow me out the door."

The thinly veiled threat hit its mark. Brad narrowed his eyes before pasting on the smile that got him into most women's panties. "Why don't you let me take you out to a working dinner and we can talk about it."

"Thank you, but no. I prefer meetings in this building and during office hours."

Not to be put off, his smile widened as if that would increase the gap between her thighs. He'd tried many tactics to seduce her during the past three years, none of which would ever work.

Her desk phone buzzed, supplying a breather from the oppressive aura suffocating her. "Excuse me, this must be important to be put through during a conference." *Mitzie deserves a raise.* Abby picked up the phone and sighed her relief. "Hello?"

A familiar hissing broken up with a telltale rattle almost made her drop the receiver. Heat drained from her face and she closed her eyes. Nothing could erase the flashback of a snake stretched out on the back seat of her car. Had it not been close in color to her seats, she would've seen it before getting in.

Her fingers trembled in hanging up the phone.

"Abby? You look white as a sheet. Who was that?" Brad leaned forward in his chair, concern etched in his furrowed brow.

"No one. You were saying something about my caseload?" Folding her hands in her lap reduced their shake.

Unconvinced, Brad let it drop as he continued his spiel. "You know, I went to bat for you just this morning."

She doubted the truth but had to ask, "Oh? How?"

"The partners don't approve of your choice of pro bono work. They're afraid you're stepping too far away from your normal workflow." Picking an imaginary piece of lint from his tailored suit pants, he added, "I vouched for you though. Told them you had it in the bag and that any limelight in your direction helped the firm."

The calculating gleam in his gaze proclaimed the fib. *He probably complained that I'm using firm resources.*

"How is that rape case progressing, anyway?"

"We got the DNA results back, finally. It matched. We also found the sample matched other victims of open cases—but outside the statute of limitations."

"Which means the DA isn't going to prosecute as vigorously without other victims or corroborating witnesses. Tough case."

"We have a DNA match. She deserves justice."

"I agree, though it took months to get the results. Bruises fade, memories dim. You look tired. I hope you don't let your work swallow you whole. You still need to have fun in life."

"I am." Royden's exuberant lovemaking explained part of her exhaustion. "I'm going spelunking next weekend. I've always wanted to explore caves. My brothers use to scout and mark passageways in the underground tunnels when we were kids, but they'd never let me go." It never hurt for a woman to reveal her tomboyish side.

"They don't realize how tough you are. Surprising since you ran afoul of trouble three months ago."

Brad's never-ending probe into her life would yield no more information than it did before. If not for the police soliciting his opinion as to her current stalker, he wouldn't have known about the near-fatal incident in New Zealand.

"I'm fine. You don't need to worry."

"But I do. Apparently, your boyfriend isn't taking good care of you. It's a dangerous world out there. Be careful."

"I'm. Fine. Thank you." In standing, he offered the patronizing smile, one probably perfected after hours of practice in front of the mirror.

Like the snake she compared him to, he slithered out of the office. His attempt to seduce failed at every turn. He'd since redirected his charisma to Mitzie. Unfortunate that it took months for the assistant to see his true colors. After several lunchtime conversations where they compared Brad's various tactics to get his way, her assistant proved resistant to his charms.

If he'd flung the last comment out as a veiled threat, she had two choices. First, she could inform one of her brothers. Matt, her eldest brother, and K9 detective would have an official chat. Lucas and Caden, PIs after leaving the force, would provide a more hands-on approach with a warning of their own. If Royden found out, he'd tear her immediate boss to shreds.

It didn't seem plausible that anyone from the firm would mean her harm. There'd be no gain, and she didn't peg any for a closeted sociopath. The only client of contention, the CEO's wife, would surely find another female attorney if Abby dropped out, probably in her home state once she arrived on the east coast. Abby had made that point clear to all.

Once alone in her office, Abby called her assistant in to inquire about the threatening phone call, which no doubt came from a public source.

"I didn't recognize the voice." Mitzie frowned. "Said the name was Blair and you were expecting the call. Hell, I couldn't even tell if it was a man or a woman but figured you'd like the excuse to get Brad moving. Why? Is something wrong?"

Abby took another deep breath and decided to table the discussion for later. "No. We're good."

The next client arrived during their lunch hour. Pro bono work bolstered Abby's spirits and reminded her why she went to law school. One day, she'd be able to accept or refuse any potential client.

Time and therapy had straightened the victim's posture and strengthened her voice. Preparing an injured party for trial entailed as many approaches as there were victims. The DA prosecuting the case appreciated the help, thanking her personally with an email directed through her boss. She'd learned early on the benefits of networking.

"Lottie, you look like you're feeling better."

The young woman lifted her chin and offered the first genuine smile Abby could remember.

"I am. I found temporary housing on the outskirts of town, thanks to the shelter's recommendation. I'm all moved in and even have a new job. Both are temporary but much better than what I had." Dark circles no longer smudged her cheeks, nor did the weight of the world hunch her shoulders. The invisible cloud which previously shadowed her personality appeared a little lighter.

"Then I'd say both agree with you. What kind of job?" Working as a waitress had been fine but having to walk through a bad neighborhood at night asked for trouble.

"I'm a secretary for a construction firm."

By the end of the hour, Abby had walked her client through the testimony, cueing her to keep answers as brief and direct as possible, never leaving an opening for opposing counsel to twist her words into an unintended meaning.

"I'm ready, Abby. I can do this. And when this is over in two weeks, I'll finally be free."

Parting advice spoken with sincerity applied to any victim. "Stay safe. Keep an eye on what's going on around you." *Words I need to live by.*

"Emilio wouldn't dare come after me now, not with the court date so close. He thinks he can beat it without touching me. I saw him a month ago in the grocery store of all places. I know he'd followed me, trying his intimidation tactics you warned me could happen. I told him I had the best lawyers in the state on my side."

"Did he do anything?"

"No. He never came within ten yards. He just gave me his evil grin. I'd never seen him in a coat and tie. It was his way of showing me he could fool a jury."

"Hmm, that was before you moved out of the neighborhood, yes?"

"Yeah. I don't think he knows where I am, now."

The smile reaching Lottie's eyes may have been tentative, but the way she carried herself spoke of confidence. She was on the road to recovery and determined to reach the end—in one piece, body and soul.

For the rest of the day, work kept Abby busy until shadows crept beyond her desk. Though she received no more phone calls, she wondered what form the next attack would take. *There's going to be another.*

Chapter Six

"People are so gullible." Time crept forward in layers of remembered instructions and small prayers. Before last month, Havoc had known little about electronic detonators, centralized blasting systems, or timing successive blast sequences. That specialty belonged to her sibling.

Having listened to an explosives expert go through the procedure of setting charges did not equate to firsthand experience. Nor did she enjoy a photographic or eidetic memory. Her intelligence stemmed more from the right side of her brain and offered talents in innovation, creativity, and intuitiveness.

Setting the current trap had been Daryl's idea, yet his analytical brain had failed to see the entanglement that ended with his incarceration. Instead of dealing fatal blows to the McAllister brothers when they interfered, Daryl used them in unethical science experiments, implanting medical microchips in one and kidnapping another.

He hadn't learned the most basic lesson; One should not play with their targets any more than play with their food. Daryl paid for his shortsightedness. His trial was still months away.

He thought to manipulate his naïve little sibling using pride, not realizing Havoc already had sufficient motivation to see him free. She wanted his knowledge to round out her skills for assassination.

Years ago, police arrested her stepfather after her mother decided parenting wasn't worth the effort. Eighteen-year-old Daryl had stepped up to keep her out of the foster system, and out of school. Their oldest sibling had left home when he'd turned eighteen.

She'd eliminate witnesses scheduled to testify against him because she loved him in a twisted kind of way. As a child, his often-cruel teaching methods consisted of various procedures for measuring her pain tolerance. He'd never pushed further than she could endure and once a test was finished, he soothed her pain with a seduction no budding teenager could resist. She'd learned more ways to bring a man to his knees than his methods of assassination. No wonder she would excel where he'd failed.

He stood a good chance of getting a fatal needle if the attorney survived. That possibility motivated her to excel in the hopes that once free, Daryl would teach her everything she wanted to know.

He'd affectionately nicknamed her Havoc due to her enthusiasm and random expressions of devotion to her intended craft. Extreme promiscuity combined with her intuitive abilities resulted in varied MOs during crime sprees.

Analytical men couldn't realize the intense high stemming from the fruits of her labors, nor could they understand the underlying motivation to reproduce a rival's results using artistic flare instead of cold calculation. *He should since he helped make me this way.*

Mind games were her specialty.

Manipulating others had proven her unique talent over the years. Unlike her brother, she'd developed a knack for gaining a mark's confidence and creating a shared purpose to guide their actions. It hadn't proved difficult to get specific details of Abby's plans. Certain electronic devices had proven very user-friendly. Timing would be the only variable.

The cave's immense chamber equaled the perfect setting for the next thrill in the McAllister saga. It was deep enough underground to avoid affectation by changing outside temperatures and big enough to supply days' worth of precious air. The addition of a few hibernating bats would ensure that once trapped, Abby and the detective wouldn't get lonely or bored. Unfortunately, it only smelled of damp and musty earth. If there'd been more bats, the ammonia odor from their droppings would've added a nice touch.

Twice, she stopped to tuck her fingers under her armpits for a little warmth. Despite the extra attention paid to detail, she tripped again, blaming the uncomfortable jump boots. The deception with footwear would prove worth the time-consuming search for the exact style bearing the specific tread pattern she wanted to emulate.

Details were important.

Interconnectivity between the caves and caverns confirmed her suspicion of a slight chance for escape after the explosion. Since her brother wasn't present to see the layout and place the charges, she'd have to settle for an educated guess. Such a job necessitated a thorough investigation of all factors involved. Time and education she didn't have, except for enduring multiple tours with a specific guide and timing their movements.

To work at night entailed a small inconvenience, a tariff paid for missing the shot in New Zealand. Strong winds had moved the damn sphere at the crucial second. Otherwise, she wouldn't be fumbling at night, fiddling with fuses, and securing the bodies of the explosives.

As long as she timed it correctly, the explosion itself wouldn't kill. No, the focus of the exercise ensured the recipients would find terror, hopelessness, despair, and then finally, acceptance of their fate. If a few bystanders perished in the blast, well, collateral damage occurred in such endeavors.

As much as she wanted to wedge tiny cameras in specific niches at strategic angles to film the coming show, her imagination would have to serve as the source of anticipation. She couldn't risk rescue personnel finding them or their signal boosters in the carnage to come. After the blast, she could film the show from a distance, watching the McAllister brothers swarm the cavern to find their dead sister.

The addition of emergency services as they worked, failed to rescue, then recovered the cooling bodies engendered warm fuzzies in her belly. The pictures would make nice mementos in her scrapbook of her time spent underground.

To slip a copy of the video through the prison system might prove tricky, but by now her brother would've bribed at least one guard who'd sneak in non-lethal contraband. The right to gloat belonged to every successful assassin, and she was ready to take her place.

It was unfortunate Royden remained glued to the bitch's side nearly every waking moment. Separating the two, if only for a while, would increase the fear and terror factors exponentially if Abby were alone in the dark and riddled with panic.

With the last of her preparations completed, she adjusted her headlamp and took another musty breath. No natural skylights through the limestone cavern would mean nothing but darkness after the explosion.

The pictures she'd taken during her guided tour filled her home's darkroom in preparation of the before-and-after display. Calcite formations lined with marble dotted the floor and stretched to unknown heights. Spurs of *cave popcorn*, formed from secondary deposits of calcite, gypsum, and aragonite deposits, added an unusual texture appealing to her artistic side. A small pang of regret for the coming destruction lasted only seconds.

Satisfaction lightened her steps in trekking up the incline to the cave's mouth. Her brother's ire also targeted the McAllister brothers, hence, they would each receive a copy of their sister walking into the cavern and rescue workers carrying her out in a body bag. They wouldn't know it at the time, but the attorney's demise equaled the initial kick-off to a campaign of terror.

If emergency personnel proved quicker than expected in setting up rescue operations, subsequent explosives ensured their mission ended with body retrieval, not rescue.

Chapter Seven

"Huh... I thought I might freak out at least a little when coming underground. The caverns have such tall ceilings; it almost feels like being outside except for the colored lights. I also expected it to be a lot darker." Abby nudged Royden in the ribs before adding, "You're multi-tasking again, cowboy."

"I figured you'd like the adventure. Arranging for the private tour was a bonus." His intention for suggesting this particular diversion ticked off several boxes on his to-do list.

The unique change in scenery gave her a new outlook on an old horror and allowed her to regain a foothold on her prior strength. This time, she wasn't a prisoner. If fate offered a helping hand, he'd also secure her agreement to move to his home on a permanent basis.

"You're helping me face my fears. The beauty of the caverns happens to be a bonus." Abby turned in his arms to ask, "Why does the term spelunking sound erotic and twisted at the same time?"

"Because you have a somber imagination crowded by lust." Royden dropped his gaze from the stalactite formation ahead to Abby's face. Her eyes radiated excitement and hope without fear. His intention to shave away a small slice of anxiety and desensitize her to enclosed spaces appeared to be working.

"Oh, I promised Kaylee I'd take a few pics with my cell." Abby extracted her cell from her purse and turned to frame a colorful shot.

"As a professional photographer, she'd appreciate a different point of view, but you'll have to wait to send them since we lost cell reception soon after entering the caverns."

Tiny LED diodes lit their path and emphasized breathtaking features along the way. Each new *room* of the massive cavern displayed a colorful array of formations at which to marvel. He used his phone to capture specific moments in time where the outside world melted away and the natural marvels surrounding them provided a backdrop fit for the particular question contained only by pure dint of will.

A secret smile played about her lips, promising a detailed description of her thoughts when their guide next wandered out of earshot. Life continued to thrust obstacles in her path, yet she faced them head-on and determined to not just survive, but also to triumph. He'd never encountered such a remarkable spirit.

The ranger who'd agreed to the private tour cleared her throat to gain their attention. "I was that way once, too. I'll be just ahead in the next room taking a break. Catch up in a few, okay?" A wistful note mingled with amusement in her tone.

"Thanks. Loitering is a natural hazard when in this guy's presence." Abby nodded toward Royden.

When he and Abby first discussed caving, he'd contacted a friend whose sister ran tours through the convoluted underground network. It was Abby's chance to experience nature as she loved it without the risk of her stalker approaching unseen. He'd arranged for security at both entrances. The three of them had the entire maze to themselves.

Despite the ever-present threat looming in her future, Abby smiled as her gaze traveled over the incredible rock formations. She ran her fingers along the ridges of a stalagmite's mineral deposits.

Flexing a knee, he retrieved the velvet box from his jacket pocket. The ring inside signified all he wanted for her, for them.

When she turned, recognition widened her eyes and dropped her jaw. "Really?"

"Not the response I hoped for..." *But something I can work with.* He smiled at her obvious case of shocked senseless. Blue eyes gazed at him with more emotion than he'd ever seen. Not all of it was readable, which gave his pulse a kick-start into overdrive. Despite the cool temperature, sweat beaded his brow. "Abby, we've talked about this—"

"But you're doing it now because you're afraid for me."

"No, I'd planned this for New Zealand, but the hospital wasn't my idea of a romantic setting."

Her face softened as she kneeled to see him eye to eye. "I love you more than anything in this world, cowboy, but I won't obligate and make someone feel responsible for me when there's a dickwhizzle on my trail. Ask me again after we catch the creep, and I'll say yes."

Her lips were butterfly soft against his own. In one kiss, he felt her desire rush to the fore. The same need slammed through his chest. He sighed, understanding her plight even though he didn't agree with her reasoning. Before he could close the box, she *tsked* and removed the ring.

"If you don't mind, I'll hold onto this until the time is right." Releasing the fastener of her necklace, she added the ring to the chain and replaced it around her neck. "For safe keeping. You tend to lose things."

He never doubted the depth of her love, only the parameters for its expression. "You're my world, Abs. I love you, and no dirtball with a gun is going to change that. I don't think we should give him the power to dictate our actions."

She brushed his unasked plea aside with her fingers sliding up his chest. "Did my brothers know your intentions?"

"Seriously? You think anyone could propose to a McAllister without the entire family knowing? I'll bet as soon as I bought the ring, Lexi went first to Katt, then to Ethan. From there, it probably took all of thirty seconds for the rest of the clan to get the news."

"Sounds about right for my family. This is so beautiful."

"Designed just for you." A grin hiked up one corner of his mouth. "I can imagine Lexi and Katt elbowing Ethan and Matt while pointing at the screen showing my bank statement." He sighed, understanding the benefits of a tight-knit family, the extent of which he'd never enjoyed. His only sibling had died when they were teenagers.

"I haven't gotten any *different* vibes from them, have you?"

"No, but I'm sure they saw it coming."

Further discussion only served to strengthen her resolve. She wouldn't budge. Knowing her family dynamics and how she grew up, he couldn't argue. It was her way of protecting someone she loved.

"Sweetheart, I—"

An explosion preceded the Earth's deep rumble by less than a heartbeat. The sound of the blast reverberated in his chest like the *whump whump* of a helicopter's blade.

Rock crashed down at the far end of the chamber as the lights flickered then went dark. Dust filling the air made it more difficult to breathe.

The ranger's scream cut off abruptly as he imagined one exit to their room filled with debris. The depth of the darkness transcended anything he'd ever experienced and wondered if it equated to what blanketed Abby after her kidnapping.

Instinct had forced him to pull her down and cover her body with his own. Details of sounds and changes in pressure registered in the back of his mind, facts he'd sort later if such a thing existed.

They were in one of the largest and most open part of the caverns, midway through the tour. They also inhabited the deepest section, which meant more time before emergency personnel could reach them. They'd have to follow specific protocols to ensure their own safety.

Unlike the intentional roof fall methods employed to control surface subsidence during mining operations, the blast preceding this disaster signaled the intent of taking lives. The large chamber's partial collapse ensured they couldn't reach the ranger. He prayed the path back to the surface remained clear.

"Royden?" Abby coughed and struggled to disentangle their limbs. "Damn. No lights. I can't see a freaking thing."

"Abby. You okay?" Royden pulled her to sit in his lap. Another near miss and his heart would give out.

"Yeah. Fine. We have to get to the ranger." Pushing to her feet, she edged away from him.

He grasped in the darkness before she outdistanced his reach. "No, Abs. There's no way to move the wreckage. Even if we could, we don't know how these tunnels interconnect, so we can't search for her. She's smart enough to keep moving." Getting Abby to safety remained the top priority. "She knows these tunnels like the back of her hand and that we're on the exit side of the damage. The best we can do is get help from those that know how to navigate this labyrinthine system."

In replaying the prior conversation with their guide, he knew she'd navigated the natural tunnels for years. "She'll keep going and find the connecting path out. Even if we were able to get through, we wouldn't know which branch to take when it bisected. It would be easy for *us* to get lost down here. She has a radio and cell phone, which means she also has light."

With slow deliberation, he ran his fingers over her head, face, and neck before smoothing his hands over her torso. "Are you injured?"

"No, no. I'm fine."

She wasted no time in assuring herself he remained physically intact. He felt her hands roving over his back and head before hugging him tight.

"We need to move it, sweetheart."

"That was an explosion, not a natural collapse. My ears are still ringing from the detonation. There may be more in store for us." Frustration mingled with anger in her tone.

"Yeah, I agree. We're gonna have to be careful on our way out. Let's find out if we have an open route to the surface."

"Hold on, Roy, I think my cell has a full charge."

"At least we won't step in any shafts."

Unable to let go, Royden wrapped one arm around her shoulders to help her up while using the light on his cell to visually assess her. "Let's go."

Abby reached for her phone until Royden suggested, "Wait, one at a time.

"Jesus. How could this happen?" She wrapped one hand around his waist.

"We'll worry about the how and why later. Right now, we need to get the hell out of here. Be careful of your step." He'd hated the fear tinging her voice and the fact he again failed to protect her. It was supposed to be the most exciting day of her life, not the last day.

Acceleration of her breathing alerted him to her increasing panic. Flashbacks and a dark imagination would send her mind back to the underground prison.

Taking precious time to calm her, he stopped and pulled her into his arms. "We'll get out of this, Abs. Nobody's gonna keep us down and nobody's gonna stop us from getting married."

"I need air."

"There's plenty here. Take a slow breath." He wanted to surround her in a soft blanket of protection. Smoothing his hand up her arm and neck until he cupped her cheek let her know he was right there. The feel of her forehead against his own, mingled breaths, and the soft puffs lengthening with each exhalation calmed his own heart rate.

Despite the urgent need to move, they'd get nowhere if she lost it. Distraction by close proximity yielded the quickest result.

"Thanks, cowboy. Give me thirty seconds and I'll be ready to roll. Keep talking."

Darkness blanketed the room except for their small bubble. Since someone preset the charges, that same evil could be lurking in any dark crevice, waiting to finish the job. "Did I ever tell you about Chacán-Pi?"

"You want to talk about food now?"

"Why not? And we're not discussing food." He brushed his lips across the crown of her head. "Chacán-Pi is a sculpture."

"Since when did you become interested in art?" Abby urged him forward, signaling her readiness to move.

"Ah, well. There's this place in Germany, the Institute for Microbiology and Virology."

"Oh, okay... It's a medical thing."

"They have this giant stone sculpture of a vagina."

"Ah. That explains it. Men always know where vaginas are located."

"No, listen. This isn't sexual. It's about caving. This is a thirty-two-ton carving. Monstrous. Back in 2014, a visiting student decided to go spelunking and got stuck. It took twenty-two firefighters to deliver him. They've been called midwives ever since."

"I always knew men would climb into a vagina if they could." The slight giggle rivaled the best music worldwide.

"No place I'd rather be." Despite their circumstances, his body's response proved her right and the fact that neither higher education nor dangerous circumstances fazed his need to connect with her on an elemental level.

"You're distracting me."

"It worked. Your breathing is under control. And we're moving."

"It's a shrink thing."

Though he couldn't see her intentions in the dim light, he noted her affectionate retaliation with the tentative brush of her fingers along his waistline before sliding down to pat his ass.

"Doesn't take much to start your engine."

"Keep that up and we'll make it out of here in record time."

He'd never thought of himself as helpless, but leading Abby toward the cavern's mouth and anyone who might be waiting for a perfect ambush opportunity reordered his thoughts. The Glock in his ankle holster lent little comfort when he couldn't see enough of his surroundings to target a hidden killer.

Each time she stumbled, he pulled her tight to his larger frame. They walked as one unit with his arm extended. His intent to light the area before them while keeping as much of their own bodies in the dark detailed the extent of his ability to frustrate a waiting shooter. Smaller rocks littered the floor and challenged their footing, but the bulk of the room seemed to be intact.

"Do you think he was watching us with infrared?" Her shaking voice drifted off as her hand tightened at his waist.

"No. If so, he would've timed it for after we'd entered the next room. Besides that, he would've needed boosters to carry the signal, and that would've left evidence behind."

"Jesus, I hope our guide is okay. Do you think she got caught under the rubble—"

Another explosion farther in rocked Abby's body into his larger frame.

"Sonofabitch! We've got to get out of here." Her voice broke as she turned and the fingers of both her hands dug into his sides.

"Abby? Listen, sweetheart. The stalker obviously thought we were farther along and sought to trap us." He wiped the tears from her face. "All we have to do is walk out. We've got this."

The phone's app cast light on their surroundings yet gave little comfort. Royden trained it to what lay ahead with the shadows trailing to their feet.

"Ah. Sonofabitch!" Abby stumbled over the uneven flooring but caught herself on Royden's arm.

"What?"

"My ankle. I've twisted it."

Royden stepped close enough to allow his warmth to engulf her. His height ensured she could rest her head against his chest, letting the soothing rhythm of his heart keep her in the moment.

"Let me see." Using limited resources, he crouched to raise the hem of her jeans. Years of playing sports gave him rudimentary knowledge to examine the injury.

The trek down had taken an hour—with stops along the way to admire the beautiful formations. Had they not dawdled, the fallen rock would either have buried them alive or trapped them. When he stood, she leaned against his chest.

The first sniffle led to another until the dam broke. She hadn't cried since the night she'd escaped a killer bent on twisting her mind.

Tears soaked Royden's shirt. Precious minutes passed until she lifted her head with a murmured, "Thanks, I needed that."

She obviously craved the contact, warmth, and reassurance. "I'm here for you, sweetheart. I always will be."

"I know. It's one of the reasons I love you. However, no more self-pity. Let's go."

A boost in spirit didn't translate into physical restoration. Her hands still trembled against his flanks. "Listen, Abs. I'm going to give you a piggyback ride out of here. We'll make better time." Instead of waiting, he turned after taking her left hand and placing it on his shoulder. Due to her shorter height, he crouched down. "C'mon, hop aboard, but be careful of your stitches."

She didn't hesitate, feeling for his shoulders and wrapping her legs around his waist. "I can hold the phone ahead of us if you lean forward just a little to help me keep my balance. Be careful with your footing."

Despite her legs wrapped around him, she still trembled. He hoped the constant connection helped steady her nerves.

Chapter Eight

Abby waited for another thunderous boom to bring the roof and walls tumbling down to crush them. A slight adjustment of her legs allowed Royden to lean forward and balance her weight. The warmth of his body seeped into her chest and soothed like a cup of hot chocolate on a snowy day.

Tears fell from her cheeks and added their moisture to his jacket collar. If not for his steady murmured conversation, she couldn't have held her focus.

Each time his footing wobbled, she cringed, knowing he carried her to maintain body contact even as his antics of bygone years distracted. Apparently, his school days included his own version of risky antics. He wasn't so different from her brothers after all.

Every so often, he'd ask a question and engage her in conversation. A check-in of sorts.

When weak light ahead grew stronger and a soft but steady stream of conversations announced the entrance near, she took her first deep breath. "You can put me down now. I'm good." Though Royden knew her weaknesses, she wouldn't broadcast them to the world. Straightening her spine and wiping her face, she felt the coils of anger tighten her chest.

Royden circled her shoulders. "That's my girl. Show no fear."

Unfamiliar voices drifted through the tunnel, men barking orders to enact emergency procedures. She listened for the familiar sounds of her brothers, knowing they would attempt to dominate the operation, despite it not being their jurisdiction. "Do you think they're already here?" Royden was well aware of her brothers' overprotective side.

"If not, they will be soon." Resignation registered in his tone and weary set of his shoulders.

"We'll face them together. I can handle them."

"Of that, I have no doubt."

The smell of clean, fresh air strengthened her determination to stand tall. "Do you think *he's* still here?" In her mind's eye, her intended assassin now lurked around every corner. Since her suffocation and near drowning in the collapsed sphere, Abby's mind formed a picture of her stalker. "It can't be Carrigan, Yet I can't think of anyone else with strong enough motive to kill. It's my testimony that will cement his fate and put a lethal injection in his arm."

"It's a possibility. There's going to be a crowd and posing as a tourist wouldn't be uncommon. First responders will know to keep an eye out."

"Royden?" A tall, well-built, and rugged man looked familiar. His approach coincided with his outstretched hand. "What the hell?"

"Hey, Tanner. Thanks for securing the entrance." Royden nodded to Abby. "We're in one piece, thanks to fortunate timing."

"It had to have been preset somehow. Either that or the bomber pretended to be waiting for a tour. I've taken video with my phone of all the people I've encountered."

"Thanks. We'll sort through it later."

EMS personnel greeted them with blankets and questions. As soon as they stepped clear of the entrance, murmurs from bystanders quieted, the hush as ominous as the trek out.

Abby searched the faces of those not in uniform. No smirks or threatening expressions declared she was life's lottery winner of the day.

Before answering the medic's questions, Abby asked one of her own. "We got separated from Sherri, our guide. Have you seen her?" The thought of dragging an innocent into her ordeal soured Abby's stomach.

"She exited from the mouth farther north, a little banged up, but she'll be fine. That's how we knew you two would probably come out here." The paramedic's reassuring smile added weight to his words.

Abby's mind numbed with the medic's assessment. Blood pressure, pulse, the cold stethoscope bell pressed against her back, all declarations of continued life but for how long?

None of the faces in the crowd struck a recognizable cord in her thoughts, but anyone could be an accomplice. On the other hand, her senses failed to register little that didn't connect to her body. Royden's hand on her arm kept her in the moment.

Billy was the first McAllister on the scene. No-nonsense was a look adopted by all the siblings, perfected by Matt, the eldest. A stint in the military had helped the younger sibling adapt to work in the police department, yet his comfort and expertise with explosives made them all edgy.

Despite all the McAllisters' involvement with law and order, either current or previous stretches in PPD, they each deemed public welfare a higher priority than the letter of the law. They'd nudged the line on several occasions, which explained why she sometimes opted out of family meetings.

When their gazes connected from across the parking lot, he blew out a breath and relaxed his stride. Still, anger and determination radiated as from a nuclear blast. Instead of addressing her directly, he faced Royden, a hand shoving hard but not budging him.

"What is wrong with you? You're supposed to be protecting her." Losing his temper wasn't a common practice for the second eldest McAllister. Poking Royden in the chest likened to a panther crouching before springing into action.

"We're alive and in one piece, *partner*. Thanks for asking." Royden stretched his shoulder muscles as if working out a kink. If fact, he resembled a rattler preparing to strike. "I had security on both entrances. His MO included a rifle, I figured we'd be safe."

"Obviously, you underestimated your opponent, *partner.*"

Abby bumped the paramedic aside and stepped between the two men facing off, a hand on each chest. "Listen up, both of you. I'll have none of that macho bullshit over me. Got it?" For emphasis, she gave her brother a small shove back.

The attempt merely rocked him on his heels but did gain his attention.

"I may be almost a foot shorter than you two, but I can still filet your butts. Do we have an understanding?"

The muscle ticking in Billy's jaw relaxed as his gaze landed on her and softened. "Yeah. I was just worried about you." Taking a different tack, Billy wrapped his arms around her tight, pulling her in for a hug. "Jesus, kid. You find more trouble than all the rest of us combined. Why is that?"

"It's my superpower. Haven't you figured that out yet?" Abby hugged her brother and prayed he didn't feel the remnants of her tremor.

"Well, you've never been one to do things half-assed."

Zeroing in on his partner again, Billy picked up where they'd left off. "What do you have so far?"

"Explosions were set. I'm guessing—timed. The guide had gone ahead to give us a private moment. I'm told she moved forward after the first explosion and got out through the other exit."

"If we hadn't dawdled, the cave-ins might have trapped us, front and rear. Either that or we would still be stumbling through the darkness trying to find the other exit. Thank heavens our guide moved quickly."

"As soon as they'll let me in, I'll go down to see what I can find. It's doubtful we'll recover any parts of the devices, but I have to look."

"Good luck with that," Royden muttered.

"Take Abby to her house so she can collect her belongings, then—"

"No. You two are not going to railroad me into leaving my home. I left for the weekend, but I intend to go back. I have to face this, Royden. Can't you see that?" She couldn't stay at her apartment, but wouldn't jeopardize her family, either. In collecting her things, she'd sort out where to go. *Where do you run when there's no place to hide?*

"Abby..."

"No, Royden. I won't. The bastard already followed us halfway around the world. He knows where I live. You think he won't find your house?"

Both men cursed in stereo.

"We'll stake out your apartment until we figure out the next step. Ethan is bringing Diego to you. He is to stay by your side at *all* times. Otherwise, we smother you in a blanket of McAllisters. And *that* is *my* final offer." Billy's jaw hardened. He'd just displayed his version of compromise.

Arguing at the moment would yield nothing. She'd learned long ago to pick not only her battles, but the timing for each. She had no intention of clinging to a dog for emotional support. "Okay, but while I'm at work—"

"He'll be registered for service duty. No one can argue the need."

"I don't recall Ethan or Lexi taking him through licensed courses."

"He'll be registered and cleared before he arrives, vest and all. He has enough training and is already protective. Trust his instincts. When's your next court appearance?"

"None on the docket this week. And if Lexi's hacking records again to push this through..." She was going to say she didn't approve, but the lie wouldn't come. Having a large German shepherd by her side would provide temporary relief, at least until she regained her composure. Ethan and Lexi trained their dogs well.

At the other side of the lot, her eldest brother's SUV skidded to a stop. Matt hopped out and clipped the leash to Damien, his K9 partner. Both appeared to be in work mode.

She glanced over at Royden, now leaning against the opposite stretcher by the ambulance. "How many people did you tell about our trip here today?"

"Really?" He kept his eye on Matt's approach, standing tall when McAllister got close.

"I know, I know. But the only people I told were my friends at work." Helplessness was an all-reaching bank of clouds covering the earth. She'd never succumbed to despair and wouldn't start now.

The expression on Matt's face declared the next hours would entail a lot of explanations.

"We'll discuss this tonight at my house. Your apartment is too small to fit everybody." Royden shrugged a shoulder, prepared to face the eldest brother. "We'll both have a lot of talking to do."

"With all my brothers present." Her sigh acknowledged the difficult conversations to come. The thought of having a dog nearby lent comfort even if it felt like a temporary crutch.

Chapter Nine

Daryl, her half-brother, would be so disappointed. He'd said from the start she wouldn't finish the task, and she'd proven him right on not one, but two occasions.

"The little black-haired slut." From her vantage point on the bluff's tree line, Havoc steadied her high-powered binoculars on a low-lying limb. Choosing a setup with an enhanced ocular lens allowed for a wide field of view where she could take in the whole area at once.

Emergency personnel dotted the scene, scurrying around like frenzied ants. Various reporters with their camera crews pestered everyone within sight. It was chaos. It was heaven.

"Isn't that sweet. They've already rallied around the little princess." A second assassination failure looked horrendous on her record, but as a budding entrepreneur, she could sweep the incident under the rug. Only her brother knew the truth, and he wouldn't tell.

Even from a distance, she saw how the siblings surrounded their sister and blocked the public and reporters' views to the attorney.

Each man, a cop or investigator living in or near Portland, scanned his surroundings. One used his phone to take video of the bystanders, no doubt sending it to Lexi, their family's hacker.

A giggle bubbled up at the thought of Lexi skimming through the facility's security footage looking for some small scrap of evidence, some blurry photo depicting the prior night's activities. *You can't see what isn't there.*

Neither she nor her brother could match keyboard skills with Ethan's girlfriend. Instead of saving the computer nerd as the last target, he should've made her the first. Men ceased to think a situation through when they knew it all.

The fact Havoc always had a backup plan proved her worthy of the task. Due diligence with preparation supplied her with the resources she'd tap into and the things she needed to learn. She'd chalk today's failure up to her brother's incompetence.

Fascination with the study of orchids would gain her entrance into her first mark's world in a place he considered safe, his sanctuary. Credlin's intelligence dictated her fund of knowledge be thorough yet curious, detailed yet eager to learn more.

Online photos depicted the soon-to-be divorced businessman a stud. She couldn't wait to find out. Every job should have its perks. The fact she found hers between the sheets made the prep work worthwhile. Traveling a good distance to obtain contact lenses was a minor inconvenience.

Once she ensnared the ex-husband in her spell, she'd press her advantage and move on to the second of three marks, using the tools gained from the prior to incriminate the next. Both the supervising attorney and one associate from Abby's firm were scheduled for mind games.

Merry goose chases were such fun. This was the part of the job she enjoyed most. The similarity of a lioness chasing down smaller game, anticipating its sharp claws and teeth tearing through its prey came to mind.

This time, the quality of deception and betrayal would rival anticipation of the final act in any scheme ever devised, and the law would be the teeth in the bite against the lawyer. How appropriate.

* * * *

Despite Abby's reassurance to her brothers, Royden insisted she ride to the hospital for examination. He wasn't about to take any chances.

"I don't like the double standard. I'm lying on a stretcher, all buckled in, and you're sitting on the other one, watching out the back. I'll bet my last dollar there's a McAllister vehicle both in front and behind us."

Royden took her hand in his. "The world is full of double standards, sweetheart. You know life isn't fair." He grinned, knowing it would infuriate her. He intended to keep her fear at bay until she regained her confidence.

Once in the ER and awaiting confirmation of x-ray results, the physician advised her ankle was probably sprained, not broken. Abby claimed it felt better and resented the testosterone insistence of the x-ray. Crimson climbed her cheeks with her brothers' ongoing conversation outside the room. She felt like a child caught in a horrific windstorm.

"Might as well lay back. It's going to be a while before the films are read." Royden claimed the chair beside her stretcher, unable to keep his heel from bouncing on the tile floor.

"Jeez. Not the way I planned to spend my Saturday."

"At least we're together." Standing once again, he felt edgy enough to need motion to contain his anger. Another outing, another attempt on Abby's life.

Various devices, from bandages to IV equipment, lined the shelves on one side and adjoining wall of the room. Behind the bed, more supplies ensured staff remained ready for any eventuality. The other long wall consisted of glass where occupants could see the comings and goings of personnel when the curtain was open. Three of her brothers stood outside, either surveying the foot traffic or pestering the staff about Abby's condition.

"I feel sorry for the nurses." Abby nodded toward Matt, who currently spoke with her doctor.

"Don't worry. McAllisters been here enough, everybody knows them." Royden paced around the foot of her bed, nodding to Ethan outside the room.

"Roy? Hey, wrangler. Long time, no see. I was going to look you up next week." The statuesque ebony-haired professional entering the room headed straight for him, arms wide. Tall and athletic, the doctor's white lab coat couldn't hide ample curves.

"Hi, Charlotte. How've you been?" Royden cast a nervous glance back at Abby, watching her mouth form a perfect O. The old nickname verged a little too close to Abby's pet name, one she'd found fitting after one of their marathon lovemaking sessions.

"Since when did I slide from Charlee to Charlotte, fella?" Confusion knit her brow when he didn't return her hug. "Just because I'm an ex doesn't make me a leper, does it?"

Royden patted her arms in a conciliatory gesture before stepping out of reach. "Of course not. How long have you been in town? And how'd you know we were here?" The slight hand gesture included Abby.

"About two weeks. I'm still getting settled. I was going to give you a call and see when you wanted to get together. I heard you'd made detective. I knew you would. Hell, you'll be running the department if you don't quit and join a private practice, like me."

"You're keeping tabs on him?" Abby's tone equaled that of calm interrogation.

"Isn't that what friends do?" Charlee turned to smile at the patient. "Hi, I'm Charlotte Nickerson." Street clothes under a lab coat included a skirt that revealed well-toned legs. She turned her mega-watt smile back to Royden. "We have a lot of mutual friends in the medical profession. I'm now part of the staff here. Orthopedics."

Heat swept up Royden's neck when he caught the severe scowl on Matt and Ethan's faces, watching and dissecting his every move. Every word of their conversation would've carried through the open door. He'd long been vetted by the McAllister clan and didn't expect the past to bite him in the ass.

"So, you finished your residency and moved back to Portland." Royden surmised in as neutral tone as possible. "Congratulations. How're your parents and Toni?"

"The family's fine. How about your folks? I spoke with them last weekend and your mom told me about your promotion. It was wonderful to catch up. She told me you'd bought a house and that I should drop by."

Thanks, mom. His parents loved Charlee and had hoped she'd stay in Portland to settle down with him. Unfortunately he hadn't told them he'd found his forever. "My dad had minor surgery last year, but he's amended his diet and exercise routine. He's doing well. His blood pressure is under control." Royden knew he was babbling, so unlike his normal demeanor. The figurative noose closing about his neck and tightening with Abby's enlightenment suffocated his thoughts.

"Huh, he didn't mention it when I spoke with him. I'll call and see if there's anything I can do for him. Well, here's my number." She pulled a business card from her jacket pocket. "Give me a call so we can catch up." With a bearing that suggested they could pick up exactly where they left off, she smiled before leaning forward to kiss him.

He turned his head to the side, so she kissed his cheek. In silent horror, he deciphered Abby's expression and knew the minute enlightenment occurred. Sweat dampened his chest and spine between his shoulder blades. He didn't dare mention catching up, not with three McAllister gazes bearing down on him. He wore his most sincere smile. "It was good to see you again, Charlotte."

"Sorry. Where are my manners?" Charlee strode to Abby's side. "I can check on those X-rays for you, Miss McAllister." Gesturing with her left hand displayed the small diamond on her ring finger. By wearing it, she'd declared her intentions louder than if she'd shouted.

Abby's slight gasp signaled recognition and placing the appropriate puzzle pieces in order. Despite the coolness of her gaze, immeasurable pain lurked within. "So, you knew Royden well, once upon a time. A lot of things have changed."

"Yes, we grow, we learn. Thankfully, some things remain the same. Royden and I had planned to marry. The last two years of my residency took me east, but now I'm back." Turning back to Royden, she added, "We haven't spoken since what, June? Well, except for the emails around Christmas. I was hoping to surprise you."

"Yep, did that. Charlotte." he was careful to use her proper name, "Things have changed, though." The surprise churned the acid in his stomach. Charlotte's assumption that they could pick up where they'd left off after not seeing each other for ten months was preposterous. In hindsight, the Christmas email he'd received and not thought much about held more significance. Apparently, she'd kept up with his parents, something he'd failed to do adequately. In respect to what they'd shared, he would explain, Abby was his future.

"I'll check back with you in a bit."

He'd long understood Abby's mindset. She wasn't one to engage in subterfuge, unless it involved trial. The pain etched in her furrowed brow broke his heart.

As soon as Charlotte left, he prayed his efforts of damage control would succeed. Her brothers could wait their turn.

"She seemed nice. When were you going to tell me you were engaged?" Abby's neutral tone failed to cover a world of pain.

Coming to the point might head off more hurt feelings. "I didn't tell you about her because—I don't know—she'd moved away. She and I are *not* and were never engaged. I'm not keeping any secrets from you, sweetheart. That ring was a pre-engagement symbol. Yet, she walked away."

"She still wears it? How odd."

"It was a promise ring, given long *before* she relocated to the east coast. I didn't ask for it back because I didn't want to hurt her. She used to keep it on a necklace because of going into surgery. I guess putting it on was her way of declaring her intentions, but Abby, it's not going to happen. I love you."

Royden's desperation multiplied. Matt, standing outside Abby's line of sight, started for the door, held back by Ethan and Lucas. Interference from her brothers could cost him the love of his life. Charlee equaled a force of nature when it came to something she wanted. Two seconds into their conversation detailed Royden on the menu. He had to be convincing to salvage what he cherished most.

"Abby, you're the one I'm with, the one I want. No one else."

"Hey, we all have a past. It comes with age."

"Yes, but when we promised each other full disclosure, I assumed it pertained to anything significant."

"And a prior engagement isn't important?"

Royden gritted his teeth. "It wasn't an engagement as such. We were waiting until she finished her residency, but she moved east. I haven't seen her or spoken with her since I met you." He had returned an email, but with general comments, as one would with an old friend.

Charlotte's obvious comfort and familiarity with kissing him and resting her hand on his chest added fuel for later fires.

"Amazing, how much she resembles me, long black hair, direct, and professional." Uncertainty clouded her gaze.

They were anything but good. *You don't know the determination of Charlotte Nickerson.* She'd set her sights on becoming Mrs. Patterson before medical residency moved her across the country and was now back to stake her claim.

The ER doctor's return interrupted further discussion. Ending a conversation on shaky ground was not acceptable. He should have told Charlee that he and Abby planned on marriage, or at least declared they were living together. Stunned disbelief that she not only wore, but also flaunted the small diamond had held him mute. He had a lot of explaining to do.

Chapter Ten

"Hey, sweetheart. Time to wake up. Your brothers are gonna be here within the hour." Royden's easing down on the bed rolled Abby toward him.

After leaving the hospital, she'd caved, agreeing to stay at his home. He hadn't given her time to mull over the conversation between him and his ex, which she still needed to do. Men may not see it, but a woman knew when another aimed for her man, and Charlotte Nickerson held more determination than most, judging by her demeanor. *Royden needs time alone to think things through.*

Abby stretched and yawned, trying to clear the remaining cobwebs from her thoughts. "Wow. I feel like I could sleep for a week."

"Maybe because you didn't get much last night?" His apologetic grin failed to register as sincere.

He'd spent hours showing her, not with words but with touch, how much she meant to him. By the time she passed out from exhaustion, he'd left no doubt that she encompassed the center of his world.

With each soft caress and slow glide of him joining their bodies, he reaffirmed their bond indestructible. When she'd closed her eyes, his featherlight touch brushed her forehead down the bridge of her nose before sliding across her cheek, demanding without words that she hold his gaze and *feel* everything he offered. Words became unnecessary.

"I'm up. I'm gonna grab a quick shower." She extended her arms and pulled him closer for a kiss.

With his quiet steps away, so went some of her assurance. Flashbacks of the speculative gleam in his ex-girlfriend's gaze, understood by any woman, declared the battle for Royden's soul had just begun. He'd detailed his previous relationship on the drive home from the hospital even after she assured him she didn't need to hear it.

Water sluicing over sore muscles circled the drain as confused thoughts wheeled around her mind. The timing of Charlee's appearance combined with Abby's affinity to danger watered the seed of uncertainty. She needed time alone, in her own home, to sort through the events and facts threatening to overwhelm her composure. As many times as she'd sorted through her brothers' antics and dances with the law, they could grant her one night of surveillance outside her apartment complex.

Coiling her hair in a quick bun, she felt ready to face her family, due to arrive any minute. Straightening her suit jacket equated to mental preparation for facing her siblings as well as removing telltale wrinkles from Royden's amorous bent when they walked through his door. The bathroom mirror reflected evidence of their tryst with slightly swollen lips, flushed cheeks, and eyes that sparkled despite the coming storm.

Royden's success in fending off her sibling's visit the prior afternoon earned him more than a gold star. After an evening of conversation, he'd spent an hour on a conference call with her siblings, assuring them of her well-being and sketching an outline of his association with Charlotte. He'd understood Abby's need for a break to gain her equilibrium and hence had run blocker, much to Matt's frustration.

Downstairs, the doorbell rang, followed by a creak and Royden's murmur. Her eldest brother, Matt, was first to arrive for the family inquisition and made no such concession in lowering his voice.

Her conscience chided her for dragging her feet while her better half took the brunt of the initial greeting. As much as she loved her family, every work-related meeting entailed walking a legal tightrope.

They'd each straddled those lines, something she'd refused to do or acknowledge. Royden didn't mind facing down five angry McAllisters, claiming it would be like just another day at the office.

Each click of her heels on the hardwood reinforced her mental equilibrium. At the top of the stairs, she cleared her throat. "Hi, guys. Glad you could join us."

Matt and Billy stared open-mouthed while their girlfriends Kathryn and Remie snickered.

"Told you they were fine." Katt elbowed Matt in the ribs and received a stern look in return.

Behind them, Hoover, Lexi's shepherd mix, plowed through the congregating group and into the great room, bouncing with Diego, who'd spent the night trying to wedge himself between her and Royden.

"Hoover, that's rude." Lexi, the family's resident hacker, tugged her McAllister inside. "C'mon Ethan, let's put this food on the kitchen table."

"It wouldn't be a get-together without a meal," Caden mused as he and his older brother, Lucas, preceded Kaylee and Megan inside, each bearing grocery bags.

Royden just nodded and smiled. "I should've expected this."

"Damn right you should've. You're family." Matt softened his gaze as he watched Abby walk into Royden's arms.

"All right. I know you guys are here to talk, but I'm setting ground rules before we start." Abby gestured for everyone to find a seat. Between the recent acquisition of extra furniture plus Ethan and Caden tugging Lexi and Kaylee into their respective laps, everyone settled.

Each woman smirked, having adjusted to Abby's style of dealing with McAllister problems by drawing her line in the sand.

"Okay. I don't want to hear about anything illegal. I value my job and I'm not adept at bending."

Katt and Lexi's gaze snapped to Royden, as if for confirmation. Royden's cheeks darkened on a chuckle.

"No, damn it. This is serious." Considering she stood shorter than everyone else present, Abby remained standing in order to keep the small edge.

"Which is why we're all here," Matt finished. "We'll stick to the law, and you don't hold back *any* piece of information, regardless of how you think it *could* be used." Matt pulled out a tablet from Kathryn's satchel.

"Let's start with what we know." Abby's world consisted of facts, consistent, comfortable, and part of a whole picture. "My stalker is a male that wears size eleven boots that could've been bought any number of places in either country."

"Or—it could be a very large female, or smaller woman who'd stuffed the toes of her boots," Royden added apologetically.

"You have some new clients with potential for gain if they can influence or eliminate your support." Royden wouldn't mention names but led the conversation from the front.

Both Lexi and Kathryn retrieved their laptops and powered them on. Each smiled at Abby's attempt to stare them down. Lexi's inclination for hacking came as natural as breathing while Kathryn had proven herself a fast learner.

"I do have several cases that you'd consider controversial." Abby took a deep breath to lighten the weight of Royden's stare and Matt's scowl. "Everybody thinks lawyers are scumbags... until they need one."

Discussing facts situated her in the center of her comfort zone, analyzing data and postulating solutions. "I have a pro bono client who was raped by her ex, a gang member with a record."

"The DA prosecutes that stuff—what's your involvement?" Matt turned his glare on Royden, as if expecting him to scrutinize and screen her cases.

"McClain is not adept at prepping rape victims to testify. My involvement entails a civil suit against the property owner where the assault occurred. It's in my client's best interest that the jury returns a conviction against the accused. Hence, I'm helping her prep."

"So, if someone took you out of the picture, it would weaken the prosecution's case." Caden flinched under Matt's scowl.

"I don't know if the defendant is aware of how much I'm helping Lottie behind the scenes."

"It's one possibility. If they do, they're trying to destabilize the victim by knocking out her support. I've seen it happen any number of times." Billy rubbed his knuckles along the back of his girlfriend's hand. Small gestures like that constituted each McAllister's approach to relationships.

"I've spoken with the DA and they've received no threats from that direction." She touched the high points of current situations, having obtained previous permission to divulge nonessential information.

"Be more specific about your involvement in the rape case," Caden demanded.

"It's civil. The perp was supposed to be working at the time of the incident. He dragged my client into a back room of a private business. The owner knew the little shit belonged to a gang and had a record yet hired him anyway. His work was unsupervised."

"So, you're shot-gunning. Name everyone in the suit and see how it all shakes out." Lucas frowned until Megan reached over and patted his thigh.

"That's pretty much how it works. There are more details that indicate the shop owner should have been more responsible, but I can't discuss it. You have it in a nutshell."

"What other situations are you handling that could be potential triggers." Billy winced with his word choice.

"I currently have a big divorce case. Both the partners and Brad, my supervising attorney, didn't want me to have it, but the client asked for me." She shrugged. "What the client wants, the client gets when they're the social elite with millions of dollars and an entire company's future at stake."

"Name?" Matt asked.

"Um, no. That information is—"

"Theodore Credlin." Lexi hunched her shoulders under Abby's glare.

"Hey, I'm an officer of the court and cannot condone meddling."

"It's public information. How many big-shot CEOs living in Portland are in the news so much due to expectations of losing their shirt?" Lexi pointed to her screen and leaned aside so Ethan had a better view.

"Damn. That's a lot of reasons for hate. Yet, why go after you? The wife is in more danger." Ethan's absentminded caress of Lexi's back induced a visible shudder. Each smiled.

"Had she received any threats from him?" Matt asked.

"No. None that she's advised, but she did make out a new will. I thought it a little paranoid to have two identical documents." Abby shook her head when Royden urged her to sit.

"Where are they?" Billy, the resident explosive expert and criminal investigator for PPD, retrieved his cell and made a note.

"One's in my office. I locked it in my safe and even changed the combination."

"Do you have the combination written down somewhere on your desk?" Lexi asked.

"Um, kinda." She'd been warned by the hacker about security on several occasions, now regretting not heeding the advice.

"How about tomorrow morning I visit and help you with electronic security." Lexi continued to type on her keyboard.

"Not necessary. I'll take care of it in the morning." Reeling from being in the proverbial spotlight, Abby simply shook her head.

"Let's discuss anyone else in or connected to your office that might have motive." Matt again leaned over to view Kathryn's computer screen again after she tugged on his sleeve. "Damn, he is worth a lot of money. Losing half of that would crush lesser men."

"I'm one of several attorneys angling for a promotion to a supervisor's spot."

"Jeez. I didn't think lawyers had to deal with that type of crap." Megan, quiet until now, shook her head. "I'm glad I'm just a vet."

"You'll give us a list of names." Matt made a notation on his tablet.

"Oh, my boss, the supervising attorney, told me to encourage the business man's wife to seek local counsel in Delaware when I wouldn't back down or coerce her to use him instead. I wasn't sure why he switched tactics or changed his mind. I'm thinking he wants to get his claws into the CEO. He also demanded to see the will and wasn't happy about receiving a copy."

"Does the wife have any family?" Kaylee, usually quiet and thoughtful, drummed her fingers on Caden's knee.

"Yes, she's from the east coast. If the husband had both original documents, he'd gain complete control of his company, assuming his wife and daughter were out of the picture." Abby closed her eyes, not liking the facts presented to light. "Brad reiterated today that he thought I should drop the case."

"What about others—anyone not connected to your firm?" Lucas murmured, lightly running his thumb over Megan's fingers. His girlfriend's intense focus remained on Abby.

The tie of each McAllister to his better half equaled what she shared with Royden, or so she'd thought. Introduction to his past love injected a world of uncertainty in their future.

In the past two weeks, he'd demonstrated through action, he was the man for her. Not just because he wanted to protect. No, he understood her on an elemental level and would go to the ends of the Earth to see her happy.

An insecure woman might move the diamond on the chain around her neck to her left ring finger, but Abby wouldn't take a win by default. She needed time to be certain his feelings remained solid. He deserved an interval to sort his feelings. She intended to give it to him.

"What about Zachery, Carrigan's older brother?" Abby glanced at Lexi, wanting to ask but afraid to know the answer. "Has anyone interviewed him again?"

The man responsible for kidnapping and terrorizing her three months prior had one sibling, a man who hadn't bothered to show up at the initial hearing. Zachery remained a question mark in her mind.

"He moved to a small town outside Seattle after his brother's arrest. As much as he declared Carrigan innocent during the initial phase of investigation, he understood the evidence was overwhelming. Kidnapping you and killing other young women apparently pushed the line for him," Matt replied.

"I checked on his whereabouts yesterday and while you were in New Zealand," Lexi offered. "I have video footage of him coming out of a grocery store in his home town. Either he's not our guy, or he has help. On the other hand, his bank account—"

"I don't want to hear about you hacking bank records, guys." Abby nipped her teeth between her lips at wanting to know yet also wanting to stay within the law's boundaries. It was the familiarity and structure that reinforced her mental walls. Yet it wasn't just her life on the line, Royden could also have been killed in the caverns.

"I don't think he's our guy, Abby. I just don't." Lexi's voice dropped to a murmur.

"So, we're no closer to having a lead than we were a week ago?" The urge to cry surfaced, but anger won the battle.

"Not quite," Billy supplied. "I spent the day and most of the night examining the cave-in. Those charges were set in strategic locations. Had the bastard taken in the topography properly, he would've been successful in burying you three alive."

"Did they recover any part of the devices used?" Matt asked.

"Not yet. And they probably won't." Billy shook his head.

Lucas picked up the thread of conversation. "What if they were after the guide and not us? If the intent focused on getting her without piling up a lot of casualties, that would be a way to do it. Plus, she was on the schedule for a private tour and your names weren't. She's the one that was almost trapped down there. Had she not worked and known the alternate route, she might've gotten lost."

"It is a possibility. One we can't ignore." Ethan pointed out. "I'll get Larrick to use his redneck charm to get more information from her."

"All right." Matt held up his hand. "Moving forward. Royden, you and I will delve further into Zachery and any recent and unsavory acquaintances. Lucas, you and Caden check with your contacts, then look into the gang members. Billy, you and Ethan scope out the CEO. Though it seems to me, if he's smart enough to head up a company that big, he wouldn't make such a public mess of his divorce." Turning his attention to his girlfriend, Matt sighed. "Katt, I know you and Lexi aren't going to stay out of this. It's in your blood. Whatever you dig up, let us know."

Kathryn gave Lexi a thumbs up.

"What about your ex, Royden?" Billy's steel-edged tone raised everyone's hackles, judging by their expressions.

"I haven't seen Charlotte in two years; she's not part of this. I didn't even know she'd returned to Portland."

"Not only did she look determined, but she sported a diamond on her left hand. Can you explain that?" Matt started to stand, stopped by Kathryn who pulled him back.

"Stop it, Matt. Royden's ex is just that, an *ex*-girlfriend. She has nothing to do with this. She's only been back in town several weeks." *If she was telling the truth.*

To divert everyone's attention, Abby tapped her toe on the floor until all eyes focused on her. "There is one other thing. I received a phone call, of sorts."

"What? What do you mean... *of sorts?* Why didn't you tell me?" Royden stood and turned her to face him.

"They didn't speak. There wasn't much to tell. It was just a, um, sound. A rattle snake shaking its tail and hissing." Abby closed her eyes against the storm brewing in Royden's gaze.

"Why the hell didn't you tell me, or your brothers for that matter?"

"Because—I'm sure that whoever it was, wouldn't call from a private or traceable line. It's a scare tactic, cowboy, and I won't scare so easy."

Matt shook his head. "That's it. Abby, you still have vacation time." A muscle ticked in his jaw as he waited for the fireworks to begin.

"Oh, hell no. Not gonna happen, mister." She stood her ground, knowing that short of someone handcuffing to a chair, she would go to the office. Home was her sanctuary, but work kept her sane.

"Let's table that discussion for now, guys. It's time to eat." Royden scowled at her brothers in urging them up and to the kitchen.

She'd hated putting him in the position of middle child, knowing he held tight to the reins of his frustration for her sake. The only outward sign, a muscle ticking in his jaw and a smile that didn't reach his eyes. He was a master at picking up subtle signs in someone's body language, pitch or tone of voice, and anything indicating stress or deception. In teaching her those little nuances, she'd learned to read him better.

He generally got his message across with subtle hints. If that didn't work, he'd put his foot down, something that would shock her family.

She wasn't going to budge.

Going back to her own home might be the hardest decision she'd ever made, but the stalker already knew her habits and agenda. With Charlee's entry onto the scene, it was only fair to give Royden time to sift through old feelings and emotions. Time and planning would sort the best way to see that happen. It was too late by the time her family left, to explain her plan, hence decided to wait until clearer heads prevailed.

She'd have to learn to take better precautions. *Like my brothers wouldn't stake out my apartment for a night or two.*

Chapter Eleven

Target # 1

Daryl once explained how assassination embodied a form of art that yielded more satisfaction with proper preparation. It all boiled down to a matter of perspective.

Meticulous attention to detail allowed Havoc to predict how the McAllisters functioned with respect to their various talents of investigating. In order to keep them off balance, she'd throw them enough witnesses from different angles so they couldn't untangle the truth. Despite previous setbacks, the games had just begun. The fact she dragged it out a little longer gave her more time to savor the coming victory.

Unfortunately, her big brother had not practiced what he'd preached. A sharper learning curve and wider array of assets gave her the advantage.

Nature blessed her with a beautiful face along with perfect curves that could turn any man's head. Intelligence and intuition sealed the deal. Sex equaled a wonderful perk.

In forming a connection with the CEO, she used every asset to her advantage. The side benefit of sack time with one other target in achieving the final outcome made her realize she should bestow a gift to the man who gave her the most pleasure. *A glimpse inside my mind.*

The convoluted path to success would dumbfound her brother with its intricacies plus satisfy the condition that she not repeat any assassination method. That little detail helped keep the feds out of her business. They tended to congregate around multiple bodies with the same MO.

Her visit to the optometrist concluded with various colors of contacts. Using a false identity and going out of state had proven a minor inconvenience compared to fiddling with the lenses.

Since her first target would suffer a fatal accident made to look like suicide, it didn't matter if he saw her without a disguise. With Credlin's final curtain call, there'd be a note blaming Abby for urging his wife to move across country, hence blame the attorney for his family's death. Abby's disappearance might even remain a delectable mystery, not that it mattered.

The CEO was an alpha male with a promising athletic build. Her guise of a flight attendant explained erratic hours along with comings and goings he couldn't easily pin down.

With any luck, the dominating personality would convey into the bedroom while making manipulation easier. It promised to be the more pleasant experience of her targets.

Careful preparation during the day ensured she'd considered and attended to every detail. A heavy sigh escaped her as the commercial carpet cushioned the sound of her heels along the hotel's hallway. Her preference for a late-night rendezvous centered on hotels a bit more out of the way, yet realized his arrogance demanded he test limits and take certain risks.

A tentative knock on the door drew a quick response.

His money bought the best in everything, and he'd acquired the determination to keep it, if not the stomach for the method necessary to make it happen. The room, like the man himself, was extravagant. A bottle of champagne sat in the bucket on the table by the leather couch. A nice touch, but one she didn't need.

Off to the right, open double doors led to a bedroom in creams and tan. Overstuffed pillows covered one third of the bed. They'd soon be scattered on the floor.

When the police eventually came knocking on his mansion's door, she'd savor the video of them dragging him out in cuffs. Only then would she be free to kill him, the despondent CEO, caught up in greed and arrogance.

The minute he snatched her inside, she welcomed his rough embrace. No tentative suggestion, just the assumption she liked it coarse, borderline brutal. Her second mark was a pansy, but not this one.

When he shoved her up against the door and pushed her stockings down, she smiled at the treat to come. His egotism stemmed from experience and a long, lean body sculpted for the runway, looks he used in his savage acquisition of smaller companies.

"I've looked forward to this." Dark stubble with flecks of pewter covered his jaw.

The weight of him pressing her against the door and his mouth skimming down her neck fueled her own need. Her fingernails raked down his back, eliciting a growl.

"Ah, me too. A friend got sick and I had to take her overseas flight. You know my job keeps me on the run at all hours." A smile teased her lips as he turned her around to face the door. Rugged hands yanked at the top button on her skirt. A quick shimmy and it slid down her thighs.

"Spread 'em." The rumbled command came on the heels of a solid slap to her left cheek.

He used his leg to slide her foot sideways before pulling her hips back. His hands seemed to be everywhere at once. The exquisite pressure of him squeezing one breast simultaneous with his other hand delving within her panties made her quiver.

She moaned at the rending of material. His command of her body preempted thought of the final outcome, letting her enjoy the moment. She would regret snuffing out such a superior specimen of manhood.

"You don't need these around me. They're cumbersome."

"When this is settled, you can be a flight attendant with a much better schedule. We can fly wherever we want."

She'd been ready before crossing the door's threshold.

The punishing grip on her hips would leave delicious bruises, a reminder of how well he'd filled her.

It was a raw, animalistic mating in the primal sense, guided by savage instinct and transcending any prior experience. She climaxed the second the pad of his finger touched her sex.

She could picture him in the boardroom with a take-no-prisoners' attitude. Bringing him to his knees would entail the epitome of role reversal, and she looked forward to it.

When he finished, he led her to the bed. A quick recovery time ensured him ready for round two before she fully caught her breath. It was going to be a wonderful night.

Afterward, he lay on his back with his hands laced behind his head, with her curled on her side facing him. Smug and self-satisfied, he offered the perfect memory for later evaluation.

It was time to get down to business.

"You know, I happened to find something out concerning your soon-to-be ex-wife."

"What? When you said you had a friend involved in the case, I wasn't sure how close you meant."

"She's made up a new will. I haven't seen the particulars, but I'm sure it cuts you out entirely."

"No doubt. I'm going to need a freakin' good attorney to get control over my own damn business. We didn't have a prenup."

"I also know—"

"I told you I can't use Salsman and Fernandez. That's the firm my ex is using. They couldn't take me since it'd be a conflict of interest."

"Ah, but your ex is moving across country, and I have it on good authority she'll be using a Delaware firm."

"I'd have to check on the legality of that. 'Sides, there are plenty of lawyers in the Portland area."

"It'll all work out for the best. Trust me." She didn't bother to mention that his wife wouldn't need an attorney, only an undertaker.

The thought occurred that he might actually care for the woman and child. Time would tell.

"What do you get out of all this?"

"Besides some rare orchids? Your body, of course. I don't mind keeping our affair secret, I just hate hiding—"

"Soon, we'll have lots of time to spend together."

The drop in his voice alerted her to how they'd spend it.

"I have back-to-back flights this coming week and won't be able to see you next weekend."

"Then we'll have to make up for lost time..." He reached over and pinched her nipple, letting her know the night had just begun.

Target # 2

Another day—another mark.

Sunday's schedule barely gave her time to get home and dye her brown locks red. When she finished the job, maybe she'd go blonde. This time, she chose green contact lenses to contrast her hair.

The physical transition of dying her hair proved anticlimactic when compared to the rush of watching a convoluted plan come together. With the third mark, she could wear a wig since he'd only *think* he'd gotten some, thanks to a little pill and a lot of booze.

Each man served a purpose and, in the end, would fear working with a sketch artist, not after she'd implicated each to the point of facing either legal charges or censorship.

She'd make it clear just how she'd played them, dragging them too deep into her web to speak up. None would stick their neck on the line to help McAllister.

The initial contact with her second mark had taken place in a small café where she'd pretended enthrallment after chatting him up online. He'd bragged about his supervisory position at Salsman and Fernandez, and practically salivated when she suggested an early dinner.

They'd barely touched on the subject of her need for a lawyer once she mentioned that it was her sister seeking counsel. His shift in attention came right on cue. From there, it was pathetically easy to guide him to bed.

Once there, he proved true opposites did exist. She'd hoped for another commanding presence but was sorely disappointed. He was all bluster and no talent.

Situated in an upscale neighborhood, the house reflected his need to demonstrate superiority. His beady gaze took on a calculating gleam the minute she'd walked through his door.

Signs of early male pattern baldness and a few superficial blood vessels across his nose declared the slow downward spiral of his life. The pathetic attempt to hide the inevitable by combing wisps over the bald spot almost invited pity.

Fortunately for her, his schedule didn't allow time to keep a wife happy or get out and socialize. *Divorced men are easy pickings.* The right smile made it clear she just wanted a little fun. In a few weeks, he'd learn just how far her version of fun differed from the norm.

Years of deskwork without regular exercise had taken its toll. His soft body contrasted the CEO's firm planes, and it took all her superior acting skills to convince him of her interest. Once he lay sated, the satisfied smirk on his face declared her talents successful.

"I knew it was only a matter of time before we met. Whoever said online dating can't bring happiness is full of shite." As if reaffirming his point, he pulled her back against his chest to spoon.

The bedroom had been a little cool on her arrival to his moderate-sized colonial. A light jacket, casually tossed on the sofa downstairs, had warded off the early evening chill and laid conveniently near the framed picture she'd take as a memento of time well spent. Now, she pulled the sheet up to ward off the goose bumps forming.

"I have to say, there's something about lawyers, not just the way they use words to sway judgements—it's the way you think. Analytical, dissecting possibilities until you find the right path."

He trailed his fingers across her shoulders then down her hip. "Oh, I'd say we've found the right path."

Unless she wanted to endure round two of his fumbling, a distraction was in order. "So, you said you're close to making partner at your firm. What's standing in your way?"

He paused his fingers on her hip before making small circular motions. "Hmm, it would help if I could land a big client. That's always a bonus."

"Like a big divorce case?"

He chuckled. "That would work." His puffy breath brushed the back of her head.

"You remember I told you my godfather is getting a divorce?"

"Yeah. You said he already had counsel."

"True, but I could sway his decision. He's not happy with his current lawyer, and he doesn't want to deal with a woman."

"Ha. My ex insisted on a female."

"Uncle Theodore was contemplating switching to Salsman and Fernandez since it's one of the largest firms in the area. Isn't that where you said you worked?"

"What's his name?" Greed and ambition crept into his voice, understood by the careful word selection and lack of humor in his tone.

"Theodore Credlin."

He sucked in a quick gasp, followed by a groan. "His wife is a client, so that would make it a conflict of interest. When you talked about him before, I didn't make the connection because his ex reverted to her maiden name. What a missed opportunity."

"Wow. But I heard she's moving across country. Won't she get a new lawyer there? Even if you couldn't handle the divorce, he's looking for new counsel to handle business affairs. Sounds like a double whammy in the promotional column..."

Since plans to finagle Abby away from the CEO's wife were already in effect, the encouragement and reinforcement of the intended path came at an opportune time.

Target # 3

Thanks to the ineptitude of the prior target's lovemaking, she wasn't the least bit sore Monday morning, only grumpy.

A corner unit in her upscale townhouse equaled sanctuary, and she could come and go without notice. It had taken a bit of time to hack into the building's security system to keep her travels private, but well worth the effort.

Looking at herself in the bathroom mirror and arranging one of her wigs, she decided the black bob suited her next *client*. If all went well, she'd never find out if his penis was equally short.

Havoc preferred her own long wavy locks, but the wigs proved useful, another barrier when gathering information about McAllister. *Hmm, blue contacts this time.*

The new quarry, Johen Claver, was an associate attorney and coworker of the McAllister tramp and appeared as a younger version of his boss according to his social media profile. Several pictures of him standing next to his wife revealed body language that made her smile. *Another sap.*

Prior digging also confirmed his penchant for snagging a drink at a chic bar one or two nights a week before going home. It shouldn't take long to get him alone, drug him, and take the appropriate pictures. *I hate cheap motels.*

She imagined the panic on his face *after* showing him photos of them in a horizontal tango. It wouldn't take five minutes to secure his part in her plan. In the end, she might not have to waste the time and eliminate him if he kept his mouth shut.

The trick entailed ensuring he enjoyed a good buzz and wouldn't remember her face, before she roofied him. Under the guise of wanting more of his body and deepening their bond, she'd give him a few flowers that would showcase her feminine side. Stringing a man along was her specialty. *Another hidden gem to make him keep his mouth shut.*

According to office gossip, he wanted the promotion to supervising attorney in a big way. She'd just happened to have put herself in a position to help, claiming leverage over one of his bosses. Once he felt the trap closing around his neck, he'd keep his mouth shut about the little B&E.

As far as the other will, the keeper of that document had indoor plumbing. It was one thing to sleep with a man, but her door didn't swing both ways. A little bribery went a long way.

A glance at the wall clock informed she didn't have time to listen to the day's recording to glean what she could about Abby's plans. It would have to wait.

After her rendezvous with her third target, she'd finagle a way to change the battery in the hidden transceiver that had yielded such specific results. Abby thought she was so smart, but Havoc knew every move before the attorney made it.

Meanwhile, a brilliant sub-plan took shape, one in which she crushed Abby's boyfriend. She hadn't enjoyed herself so much in years.

A final pat to her wig and she was off to the bar.

Chapter Twelve

For the second time, the lock refused to open. If forced to use tools, he'd also leave behind evidence of theft. The night's goal included stealing with the hope Abby would blame herself for misplacing the precious document.

Johen's nonverbal scream echoed in his mind, increasing the tremor which might account for the error. Taking the small penlight between his teeth, he hunched down to get closer to the dial.

He'd never suspected the conniving bitch last week capable of such devious standards. *Never thought I'd be blackmailed.* He either came up with the document or forfeited his marriage and career. He didn't even have the satisfaction of remembering the sex, only a fuzzy haze surrounding the evening and one hellacious hangover the next morning.

When his wife questioned him about the orchids in his car, he'd elaborated on how she'd love to grow some flowers in their sunroom. He even found a special medium in which to grow them. It hadn't made up for not coming home the prior night, but they'd weathered tougher storms.

If wishful thinking could conjure a sledgehammer, smashing the poor excuse of a safe using all the pent-up anger would make the night's risk palatable. It might've helped if he'd foregone that last expresso before setting out to commit B&E and theft.

The holes he'd cut in the knit cap for sight and breathing had imparted a certain comical appearance when assessing his reflection in his vehicle's vanity mirror. Another sneeze threatened to shatter the silence.

His nose kept poking through the lower hole, its misalignment due to the repetitive need to scratch his head. The urge stemmed from nervous tension, as when he prepared to face a jury in a case destined for failure. Had he been one to wear glasses, they might have kept his cover in position.

Placing his trust in a blackmailer wasn't the smartest option, but it appeared the only one that kept his life intact. He'd never considered himself as shrewd as some of his colleagues but took a step back after realizing the degree of calculation that had gone into his puppet master's plan. Underestimating her would not happen again no matter how tempting the package.

She said she'd looped the security feeds. A silent prayer embraced the hope she was as good with security systems as she was with drugging her victims. He didn't care as long as his life moved forward and not in the direction of prison and divorce.

Moonglow through the budding trees outside cast shadow arms along Abby's desk, mocking his slow progress. Tonight's success would herald the next phase of his career. Too bad McAllister had to suffer in the process. From the first week of employment, she'd shown him and the other new hires she meant business. It became quickly apparent she was too good to associate with anyone outside of work hours.

Unlike wall safes situated between vertical studs, the freestanding model before him remained bolted to the floor inside the closet. Had he not known specifically where to look, he would've missed it, hidden behind a false box front.

Knowing in advance he'd find a compact model didn't assure him he could open it, but a few hand tools tucked in his backpack guaranteed he wouldn't leave without his prize. It came down to finesse, which he normally lacked.

In frustration, he stood and searched the unlocked drawers of her desk, confirming McAllister the dumbest smart person in the firm. It didn't take long to find the lock's combination. She'd written down several sets of numbers on the back of her calendar. He used his phone to take a picture, not trusting his memory.

Nervousness didn't agree with him. Sweat popped up on his brow, absorbed by his mask in the moderate temperature. Each thud of his heart coincided with the imaginary clock ticking down the seconds until someone flipped the light switch and caught him mid-search. Lack of night security didn't prevent one of the restless senior partners from making late-night appearances.

His keycard gained him entrance to the building. Determination would see the job done. Once he found and delivered the damned will, he'd sit on top of the world. No doubt, his conspirator knew about the other located in the county office building.

The fruits of his labor would yield a sweet reward, and the bitch who hired him would get—he didn't quite understand her motivation. Why did she hate Abby? She had such a sweet face. Hell, he wouldn't turn either her or the McAllister bitch from his bed, though he'd have to gag the lawyer. Both were too damn smart for their own good.

At least tonight, he'd outmaneuver one and appease the other. Maybe when it was over, she'd slide between the sheets with him.

The faint click of the lock inspired images of him and all he wanted in life. Ironic that a few sheets of paper could make such a big difference. A promotion, better office, and more money.

Inside, several folders occupied the file organizer. If his nerves had allowed the time, he would've rummaged through each in search of anything useful. Unlike the black-haired McAllister, his moral compass never made it to true north. Then again, he didn't come from a family of pigs, either.

A sigh of relief whispered in the dark as he found the will. After tucking it inside his coat pocket, he returned the folder to its place and closed the door. He didn't know enough about Abby's habits and hadn't thought to ask his colleague if she checked her safe every day. If so, tomorrow might rival the fourth of July. Fireworks in March had a nice ring to it.

With attention to detail, he wiped every surface his gloved hands had touched. A loose hair wouldn't point investigators in his direction since he'd sat in her office and hashed out issues many times. Caution around a bunch of determined cops was smart, not paranoia. That same preparedness had urged him to cover every inch of skin, sans eyes and nose, along with carrying a small spray bottle of cleaning solution.

He could practically taste the sunny island vacation in his future, assuming his blackmailer followed through in coercing Abby to leave the practice. He had seniority over the others vying for the promotion.

Considering the night's success, he decided to leave a non-traceable calling card, one his colleague should notice but not be able to pursue. Before leaving, he broke off two lower leaves of her prized African violet sitting on the desk.

Chapter Thirteen

Abby opened her eyes but froze every muscle to listen for the sound jolting her from a deep sleep. The thunderous gallop of her heart and a respiratory rate she couldn't control increased when Royden's hand on her waist tightened.

"Hey. You all right?"

Diego, her brother's dog, lifted his head at the foot of the mattress, a low whine in his chest. Buttery bars of yellow from the attached bathroom's nightlight revealed his steady gaze.

"Yeah, I'm fine. I just need to move around a bit."

"Let's make some hot chocolate." Royden lifted the covers but stopped when she covered his hand.

"No. It's all right. Really. I'm okay. I'm just gonna grab a drink of water."

As if knowing she'd head downstairs, he urged, "Take Diego with you."

Before she could reply, the dog jumped from the bed and trotted out of the bedroom with his ears perked. Upon arrival at Royden's two-story country home, he'd examined every room as if claiming the space as his own.

The temperature had dipped when the drizzle started at sundown. Downstairs, the rain-washed countryside yielded a silvered view of forest and wild grasses. If not for the home's isolation and Royden's strict detail for security, she'd crack a kitchen window for a wisp of the clean, crisp air.

Diego sat in the living room, his gaze roaming outside and his head tilting to the side. A keener sense of hearing allowed him to easily pick up subtle sounds that only whispered through her thoughts.

Mechanical actions of filling a water glass allowed her mind to filter repetitive flashbacks and ponder her predicament, until the shepherd's whine snapped her attention to the front of the house. Setting her glass on the granite island, she padded over to see what perked his interest.

Was the killer watching them, planning his next attack?

"You want out, boy?" His signal to go out was to paw the door, hence, Ethan and Lexi kept his nails trimmed.

He barked but not the typical intruder's warning. His ears swiveled, and he remained alert with no sign of aggression. Ethan had warned that the dog sometimes chased deer.

She waited. If someone watched the house, they'd know they couldn't sneak too close. If not, there was no problem.

Minutes passed as she weighed her options. Waking Royden would flag her fear and weakness. *Not an option.* Frequent sleepovers lessened the feeling that she was in hiding.

When the shepherd lost interest in whatever had caught his attention, he padded to her side and nudged her leg.

"You're such a good boy." Abby took a deep breath, satisfied with her decision.

In returning to bed, she felt Royden stir and pull the covers back. The question hung between them, so she spared him the anxiety.

"I'm fine. I think he just saw an animal or something."

With Royden's arm around her once again, she snuggled against his chest, content and secure.

Diego hopped onto the bed and plopped down, facing out, ever watching.

Sleepless nights usually coincided with physical activity and sated bodies before morning. Abby sighed; the past two months' changes initiated alterations in lifestyle not consistent with her desired future.

Come morning, she was due for a serious round of introspection.

ABBY WATCHED Royden grit his teeth before narrowing his eyes. "Sweetheart, I'm taking you into work, end of story."

"Not unless you tell me why. Something's changed and I'm not budging until you spill."

She'd gotten up early after hearing him exit the shower. When she'd come downstairs, he'd been waiting. It didn't take long to see through the calm façade. He'd remained quiet during breakfast, his mind burning through various possibilities of whatever concerned him.

"Abby."

"No more secrets. Remember? That's what you swore."

His lips thinned as he removed a small evidence bag from his jacket.

"What's in it?"

"A round from a sniper's gun."

"Damn. Where?"

"On the front stoop."

"Before you ask, I'm not going to hide out in some safe house. This prick found me halfway around the world. He can find me anywhere. We just have to find *him* before he makes another attempt."

Dropping his chin to chest, he sighed. "I know, sweetheart. I know."

When he held his arms out, she stepped forward and snuggled close. It was the warmest, safest place in the world.

ROYDEN SMILED in passing several clerks along the corridor. His best effort received frowns from two out of three.

"Loosen up, cowboy. We're in the office and plenty safe." She'd never been one to accept hovering and would've found his presence cloying if a strange foreboding hadn't set up shop in her chest. The prior night had rattled her more than she'd admit.

"Abs, I'm gonna bring you lunch today. It's nice outside, and we can sit at a picnic table in the courtyard." The firm's office space encompassed the entire second floor of the horseshoe shaped building. "How about a sandwich from the new pub on Fourth and Main."

"Sounds great. I'll need a break by then, I'm sure." Abby nodded to her assistant in passing. "You really didn't have to walk me to my office, you know. I learned my way around years ago and you're getting curious stares." Half the women they passed undressed him with their gaze.

"Not worried. I have you to fend them off."

"It's why I carry pepper spray."

The intended joke died a quick death when she stopped in front of her desk. The blotter sat askew. *Unusual.* She narrowed her gaze while scrutinizing her personal space. Though not admissible in court, her instincts served her well and had pointed her in the right direction on many occasions.

Royden scanned the space then stepped to the window to survey the exterior. Tension tightened his shoulders before he turned to face her. "What is it?"

Although she'd previously enjoyed having a glass wall to her back, now it provided visual access to anyone wanting to catalogue her movements or take a shot from the wooded area. Of a sudden, she felt exposed, vulnerable.

"What's wrong, Abby?" No one occupied the courtyard below. The small shrubs hid no apparent threat. No one sat at the benches chatting or taking a break.

"This plant is facing the wrong way, two leaves have broken off, and my calendar is crooked." Opening each drawer in succession, she checked the contents. Nothing appeared missing or out of place.

"Maybe you moved it accidently before leaving, and don't plants lose leaves occasionally?"

"No, this is a perfectly healthy plant. I turn the blossoms to face the sun each morning. This section should be facing the door, not the sidewall." Pointing to the young plant, she added, "Look here. Someone has broken off the leaves."

"Maybe your assistant did it by accident?" The dubious brow raised declared his confusion.

"No. She wouldn't. She knows better than to re-order anything in this office." Her peculiarity and affinity with organization and consistency concerning work life baffled even herself. It was one reason she loved being with Royden, who was slightly disorganized.

He'd been the first man to coerce her from her shell and become somewhat spontaneous. He'd thought she'd taken things too far with what he called her adrenaline junkie phase, but in fact, each feat was an affirmation of life after her abduction.

"Is anything missing?" Unable to remain still, he paced in the small area, alternating scanning the courtyard and the infinite space beyond.

Apprehension filled her mind and dropped her stomach. "My safe. Let me check it." Her heel snagged on the institutional carpet in her haste to get to the closet. As usual, the door remained closed. Yet a small ridge of dirt contrasted the off-white fibers near the doorframe.

Royden pulled her back, his grip on her upper arm tightening.

"Hold on, Abs." Nudging her aside, he opened the door, one hand on the knob, the other palming the gun at his hip.

Abby stepped back, the momentum of her earlier self-assurance fading. It was a mental retreat into a dark room below ground, quiet, with no subtle noise other than the steady thrum of her heart to reaffirm life.

Royden switched on the small light. "Appears nothing's been disturbed. Take a look, Abs, but don't touch that dirt."

Growing up with five brothers educated her on the fallacy of showing weakness in the face of fear. Two steps brought her to the threshold.

"Let me open the safe and see if everything is there."

"You remember the combination?"

"Yeah, it was the date of our first kiss."

Royden's jaw dropped. "All this time, and you're a closeted romantic. How did I miss that?"

"You've been blinded by my devious mind and rigid self-control."

"More like your honesty, stunning beauty, and integrity... Not necessarily in that order." He crouched beside her, careful not to disturb the ridge of soil that had caught his attention. "Wait, put these gloves on and only touch the outer edge of the dial. Don't contact the shackle or exterior case."

Doing as requested, she opened the safe, her breath locking tight as it swung wide. Inside, one of her worst nightmares as an attorney took form, an empty folder.

"Damn. There's a file missing." Abby reeled back, balanced by Royden's arm. The ramifications of losing such critical documents would echo through her career. Besides Salsman, Abby's assistant was the only other who knew about the safe.

Brad locked the common file room containing the firm's confidential information each night, but anyone working at the firm had access during office hours. Current events supported Phyllis Rollison's paranoia and Abby's lack of due diligence.

"Which file?"

"Phyllis Rollison, wife of CEO Theodore Credlin. How'd they know where to find the combination?" Keeping the safe a secret reaffirmed her notion of a pipe dream.

"Actually, it's common to hide a password somewhere on one's desk, easy access and all that." Royden stood and held out his hand.

"C'mon. I want you to sit with your assistant for a bit. This is now a crime scene."

* * * *

Royden cursed even as he breathed a sigh of relief. They finally had a string to pull. The missing file and the attempts on Abby's life couldn't be a coincidence. They now had a thread to unweave the shroud leading to the right direction and a possible motive.

It wasn't the first time his hand shook and probably wouldn't be the last, not when his heart belonged to a five-foot-five dynamo who'd proven herself hell on wheels in the courtroom.

His first phone call went to Mathew McAllister, not because he was Abby's oldest brother, but because the family networked both in and out of the police force like nothing he'd ever witnessed.

Whenever a sibling found trouble, the entire crew involved themselves. On frequent occasions, Abby was the one who disentangled her brothers from sticky situations, her knowledge of law as sharp as her nose for trouble.

By the time he'd called a crime scene tech, several staff members surrounded Abby, each posing questions. She'd shaken off the tinge of uncertainty that earlier mashed her lips between teeth. Now, she stood determined and strong.

"Hey, what's going on here?" An air of pompous authority surrounded the shorter man's approach while the expensive suit failed to hide the slight bulge at his waist. He pulled himself up to his full height but had to tip his head back to look Royden in the eye.

"Waiting for a tech to arrive. You're Bradly Thempkin, right?" *The man who badgers Abby to no end.* Returning the favor seemed appropriate.

"Yes. I'm the supervising attorney for this section. What's going on here?"

"This office is a crime scene, and until I'm finished, no one is going in."

Bradly made a show of peering around Royden and into the office. "I don't see a dead body in there... I thought you worked homicide. What has she gotten into now?"

"I'm not at liberty to discuss details, though I'll take your concern into consideration."

"If she's putting the rest of the employees at risk by being here, maybe she should consider taking a leave of absence."

"Your coworkers are not in any danger, Mr. Thempkin."

As much as Royden wanted to crush the man before him, his priorities included finding Abby's stalker. A mental breath cleared the haze of anger and forged a more pleasant expression. Relaxing his shoulders, he reverted to his training.

When interviewing witnesses, Royden initiated a pattern, an approach to put the subject at ease and establish a rapport. Information came easier when the interviewee didn't feel the bite of interrogation. Years of practice allowed him to get a feel for a person's default expressions so that later he could separate truth from deception.

Experience helped him pick out nonverbal tells that guided his conversation. A soft change in pitch, nonessential information added to a story for the sake of cementing the lie, or clusters of body movements indicating stress, all combined to round out his assessment.

After manipulating the conversation enough to draw a mental bead on Bradley's normal response patterns, Royden went for the jugular.

"Tell me, what is your interest in Theodore Credlin?"

A tic at the corner of the older man's right eye preceded the attorney's gaze sliding back to Abby.

"Hey. If she's divulging information about our clients, she's violated more than a few laws that can get her disbarred."

"He's not a client that I'm aware of. Has he contacted you in reference to his divorce?"

"That would be unethical. I've not contacted the man." The attorney looked away again, his mouth set in a firm line. When his gaze returned to the office in question, fury radiated an unspoken threat. "What was taken?"

In making a statement, he'd not answered Royden's specific question.

"Now why would you assume something was stolen?" Royden couldn't determine if the angry aura was directed at Abby or life in general.

"Because there's no dead body. Unless you can see something I can't."

A review of the prior discussion during the McAllister's family get-together affirmed the supervising attorney's keen interest in Abby's case and the veiled threats meant to influence her decisions. "Tell me, Mr. Thempkin, where were you last night?"

The half-sneer curling one side of the attorney's mouth preceded his muttered, "Home. Asleep. And alone. It wasn't the night to snare the little witch." The nod in Abby's direction indicated his intent.

Before Royden could snatch the man up by his expensive lapels, a strong hand latched onto his forearm.

"Detective Patterson, what d'ya have for us?" Mathew McAllister's not-so-subtle tug edged Royden away from the confrontation. The formality of the greeting declared the detective's businesslike nature and determination to continue along the same vein.

"Someone broke into Abby's office last night." Royden watched as his quarry walked toward Abby with angry sputters. They were due to have a meeting of the minds in the near future.

Matt turned to face Abby, who held up her hand with a small smile. Her expression declared her ready and willing for a verbal sparring with her supervisor.

Turning back to Royden, he gestured for them to step aside for a quiet conversation.

"What was taken?" Matt checked out the small gathered crowd, confusion knitting his brow. "I know damn well she wouldn't touch anything after realizing that."

Royden nodded. "Phyllis Rollison's will was taken from Abby's safe. The intruder left behind some dirt. Abby swears it wasn't there yesterday when she left, and there was no cleaning crew last night."

"Her office is always spotless, so I'm inclined to believe it's our first piece of solid evidence."

A soft shuffle signaled the arrival of the crime scene techs. "Hey, guys. What's up? Somebody nail a lawyer?" Like his partner who also carried a case, the lead tech wore a blue jumpsuit.

"Conlin. Thanks for the speedy response." Royden gestured to the office and explained the situation and that it tied into a larger case.

Conlin jutted his chin toward Abby. "Hey, we try, but when it's one of our own, we damn well step it up a notch."

As the techs entered the office, Abby strode to Royden's side. "How long before I can get back to work?"

"Not until they're done." Royden began, hesitant to say the words guaranteed to piss off his better half.

"Until we clear the employees here, you're off." Matt's face set in hard lines, as if preparing for an inevitable battle.

"Um, no. I am going to stay—and work."

"Abby, listen to me." Matt held his hand out, his index finger inches from his sister's nose. "You can't go in your office."

She matched him stare for stare. "I can work in Gena's office. She's out on maternity leave for another month. Think they'll be done in there by then?" Her sarcasm indicated she'd wait Matt out as long as it took.

Royden blew out a breath, knowing he needed to prevent the argument from escalating. "Why don't I take you out for a big breakfast, Abbys? It'll give the guys time to take pics and collect evidence."

Matt nodded his approval.

"All right, cowboy. Let's go." Turning to her older brother, she added. "I am not taking time off. I will not be secluded. And I will not hide. So put that in your pipe and smoke it while I'm gone."

If he hadn't known her so well, Royden might have missed the slight tightening about her eyes and mouth indicating she wasn't as confident as she appeared. Circumstances presented challenges she accepted at every turn, regardless of the inner demons gnawing at her insides. The cave-in and scar on her upper arm proved a reminder of life's fragility.

He admired her strength and courage. She was a partner he'd cherish for a lifetime, but even partners needed help on occasion. Sometimes, they didn't realize they needed it. Try as he might, he couldn't get her to see that she didn't have to carry the entire load alone. It was one part of their relationship she didn't understand.

Instead of hammering her with questions or providing distractions during their drive, he waited until they seated themselves in a cozy café to speak. Her knowledge of his usual methods of approach necessitated frequent changes.

"You okay?" Royden murmured after the waitress poured their coffee.

"Yeah. Thanks for giving me space. It's like you know my mind."

"I should. We're flip sides of a coin. And I appreciate how your mind works." He waited, understanding she'd realize which questions came first but also needing to process events and sort facts.

"My gut tells me Bradley, my immediate supervisor, didn't do it."

"Why?"

"Can't put my finger on it."

"Gut instincts usually come from accumulated facts we're unable to define. You said he wanted to see the original documents."

"Yes, but that isn't new. He *always* wants the originals. As my boss, he has every right to inspect any and all of my work."

"But the safe was hidden." Throwing that out there gave her another piece of the puzzle to consider.

"Yes, yes it was. Only someone who knew I had one would know to look for it. To my knowledge that includes Salsman, Mitzie, my assistant, and the company that installed it."

"What about Mitzie?"

"No. That wouldn't make sense. She has no motive. She's slept with Bradly in the past, so she understands what a classic asshole he is and wouldn't succumb to false charm."

"Maybe there was talk between the sheets at that time. Unless someone else coerced her to reveal secrets. We'll be looking into everyone there, along with their associates."

"I can't believe this is connected to my stalker. If the killer wanted me dead, why steal? Seems to me they would've taken that road first, unless they intended to create confusion and widen the suspect pool. Hell, with the way rumors fly around that building, everyone could know about the safe. I seem to remain a hot topic." Abby snorted in disgust. "The cleaning crew could've discovered it."

"At what point was it known that your client made out a new will?"

"Mitzie, my assistant, knew as soon as it was done. Brad, my supervisor, well, I sent him a memo when I filed the document. Whether he or his assistant read it is anyone's guess."

"Has he hit on you again in recent weeks?"

"I don't think he can look at a woman without doing so. He asked me out to dinner."

Royden scrubbed a hand over his jaw to hide the muscle flexing. In the back of his mind, he added several bruises to the intended conversation with the man needing an attitude adjustment.

"Thank you for understanding my work keeps me level-headed."

"Thank you for understanding that my need to see you safe includes taking you to and from work until we've resolved the threat."

Abby sighed, resignation written in the slight twist of her lips.

It was the closest he'd get to an agreement. He couldn't tolerate any increased risk but intended to see adjustments made to her office before her return, including window coverings and rearranged furniture.

Chapter Fourteen

Abby studied her client as she settled into the chair at the head of the large conference table. It was obvious the young woman had something to say yet hesitated.

Instead of breaking the solemn silence, she opened her file and ordered her papers. Mitzie, her assistant settled in the seat opposite and prepared to take notes.

"I appreciate you calling me with the news. It seems the State's Attorney's office takes their time with filling in details." Lottie tucked a lock of hair behind her ear and exposed the thin scar marring her cheek. A new confidence emphasized the set of her shoulders.

"They get busy and delays happen. However, I wanted you to know we got a DNA match and the shop owner has hired counsel. It seems everyone is now aware of the seriousness of the situation. What is it you wanted to tell me?"

"If someone hadn't erased the back room's video..."

"Not as important now. We have forensic evidence. Let's focus on what's happening now."

"I—I'm sorry I didn't call you last night. I received a—sort of message and it freaked me out a little bit."

"What? You should have alerted me right away. What happened?" Abby didn't want to alarm the girl by voicing the dark thoughts filling her mind.

"When I got off work and went to my car, there was a small skeleton of a dead animal along with a wooden gavel sitting on the hood. They sat on top of a deflated plastic ball along with a few colored rocks. I get the skeleton; it's a reference to killing me. The gavel was directed at you being a lawyer. I don't get the colored rocks or the plastic."

Her assistant covered her gasp with a forced cough. "Excuse me. It's allergy season."

"My boyfriend and I recently took a trip and spent time in New Zealand. I was a bit fascinated with saltwater aquariums. I had an—accident while zorbing. Zorbs are plastic spheres that you get inside of, for sport."

"Which means they've lumped us together, the same fate." Lottie's gaze jumped from Mitzie, to Abby, then to the door, as if expecting an imminent threat.

"Did you call the police?" The warning to Abby was clear enough. The representation of a sphere that almost suffocated her symbolized an ongoing threat. Her support of the victim and encouragement for her to seek justice now linked their fates.

"Yeah. They made a report, but since there weren't any video cameras nearby, there's little they could do about it. They gave me the same spiel about safety."

"Any luck in finding work with better hours?" It seemed unlikely the gang member would target Abby before going after the victim. Lottie constituted a lower risk, her lack of family and prior record making her the more likely target.

"No, but I have an interview tomorrow that looks promising. It doesn't pay much, but it's enough to get by."

"Safety trumps money any day," Her assistant spoke up, a rarity and sign of commitment to the case.

The rest of the meeting progressed as expected. The client reiterated steps taken to increase situational awareness and reviewed upcoming testimony without faltering. Unfortunately, she had to survive to testify and lacked support or protection.

"Where'd you park today, Lottie? I'll walk you out." Abby could do little to help, but something as simple as escorting a client to her car would also offer a reprieve from the stifling reminder of her own predicament.

"In the parking garage, middle level. Oh, and I did get some pepper spray like you suggested. Not as good as a gun, but it'll do."

The easing of her client's tense expression brought a smile to Abby's face. This was why she became an attorney. Even though she wasn't prosecuting the case, she could support victims through the process and help them find justice. The civil suit may or may not yield much of a result financially, but her client stood taller, with shoulders straight and head held high. It was worth the effort.

"Want me to come, too?" Mitzie folded her notepad and looked at Abby expectantly.

"No, why don't you file your notes. We've run into your lunch time." Concluding the meeting, Abby pushed to her feet and turned to her client. "Does the apartment complex you're in allow dogs?"

"No, but it's a monthly lease. I'm going to look around for one that does."

"Good." Turning to Mitzie, Abby advised, "We'll be back in a few minutes."

Every lawyer worth his salt went through a phase of self-doubt. Was he good enough to argue his case? Did his opponent have information that would derail the jury's thoughts? Time and experience offered each individual the tools to excel at the former and roll with the latter.

Midday sun failed to penetrate the depths of the concrete structure as Abby strode beside the younger woman. Row after row of vehicles filled the space, each with the potential of hiding a stalker.

The rhythm of her heels echoing in the large space equaled a fraction of her heart's pounding beat. Beads of sweat dotted her upper lip and collected between her shoulder blades. Concentrating on small talk didn't keep flashbacks of her time in the hospital bed or trapped underground from invading her mind.

"Here I am. I parked as close to the exit as I could, but the place is crowded." Lottie unlocked her car and dropped into the driver's seat, twisting to offer Abby a smile. "Thanks for the company. I appreciate it."

"Hey, sweet cheeks." Arrogance accompanied the slur from behind them. Thirty yards and closing, a young man's features sharpened on approach. Several long strands of black hair escaped the knot at his nape. A gaze narrowed in warning belied the smile curving his lips.

Lottie twisted to see the speaker then startled and dropped her keys on the floorboard. "Oh, crap. I know him. Burn is an enforcer in Dominique's gang."

"Shut the door and lock it. Now." To encourage the girl to move, Abby hit the lock button and slammed the door closed before gesturing for her client to leave. Lottie didn't need any more reasons to be afraid.

"That's no way to greet an old friend." Ten yards away, the young man widened his smile.

Abby closed the distance, wanting to be clearly visible to the structure's video surveillance in the middle of the open space. Though no one monitored it during the day, the recording would reveal the confrontation to come. She canted her body to a slight angle, so her face remained in clear view.

"What do you want?" She stood nose to chest with hulking creep.

Clad in the reaper's colors, the man held both hands up, his right fingers clenched around a small cylinder about three inches long with a narrow protruding barrel. He towered a good ten inches over her. "I just wanted to see how things were going. You must be the McAllister lawyer."

"My name is none of your business. Get off this property." It took a minute for the item in his hand to register. A butane lighter.

When he leaned forward to whisper in Abby's ear, she didn't flinch or withdraw. Matt would be proud of her standing her ground. Royden would encourage her to reduce the prick's chances of procreation.

Show no fear.

"That's no way to treat a future boyfriend. That cop of yours can't possibly match what I've got." He moved his hand to his crotch and adjusted himself. His intent to intimidate worked.

"Since you seem to know me, you must also know I have five very protective brothers and an overprotective boyfriend." The forced smile plastered on her face didn't waver as she pointed to the video camera off to his side. "Now, get out of here."

"Aw, sweets, I don't mean you no harm. I just wanted to get acquainted. I hear you already have someone tracking your every move. I won't have to lift a finger, unless you ask, real nice like."

Behind her, the *whoosh* of Lottie's window sliding down surprised her.

"Burn. Leave her be. She's one lady you can't intimidate."

Abby pivoted to look at Lottie, relieved to have any reason to break eye contact with the asshole making her heart race. "Call me when you're settled in your new apartment. I'll let the DA know about today."

"I've already called the police and taken his picture holding that lighter. They're on the way."

"Haven't you heard, babe? Response times are at least, what, fifteen minutes? That should give us plenty of time to get acquainted."

Abby returned his grin with a thin smile. "I wouldn't count on that. You've stepped into a different world, now. My world."

"Freeze!" The sound of rushing steps echoed in the confines.

From the open stairwell, Royden raced between vehicles, his gun drawn. The surprise on her adversary's face was priceless.

"I didn't break any law. You can't arrest me." Arrogance added volume to his voice.

"Who said I wanted to arrest you?" Royden snatched the twenty-something thug by the upper arm and slammed him against the nearest vehicle, a white SUV. "You know the drill. Do it."

"You got nothing on me."

"I witnessed you threaten this lady with a weapon. That's enough to hold you for assault." Royden's applied pressure yielded the lighter dropping to the concrete.

"I didn't touch her!"

"Assault comes in many forms, verbal and physical to name a few. And who do you think the judge is going to believe, a gang punk or a veteran detective?"

"Royden, how did you get here so fast?" Abby concentrated on the facts, sorting time and conversations.

"I was bringing you a late lunch."

"You were staking out my office, weren't you?"

"Abby, we'll settle this later. Right now, I've got my hands full." After the clink of handcuffs secured his prisoner, Royden pivoted to face her. "Who is he?"

Tires squealing up the ramp drew their attention. Matt's pickup screeched to a halt before his door swung open and he leapt out.

"Ah, one of the McAllister brothers, I presume. Looks like they are as protective as you say." Burn's expression turned sly. "Shame they won't be able to protect you, isn't it?"

Royden slammed his prisoner back against the vehicle. If Abby hadn't understood the cold rage in his expression, she wouldn't have been able to grab Royden's fist before he broke the thug's jaw.

* * * *

Royden's gut tightened. When the call went out over the air, he couldn't move fast enough. In his mind's eye, all he could see was

Abby lying on the concrete in the same position as the aftermath of the cave-in.

How could one woman find so much trouble? In receiving his psych degree and joining the force, he figured life would prove eventful but hadn't counted on this extreme. Deciphering the convoluted mind of a criminal couldn't compare to keeping up with his almost fiancée.

Her mind wouldn't fully process recent events when life threw more shit in her direction. Like the rest of the McAllisters, she was a magnet for trouble in all its twisted varieties. Yet he'd fallen in love and couldn't imagine life without her in it.

"I got him, Matt." Deep breaths calmed the murderous intent as his fingers itched to throttle the assailant. Nodding toward the long barreled instant lighter, he added, "Looks like he was going to burn her. If you'll take that and this little shit in, I'll be there for paperwork after I see Abby settled."

"I don't need *settling*. I'm fine, Roy. I can take care of myself." Abby's voice proved steadier than her fingers as she clasped them together and straightened her shoulders.

Matt's heavy hand on the prisoner's nape signaled the warning to come. As long as Burn didn't get thrown in the caged section, he'd make it to the station without matching crescent-shaped canine bruises.

The eldest McAllister accepted the role of protector and monitor of sibling troubles. He was also the one with the greatest self-control. Royden sighed. A day came in everyone's life where they *let go*. Fifty-fifty odds were as good as the day's possibility would get.

"Where's Billy? I thought partners stuck together." Abby frowned, waiting for an answer.

"He's—" Royden's gaze slid to the street traffic.

"Let me guess. He's shouldering the workload so you can babysit me." Abby nodded to her brother Matt. "And what were you doing so close?"

"I was going to stop by with a snack. You look like you've lost weight."

"Sweetheart, this is nuts. If you had a client who'd survived two assassination attempts, you'd stash them in a safe house until we caught the killer."

"Not now, Roy. I'm working, and you can't put me in a protective bubble." Abby turned to her client, huddled in her car. "We'll handle this, Lottie. Why don't you head on out?"

"You don't need a statement or anything?"

"No. I'm the one he tried to intimidate, and since the police witnessed the incident, even I can't stop them from filing charges."

"Damn straight," came the mumbled agreement behind them.

The engine coming to life drowned out the swish of the car's window rising. Once Lottie pulled out, Abby turned on her heel.

Before Royden could state his case, she held up her hand and stopped him. "Lottie had nothing to do with this. Her window was closed for most of the conversation and she couldn't have heard my discussion since I'd moved away from the car. She is not a witness."

Royden shook his head. His little firecracker bottled so much tension in her tight frame that when she exploded, the result might include a nuclear winter.

"I assume you're going to file charges even if I refuse to do so."

"Yup. I witnessed an assault and will see it through." Royden fell into step beside her, his sidelong glance assessing the exasperation in her body language.

"I know better than to try and out think a shrink but realize this." She stopped and pointed a finger at his chest. "That kid doesn't have the intelligence nor the money to follow us halfway around the world *or*—" The rest of the words died on her tongue.

"No, but he might know how to rig explosives—or know someone who'd help. Emilio holds rank in a gang that could finance the effort. His buddy, there, was just a messenger."

"Okay, but how could they've known where we'd be in New Zealand? I can understand how they'd find Lottie. She stays in the city." She sighed her frustration. "But we've been all the hell over the place. Those explosives were placed *ahead* of time."

"Which means someone close to you is supplying information. *That* is why I want you to take time off. You've talked about going into private practice. Now's a good time. Let's take a few weeks and look for some office space." He'd use any coercion technique at his disposal to keep her safe. She crossed her arms under her breasts, thereby hiding the tremble in her fingers. If he pushed too hard, her defensive position equaled a swift and decisive offense.

"I spoke with Larrick. He said the cavern's guide has had problems with a jealous ex. She might have been the target."

Royden hung his head. His counterpart proved as stubborn as every other McAllister. "Abby, you shouldn't be talking to Larrick."

"I-I'll think about the private practice, Roy. But I can't stop now, not in the middle of these big cases."

"The CEO's wife has relocated. No doubt her family will recommend a local attorney. This pro bono case, you can take with you."

"I didn't want to tell you until I got home, but I guess now's as good as ever. I got a call from the CEO this morning. He said since I was already familiar with his holdings, he'd like me to work for him."

"What?"

"Don't blow a gasket. I told him no, that it was a conflict of interest. Hell, even through the phone line I could tell he was a shark. He was testing the waters." Abby cocked her head to the side. "Which leads me to believe he either has inside information about what his wife is doing or knows about the theft from my office. Neither would surprise me."

"If someone else took the will, maybe it was for leverage or blackmail against you. Maybe someone wanted you to appear incompetent, either to your boss or to the client. Wearing two hats left Royden's thoughts divided. It remained difficult to think like a lover and step into a potential criminal's mind at the same time.

"Without more information, who could say?"

"C'mon, Abs. Be sensible. You need to take time off. I'll take care of you. You'll be on your feet in no time."

"I don't want to be a *kept* woman. I've worked too hard to get where I am—or was. It takes time and lots of money to build an independent practice. And I'm already on my feet. And before you bring it up, I'm not standing aloof because of your ex. This is not about Charlotte. I need a modicum of independence."

"You're still mad. I know it."

"I was hurt, yes, because you didn't tell me. That's not the same as being mad. I've already explained. I'm not going to marry someone for the sake of safety, and you shouldn't push the issue because you're afraid for me."

Remnants of their early morning discussion would haunt him forever, the hurt in her eyes before she rolled over in bed, declaring she needed more sleep.

At present, the set of her jaw, one hand on her hip, and her toe's steady tap on the concrete declared her mind set. Further conversation would alienate her to his cause.

Chapter Fifteen

Facing off with a street punk didn't make Abby's list of smartest career moves. For appearances' sake, she'd tried to pull her courtroom façade over the thick veil of stark terror. From Lottie's description of gang retribution, the street punk could've killed and left her body to rot where it fell with no more concern than if he'd squashed a roach.

Had she not pointed out the video camera, the thug would've assaulted her. She'd seen the intent in his eyes. Circumstances raised the question of a new bull's eye on her back.

A deep breath and gazing out at work cubicles in the main area helped center her thoughts away from the new confrontational approach. Mitzie had buzzed her when she saw Bradley heading her way. How he kept his fingers in every pie, she hadn't figured out.

Abby smoothed her expression to cover the frustration of the micro-managing technique. Per his usual arrogance, he strode in and sat, as if she didn't have a pile of work on her desk. A subtle cough before a sip of bottled water refocused her attention.

"What can I do for you, Brad?" Abby clamped down on her anger.

"You can tell me why the police are swarming in the garage worse than a locust's new hatch."

Since the incident stemmed from her pro bono work, she didn't want to give him more ammunition to wedge between her and the managing partners. "Two cops don't make a swarm... A simple misunderstanding. That's all."

"That's not what I hear." Brad laced his fingers behind his head and leaned back, one ankle resting on the opposite knee.

Sharks had a friendlier approach. She matched his smile with a smirk and waited. She knew the game as well or better than her boss. The silence drew out until dawning crossed his features.

"I spoke with Salsman. He agreed that you need some time off, though he's not willing to force the issue just yet."

Abby grinned. "Not when I have trial next week and the client won't accept a substitute." Loyal clients were worth their weight in gold.

"Frankly, I don't care. Theodore Credlin is going to offer me a job, or so I hear. He called Salsman and asked about my credentials and performance."

"Well, well. Isn't that odd. He called me direct this morning and asked if I would handle his personal affairs since I have knowledge of all his holdings."

Brad shot out of his chair, fury burned in every line of his face. "You can't do that. It's a conflict of interest even if his wife drops you! The firm wouldn't stand for how it would make them look."

"Which is what I told him." Though her chances for a promotion dwindled with every beat of her heart, Abby held her head high, letting her confidence shine through her steadfast gaze.

"And what did you offer him?" Brad's dig at her ethics hit below the belt. He knew her standards and morals were solid.

Abby's retort died in her throat with the appearance of her friends, Lexi and Katt. Each walked through the open door as if they belonged.

"Hi, Abby. How's it going?" Lexi circled the desk and pulled up a chair beside her.

Katt sat in the chair beside her supervisor. A once-over declared him equal to sludge. "Hi. Did I hear a slur against one of my best friends? You know—it's not nice to smear someone's character. Didn't your mom teach you better manners?"

"Who the hell are you? You can't just walk in here like you own the place." Brad retrieved his cell from his pocket.

"Actually, Brad, we do belong here." Lexi smiled at her accomplice.

"How so?" Brad looked from Katt to Lexi, his jaw dropping when each pulled out a laptop.

"Girls..." Abby's soft warning went unheeded. The last thing she needed was for her friends to give the man a raging case of e-venereal disease.

"Some guy named—oh yeah—Salsman wanted us to update your electronic security, starting with Ms. McAllister." Lexi grinned at the man's indignation.

"That means you have to leave, per *your* boss." Katt waved her fingers in a shooing motion. "Oh, and don't forget to have a nice day. I hear smut magazines are on sale on the street corner."

Abby groaned.

Before he could get out the door, Lexi spoke loud enough for all to hear. "What is meathead's problem?"

Brad turned, his gaze narrowed. "It's a bad idea to make an enemy of your boss." It was the first time he'd shown his true colors.

"It's also a bad idea to piss off digital prodigies, prick." Lexi's gaze didn't rise above her computer screen, but the determined set of her body language indicated acceptance of a challenge.

Abby waited until Brad stomped out. Maintaining a straight face when knowing her friend's intentions equaled not smiling while delivering a decisive closing argument.

"Katt, you will not subscribe him to every dirty magazine known to man." Closing her eyes to find her center failed to wipe the grin from her face. "My yoga exercises aren't working."

"Okay." Lexi exchanged a measured look with Katt before a grin split her face.

"Ladies, that's my boss, well, one of them."

"He needs to learn some manners." Katt snickered as she typed on her keyboard. "Thanks for the compliment, Lexi, but I know I haven't reached prodigy status."

"You'll get there, Katt. Besides, he doesn't know that." Lexi nodded in Katt's direction. "Gay pornography?"

"And fetish," Katt replied.

"Oh, no. No, no, no. You girls will not do this. Please?" Abby swallowed hard, trying not to laugh.

"But if he has so much time on his hands, we should give him something useful to do with them." Katt's innocent façade didn't quite make it.

"And don't forget pleasurable," Lexi added. "Damn, he's not married."

"But he does appear to like the XXX sites." Katt smiled, lacing her fingers, extending her arms, and flexing her hands. "Damn, I love my work."

Abby bit her bottom lip, torn between the mental images of Brad soon receiving countless *gifts* and the fact that either friend could digitally erase him from existence. Flashbacks of when Lexi met Ethan and sent anonymous flower and candy baskets with furred handcuffs and lacy unmentionables came to mind. It took him months to live it down, walking into the squad room to find one or the other dangling from the ceiling above his desk.

"Did you guys really talk to the managing partner?" As much as she wanted them to wipe the floor with Brad, she subscribed to the notion of staying within certain boundaries. Legal if not moral ones. These were her friends, her family, and wanted to protect her in whatever fashion they could.

"Yup. I contacted him first thing this morning and let him know of critical weaknesses in his firewall. Offered him a discount to fix them. He jumped at the chance after I told him I'm a consultant with PPD." Lexi continued working without looking up.

"Which means you'll spend it all on dirty magazines and *devices* sent to Brad's office." Abby groaned at the thought of daily deliveries, along with a few not-so-subtle toys in conspicuously marked boxes deposited on the front desk for Brad.

"Abby?" Mitzie padded into the office and stopped. The assistant's appearance earned her a minute of quiet speculation from the hackers.

"Hi, I'm Lexi, the new IT consultant. This is Katt." Lexi nodded to her colleague. "You must be Maria? Abby's assistant?"

"Yes, but call me Mitzie." Turning to Abby, she continued. "Do you want the files on Jameson now?"

Abby side glanced at her guests. Giving them any information at all was dangerous, despite their good intentions. "No. That can wait for a bit."

"I'm sorry I didn't go with you when you walked Lottie out. I should have. That creep probably wouldn't have bothered you if there were three of us."

"Nonsense, Mitzie. I'm fine. He wasn't going to hurt me. Not once I pointed out the video cameras."

"It seems we attract the worst of the worse. Are you sure you don't need to take a break from—all this?" She held her hands out to indicate the outer office.

"What a great idea. Why don't we have a night out on the town?" Lexi nodded to Mitzie. "You up for it?"

"Absolutely. My friends and roommate were going to the Irish pub down on third and Clover tonight. Wanna join us?"

Katt nodded her acceptance, as did Lexi before Abby could think of a reason to refuse. Knowing her family, they'd have numbers rivaling the National Guard surrounding them.

A NOW-FAMILIAR itch pricked the skin between Abby's shoulder blades, yet no faces appeared familiar in the dimly lit bar. She searched among the room's patrons, certain her brothers and Royden had stacked the deck by placing several undercover or off duty officers among the crowd. Arriving a little early with Lexi and Katt, she waited for Mitzie and her friends to arrive.

"What's up, Abby? You look nervous." Lexi's gaze scanned the throng of young professionals before returning to the can of soda before her. If the server had thought the request for an unopened can strange, she'd given no indication.

Abby sat between Katt and Lexi. Upon arrival, her friends directed her to a table at the back where they'd face the room with a wall at their backs. Both girls were street savvy and self-sufficient.

"Nothing, well, I keep getting the vibe somebody's watching me."

"You mean besides Dereck in the corner?" Katt nodded toward the young off duty officer. "Don't worry. He's harmless. He asked me out several times but gave up when I told him I was with Matt."

"Royden says this used to be his favorite watering hole during his college years." She needed a distraction. It wasn't just in the bar Abby felt like a specimen squeezed between two slides under a microscope, but tonight, the demons on her left shoulder had stepped it up a notch. Her gut twisted with the need to define the threat.

"You two don't go to bars much now, though." Lexi's question came out as a statement.

"No, I'd rather spend my time in physical pursuits than finding the bottom of a bottle."

"Lexi, wasn't Ethan pissed at you for coming out tonight?" Katt twirled the straw in her fruity drink. She'd yet to take a sip. A casual eye would suspect the little PI had not a care in the world.

Abby knew better. Katt was every bit as sharp as her brothers and Royden. She'd probably stored a mental picture of everyone in the pub if she wasn't wearing a body camera.

"Yeah, until I told him I had a private investigator to watch my back." Lexi held her hand up for a high five.

The light slap earned the attention of two men at the next table. Each had watched the three women enter and settle. Heated interest kept their gazes locked onto the new arrivals. Their smirk detailed a lesson on how not to pick up a woman.

"Matt thinks Abby's trying to draw out the stalker tonight." Katt caught the eye of a server in passing. "Can we place an order for snacks, please? Also, I'd like a bottle of water."

Abby turned to her friends. "I know damn well each of my brothers and Roy are lurking very close. It's the only reason I'm not handcuffed to my bed."

Lexi sputtered her soda and grabbed a napkin. "O-kay. That was unexpected. I guess we really don't know you as well as we think. Maybe there's hope for Royden after all." Palm up, she waved her fingers in a *tell-all* motion.

"He *is* a shrink. Bet he can anticipate everything she needs," Katt agreed.

Heat twined up Abby's neck. "I'm not talking sex with you guys, simply because I know the facts will eventually make their way back to my brothers. Can you imagine how that would—" Abby covered her mouth, realizing she'd need a big distraction to alter the course of conversation.

A deep breath prepared for the verbal onslaught to come. It wasn't an exaggeration to toy with the ring on her necklace. The back and forth motion soothed her nerves.

"Ohmygod! Is that a diamond, Abby? Katt bolted to her feet to examine the ring.

"Oh, yes. It is," Lexi confirmed.

"Hey, sorry we're late." Mitzie pulled up a chair with her back to the room. "This is Jenna and Linda," indicating her friends who also took a seat. "The place is busy tonight—holy shit, Abby. Royden gave you an engagement ring? Why didn't you tell me?"

"Because we haven't set a date yet. However, Royden insisted we fill out the marriage application."

"But it's only good for..." Mitzie tilted her head in confusion.

"Sixty days. Congratulations. Where is your guy?" Jenna's upper body swayed to the beat of the music. Long blonde hair brushed her bare arms as she swiveled her chair to see the room at large.

"Not here tonight. He doesn't want to see us all get blitzed." Katt shook her head.

"I hope you cleaned your toilet before we came since you may be hugging it later," Lexi replied.

Jenna squinted in the dim light and leaned forward to see better. "Wow. That's nice. Lucky lady."

"Then why aren't you wearing it?" Lexi slid her fingers under the chain to dangle the ring for all to examine. "Is it because of Charlotte?"

Conversations stopped when the server took the new order and returned with drinks.

"How do you guys know about Charlotte?" Abby's defenses rose, but she couldn't stop from showing her pain, even if obscurely. She briefly closed her eyes to get a handle on her emotions.

"McAllister grapevine, of course. Ya know, you really don't have anything to worry about from Royden." Katt chimed in to add support.

"I know she's an ex and he's long since over her, but you didn't see the determination in *her* eyes. She wants him back. I don't know enough about her to fight it, but I don't want to start a marriage with that or any other threat over my head."

"Then let's relax tonight and deal with the rest later." Lexi held her soda up for a toast. Mitzie, Linda, and Jenna raised their glasses in agreement.

"Here's to new beginnings and a future filled with laughter and love." Katt had as much to celebrate as Lexi if Royden's assessment of her brothers' intentions were correct.

"Mitzie says you're an attorney?" Removing the elastic from the messy bun, Linda shook her head as her long hair draped to her waist. She appeared every bit the twenty-something roommate out for a good time. The deep V of her snug t-shirt revealed an ample amount of cleavage.

"Yes. I work for Salsman and Fernandez, family law." Abby took a sip of her drink and relaxed. There were too many people for an assassin to make his move. "Mitzie said you're employed as a Virtual Travel Agent. How does that even work?"

"Oh, it's great money *and* with fantastic perks. I get to take advantage of the discounts and travel when I like. Not the dream job I hoped for out of college, but it pays the bills and has nice benefits."

Linda's gaze roamed the room until landing on the young officer Katt pointed out earlier. Speculation and a certain come-hither smile stretched her lips wide. "Nice pickings tonight, yes?" Hiking her brows up several times, she chuckled and glanced at Jenna. "I call dibs on him later."

"What kind of work do you do, Jenna?" Katt smiled but her gaze remained on her cell as she continued to fiddle with it.

Abby sighed, knowing her friends had good intentions. *She's recording conversations.*

Jenna brushed her curly blonde hair off her shoulder. A little more sophisticated, she turned to face Katt. "I'm a magazine freelancer. Once I got my foot in the door with *American Outdoorsman,* I got acceptance letters for other jobs. It's a great way to travel and have your own schedule. My parents did a lot of traveling, so I guess that helped."

"What's your latest gig about?" Lexi asked, obviously intrigued.

"I covered the upheaval near Atlanta. It was pretty intense, enough that I'm thinking I'll stay close to home for a while. Maybe do a stint working for a newspaper."

"Wow, sounds adventurous." Lexi shook her head. "And here I just play with computers."

Jenna flipped her hair then smiled at a man sitting at the next table. A bit younger, she also wore jeans, and a low-cut t-shirt. "This is great. I so needed to relax tonight." With a coquettish tilt to her head, she swiped her tongue along her bottom lip. An invitation. "I don't get out to socialize much, so I really appreciate this."

"It's a bit crowded, but I like it anyway. It's cozy." Abby hadn't expected many customers and was surprised at the number of couples on the small dance floor. She wondered how many carried a badge and gun.

Country music blared from overhead speakers, originating from the jukebox by the door before a change in tempo brought an upsurge beat. The current song detailed troubled relationships and revenge, a definite switch from the traditional Irish lyrics previously piped through the speakers.

Chair legs scraping nearby turned the girls' attention to the two men snaking their way toward them.

"Hello, ladies." The taller man in front resembled a linebacker. Thick shoulders narrowed to a trim waist, but a slight beer belly bulged over his jeans. Turning his attention to Abby, he asked, "How about a dance?"

"No, thank you." Not since law school had she been out with this large a group of women. She found security in numbers, yet a doubt niggled at the back of her mind. Her would-be killer had been careful to date in not leaving evidence despite changing his MO with each attempt. If he grew impatient, a room full of semi-sober patrons might provide the perfect cover for another run at her.

Without hesitation, Katt stood and faced the hulkish man. "She's spoken for, but I love to dance."

Most people underestimated Katt. A delicate bone structure, waist-length hair, and a sweet smile disguised a mind whose speed of thought competed with the electronics she loved. After earning her degree and private investigator's license, she'd turned her talents to building a business and joining forces with the family's resident hacker, Lexi.

The second man turned his attention to Mitzie. "Would you do me the honor?" A certain sleaziness leached from his gaze, matched by the tone of his request.

"No thanks. I'm just here to enjoy time with my friends." Mitzie shuffled her chair a little closer to the table in turning down the advance.

"I'll dance." Not waiting, Jenna jumped up and held out her hand expectantly. It was unfortunate that some young women lacked the caution earned from experience. When her partner slid his arm low on her back, she sidled closer and smiled up at him.

"Ten to one odds—Katt knows everything there is to know about that guy before she returns. But please don't tell me she's gonna pick his pocket. I came here to relax."

"Fun is what tonight is all about." Mitzie held her glass up for a toast. "To hell with men and their diabolical plans." A puzzled glance at the dance floor and she looked expectantly at Abby. "*Katt* is a pickpocket? Has she been arrested before?"

"No. she just has a curious mind and the determination to see her theories through," Lexi supplied. "She's actually a private investigator."

"Wow. Really? A woman PI? I've never met one." A new appreciation lit Mitzie's face.

Linda caught the eye of a young exec type sitting at the bar. When he strode over and invited her to dance, she accepted. Her flirtatious smile received a shy grin.

When the music changed tempo and Katt returned, Abby detected the slight headshake to Lexi along with a slight flutter of her fingers. The girls were working behind the scene despite the night's purpose.

Jenna continued dancing with her partner, as did Linda. Apparently, they both hit it off from the start.

"Mitzie, I'm not so sure about that guy with Jenna. He registered kind of high on my creep meter." Abby didn't want to see the girl's night ruined because of inexperience.

"It's okay. I'll make sure they get home okay." Mitzie spoke with assurance, as if it was common procedure among the trio.

The music changed genres several times, a reflection of the eclectic crowd. A few men in suits sat at the bar, a few cowboy types dotted the tables, and then there was the younger crowd. Old enough to have graduated college but young enough that life hadn't worn the edges off their shiny outlook on life.

Several other appreciative glances in Abby's direction received a frown. She hadn't come to dance or hook up. She just wanted a mental pause where death nor brother hovered over her shoulder. Yet the niggling doubt of someone monitoring her every move filled her mind despite the fact she couldn't put a face to the suspicion.

"What's it like to be a private investigator?" Mitzie turned her attention to Katt. "That sounds so exciting."

Katt shook her head. She'd recently had experience dealing with the business end of a killer. Caution blended with street smarts kept her wary. "Most of the time, it's just sitting and waiting for something to happen. At other times, you wished you were just sitting on a house."

"Do you carry a gun?" Mitzie asked.

"I carry a stun gun." Katt avoided a direct answer.

To Abby's knowledge, Katt didn't have an LTC permit, which didn't mean there wasn't a Sig Sauer tucked under her jacket. Like the rest of the McAllister family, she sometimes made her own rules.

"What's the scariest thing you've ever been involved in?" Mitzie pressed further.

"An angry husband who didn't like the idea of being captured on film during a, shall we say, delicate moment?" Katt avoided describing her ordeal of having to dig her own grave. The psychopath who'd drugged and kidnapped her would never see the outside of prison, but that wouldn't make the nightmares go away.

It wasn't so much the question, but the way the assistant asked that drew Abby's attention. Additional questions probed Katt's knowledge and competency in her field. Types of preferred cameras, special lenses, infrared, and long-range mics fleshed out the in-depth curiosity.

The slight warmth derived from her drink faded into a light buzzing in Abby's head. She'd never suspected Mitzie of anything more than being intensely curious. The fact Linda picked up the trail of questions after returning to the table led to the conclusion they probably had many late-night conversations about narrow escapes and imagined scenarios. *Living vicariously through others.*

Paranoia was a bitch.

Abby gasped with the recognition of a tall slim woman entering through the front door and making her way toward a side table. Karma took form as Charlotte Nickerson.

Their gazes locked before a predatory smile overtook the newcomer's face. A few steps in a new direction lent little time to brace for impact. Abby steadied her nerves, remembering she held the upper hand—and Royden's engagement ring.

"Well, hello. Abby is it? I'm surprised to see you here, alone." An exaggerated show of looking around defined her mockery.

"She's not alone. She's with friends. And you are?" Steel tipped Katt's tone.

"I'm Charlee Nickerson. It seems Abby and I have a mutual friend."

"What do you want Charlotte." From conversations with Royden, Abby knew the woman detested her first name.

"He will come back to me, you know. Eventually, he always does. Can't help himself." She sighed, as if burdened knowing the future.

"Odd, since he proposed to Abby." Lexi swiveled to the side. "You really should put the ring on your finger, Abs. It'll help keep away the riffraff."

It was Charlotte's turn to inhale quickly as crimson spread up her neck. "It's not over, yet. He will be mine." Turning on her heel, Charlee stalked out.

Abby was drained, physically and emotionally. "Guys, I think I just want to go home."

Chapter Sixteen

Royden's frustration lingered like a possessive ex-lover, stalking his every move, and rearing up at random times to interrupt his thoughts. Understanding Abby's need for independence forced him to straddle the line between encouraging her quest for equanimity and keeping her safe. Her brothers wanted to smother her at every turn.

The prior evening, he'd seen his ex enter the pub and cussed a bloody blue streak. Like Billy and Luc McAllister, he also kept watch on the patrons coming and going, waiting to assist the undercover officers inside should there be a need.

Since he was alone in his car and the McAllisters had parked up the street, he spent twenty minutes answering angry text messages. The family networked better than any group he'd ever seen. With Lexi and Katt's hacking skills, the brothers would know as much or more about Charlee than he did.

Again, complete transparency involved many explanations; yes, he and Charlee use to frequent the bar, and no, he had no idea she'd show up at that time. According to the undercover officer, the situation had looked tense for a few minutes.

To make matters worse, he'd arrived home minutes before Abby walked in the door, completely drained. She wouldn't talk about her evening but did accept his embrace to hold her throughout the night.

Their morning routine had been quiet and subdued after she insisted on spending the night in her apartment tonight. It wasn't clear whether the invitation extended to him or not. Her insistence that he needed alone time to think things through held no merit.

Throughout the day, his partner, Billy McAllister, had drilled him with questions, defining his intentions, and offering thinly veiled threats.

By the time he and Abby arrived at her apartment after work, the wedge between them had solidified. He was drowning in uncertainty.

Doubt and hesitation tightened the smile that didn't reached her eyes. If he couldn't penetrate the shields she continued to strengthen, their marriage was doomed before they spoke their vows.

The doorbell rung before he could hang up his jacket.

Opening the door, he sighed, standing back for the first of many visitors.

"Leave it to the only female sibling to not have food for a family meeting," Lucas complained as he strode to the large easy chair and pulled Megan to sit on his lap. They rest of the crew entered with the expectation of dinner, or at least plenty of snacks.

"Guys, in case you haven't noticed—Abby and I have been a tad busy." Royden understood her brothers' displaced irritation.

"Yeah, you need more furniture, too, half-pint. Your apartment is crowded as hell." Caden sat with Kaylee in his lap at one end of the sofa.

The rest of the McAllisters doubled with their other halves to find seating in the moderate-sized space. Lexi and Katt had already booted up their laptops as they perched on Ethan and Matt's thighs.

"Listen. I like this place. It's comfortable and secure. Plus, I have a wonderful view." Abby set a tray of chips and finger foods on the coffee table and took a seat beside Royden.

Royden cleared his throat before anyone could point out the flaws in the security Abby found comforting. He'd already elaborated on each one. As much as he wanted her living in his home, he wouldn't use fear as coercion. At times, it appeared to take all her self-control to maintain the window dressing of serenity.

In turn, each brother had hounded him, wanting to know how he intended to fix the situation. Unlike them, he refused to bulldoze through her emotions. It wouldn't work for the long run.

"Now that we're all here," Abby began, "Let's go over what we've got so far."

I hear Theodore Credlin offered you a job," Matt murmured, then rubbed Kathryn's shoulders when she gave him a dirty look.

"Girls..." Abby's gaze bounced between Lexi, Katt, and Royden, her mouth thinning and a muscle ticking at the corner of her eye.

"Sweetheart, you know you can't keep secrets from these guys for long." Royden reached for her hand, grateful when she didn't pull back.

Her penchant for erupting like a volcano became more prominent when family members skirted the law. It was times like the present when his calm assurance helped the most.

"Oh, hell." Kathryn sucked in a sharp breath, leaning back against Matt. "Lexi, pull up Phyllis Rollison in connection with Ohio state police." Continued tapping at her keyboard didn't slow as Matt leaned around to view her screen.

"What?" Abby's patience had shortened. They were all familiar with Kathryn and Lexi's disregard for any and all electronic barriers, their skills commensurate with their curiosity. The fact they both used gathered information wisely, if not legally, was one of the reasons she'd accepted each.

"What the hell did you find? Wait, if it's obtained illegally, I don't want to know. Roy?"

As a psychologist and working detective, he understood her position and rationalized the usage of information.

"It's okay to see, Abby." He read the screen that had been swiveled around. "This is on the news. It says Phyllis Rollison and her daughter were involved in a motor vehicle accident while traveling east on I-70 outside Columbus. Both were killed."

Abby covered her mouth as if afraid of what she might say. When Royden stood and pulled her into his arms, she went willingly. After a few deep breaths, she swiped a bottle of water from the coffee table. Her hands still trembled.

She accepted Royden's motion to sit beside him and his arm around her shoulders.

"Oh, god. They were heading to Delaware to be near her family. She wanted a new start." Abby blurted out the truth.

"I'll get the reports—" Billy retrieved his phone to take notes.

"Don't bother. They're being distributed to each of your work computers now." Lexi didn't look up from her keyboard, engrossed in her endeavor.

"Looks like Credlin just moved to the top of the suspect list," Kaylee surmised.

"He's too wealthy to get his hands dirty." Katt grimaced at her screen but continued to work.

"We'll look further into his records." Lucas arched a brow at Lexi, a silent signal to send him *all* her information. As a private investigator, he had little compunction about splitting hairs, or laws.

Royden's first month of partnership with a McAllister equaled a cold shower. Like the rest of the family, Billy held ironclad beliefs in right and wrong. As long as no one was hurt in the process, some laws became more akin to guidelines.

"Have the reports come back on the dirt sample from Abby's office?" Caden asked.

"Preliminary shows traces of sphagnum peat moss along with what they think is a fertilizer used in growing orchids." Billy murmured as he toyed with the seam of Remie's jeans. Side by side, they formed an impervious shield against any that would consider pitting one against the other. When apart, they remained equally strong.

It was the kind of relationship Royden enjoyed with Abby. Despite her insecurity stemming from recent events, she'd stand firm in her commitment to their relationship. The fact she wanted to protect him endeared her all the more. He'd spend every available minute erasing the threat of Charlee from Abby's mind. "Plenty of people raise orchids as house plants. You can buy the growing medium at any big box store."

"Not this stuff. The lab can't match it to a brand," Lexi refuted. "I'll bet it's expensive as hell."

"Uh, we know someone who has a large greenhouse full of them. Our CEO buddy is a busy man. He's producing hybrid flowers and registering them with the Royal Horticultural Society." Lexi leaned to the side and pointed to her screen for Ethan to see.

"True, but look, Lexi. He employs quite a few workers. Even if you could pin the sample to that location, there're too many possibilities. Any one of his employees would carry the dirt on their boots or sneakers." Katt's shoulders slumped with the finding.

"Do *not* hack private files, ladies. Please?" Abby covered her face with one hand as if to wipe away the knowledge of illegal searches.

"The orchid information is on his webpage. Look for yourself." Katt shrugged a shoulder but kept typing, ignoring the obvious illegal search into Credlin's personal files.

"The techs didn't come up with anything else in their search of Abby's office," Ethan added.

"Nor was anything else discovered in the caverns." Billy glanced to Lucas. "Did you or Caden find anything else about the gang, Blood Eagles?"

"The rapist, Emilio, is backed by money. A good bit of it. The gang leader vows that Burn's advance on Abby wasn't sanctioned and claimed her a victim of opportunity." Caden's apologetic glance toward his sister spoke volumes. His brief explanation spawned a deeper discussion of future approaches to the gang and the risks in doing so. "Yet they knew about her and her ties to the victim."

"He also assured us that he'll deal with the splinter group formed over this legal issue," Lucas added. "On the other hand, they do have access to the money needed to pursue whatever ends desired. Rumors have it their drug trade is thriving."

"What about Carrigan? His trial isn't for another two months, but I imagine our twisted psycho is anxious to get out of jail. He could have enlisted the help of his brother or any number of friends." Abby's tension took shape in fingers thrumming on her knee. "After failing to frame Billy and kidnapping me, the psychotic genius has plenty of motive to end any and all McAllisters."

"I checked on the brother, Zachery. He said he never left home over the weekend. He has no alibi, but I can't prove him a liar." Matt sifted his fingers through his better half's long hair, an unconscious affirmation of her help.

"Isn't that the hand you wipe with?" Katt leaned forward and frowned. Guffaws erupting around the room lessened the tense atmosphere.

"How about Brad? He was pretty pissed off with the fact the CEO both called you and spoke with Salsman, your boss." Ethan's question, directed at Abby, included the nonverbal request for information from Lexi and Katt, who both went at their keyboards with a new zeal.

"Oooh, wow. I don't see purchases for any type of gardening supplies, but he's really into some heavy shit..." Katt's mouth twisted into a semblance of having sucked on a lemon. "Didn't see this earlier." Tilting her head to the side, she added, "I don't think I could manage that position."

Behind her, Matt covered his mouth on a choking cough. "Damn. Never saw that one before either. How'd you get to his personal video—never mind."

"Stop! Do not tell me anything you've found through hacking. I don't want to know." As if confirming her neutral ground, Abby turned to Royden. "See what I have to put up with?" Curiosity mixed with desperation in her silent plea to sort the issue.

"Hey, Katt, catch this link back to Credlin. Did you see his—playroom?" Lexi asked, excitement in her voice belying her dropped jaw and heavy frown.

"Twisted millionaire. People think because they lock videos behind closed doors, no one can gain access or view them on their computer. The dumb shit thinks his firewalls protect all. Guess that's what happens when you have more money than brains." Katt leaned to the side, supported by her boyfriend's strong hand. "How do they do that, anyway?"

"Bet he wouldn't want that made public." Ethan chuckled over Lexi's shoulder.

"Enough! Ethan, you're supposed to be the voice of reason for her." Abby took a deep breath. "I do have a thought, however. Since we're not any closer to narrowing down our list, I could meet with Credlin under the pretense of discussing terms of employment and maybe even feed what he tells me to Brad, my supervising attorney, who's asked me out to dinner a hundred times."

"No." Royden's emphatic declaration echoed among her brothers. "It was bad enough when you had a girls' night out. I can't take any more."

"Royden, she was fine Monday night. The guy who tried to pick her up—turns out he works for Parks and Recreation." Katt's matter-of-fact explanation continued. "He's got a place on Wharf Road. Considers himself a survivalist and is prepared to live off the grid for years. He just doesn't seem the type looking for that kind of trouble."

"And you learned all that during a couple of dances?" Abby arched a brow at her friend.

"Well, that and his wallet might have accidentally slipped out of his back pocket."

"Wait, what? You danced with a suspect? What the hell? You were supposed to stick with Abby and observe." Thunderclouds appeared less ominous than Matt's expression.

"Lexi was with Abby while I checked out the *potential* suspect. I was fine, Matt. I *am* a licensed private investigator, remember?" Katt's answer did nothing to placate her mate's ire.

"Besides, if we don't find the creep who's after her, she's gonna keep putting herself out there. It's what any of us would do." Lexi's explanation stirred a round of grumbles from all present.

Subsequent bickering halted with Royden's sharp whistle. "Enough. This isn't helping." A deep breath strengthened his resolve. "First, Abby, you are not *putting yourself out there* anymore. I know you need breathing room and feel like your brothers are smothering you, but they love you. We all do."

Royden paused a second to let his words sink in. "Second, you have to know that any of us would go to any lengths to end this nightmare and see you safe. We all want to move forward in our lives, but we have to deal with this situation." His next proclamation would receive the most resistance. "We cannot continue to take unnecessary risks as we have been." He'd been as patient as possible, but the time had come that his heart's desire understood the difference between testing limits and foolish, dangerous behavior. "Staying in this apartment is one of them." What she'd considered security was a flimsy excuse to prove her courage.

"I need a night in my apartment to think things through."

"No, you don't. You can come to my place." Matt's firm tone left no room for argument. As the oldest, he'd always drawn the line when it came to sibling safety.

Abby groaned when Royden remained quiet. He wanted her in his home for all the right reasons, yet she still balked. He realized losing her independence felt too much like giving in. She was a fighter.

Either of her brothers would gladly accept responsibility for her safety, but she wasn't their responsibility to accept.

Selfish as it might be, he'd rather she argue and hold her eldest brother at arm's length than himself. There was a time to speak up and a time to let the cards fall where they may. He'd long understood the family dynamics and chose the timing of his battles.

Matt continued, unfazed. "Failure to move will result in some very unpleasant circumstances. I'm sure there are building code violations that could be found, perhaps some type of hazard?" A glance in Lexi and Katt's direction received affirmative nods. "Not only that, but we could each make it our business to make our presence known. I think folks would get mighty nervous if they thought they were living in the middle of a hot zone. Wouldn't you?"

"Damn it, Matt. This isn't fair."

"Life isn't fair, half-pint. Get used to it. The question remains, which one of us are you going to stay with?" Matt arched a brow and waited.

Abby twisted in her seat, tears brimming her eyes. "Sometimes I hate coming from a large family."

Royden accepted the hand she held out.

"I'll spend tonight here to pack some things. I'll be at Royden's house tomorrow. Okay?"

He didn't mind another stakeout. He'd done many over the years though never with a loved one. "Sounds good, sweetheart." It wasn't the way he wanted her to come to him, but safety trumped everything else.

Chapter Seventeen

Since Royden's reluctant goodbye kiss, Abby muted her apprehension by perusing the online TV guide. She wasn't in the mood for a thriller, romance, or even the documentaries she and Royden usually enjoyed. Nothing sparked her interest.

Her suitcases were packed and ready to go.

Alone and in the dark except for the screen's white noise, she'd sat on the couch and pondered what other things she'd take with her the next day. If not for her pride, she'd be tucked against Royden's side, sated, and discussing the upcoming weekend plans. She'd argued her point of the second-story apartment's safety, gated community, alarm codes, etc, but in the end realized none of those measures could stop a bullet.

When she'd first seen the complex and amenities, she'd wanted a first-floor unit to take advantage of the space out back. Now, the second floor felt safer, to a point.

Moonlight seeping through the vertical blinds over her slider created thin bars that reminded her of her predicament. The twisted psychopath who'd kidnapped her might be the one in jail, but Abby was the one held hostage. Until she testified and her family found her stalker, she wouldn't be free to continue life on her own terms. Another form of imprisonment.

Claaang.

The strange metallic clink outside diverted her attention to the dining area and balcony beyond. *A killer isn't going to announce his presence.* She wished she had Diego by her side but having to take the dog for a walk after dark held no appeal. At Royden's house, they could let the animal roam, but not around an apartment complex.

Fate threw out pivotal moments on occasion, whether to test a soul for worthiness or challenge a person's courage didn't matter. With no other sound louder than the heartbeat thrumming in her ears, she pushed to her feet and padded to the side of the glass door.

Another jangle of something solid, metal striking metal, forced a small whimper from her throat. *The balcony's railing is wrought iron. But what loose item could strike it?*

Excess salivation and the lump sliding up her throat denied the ability to clear her airway. Shaking fingers halted midway to the vertical barrier hindering her view. It galled the crap out of her she couldn't force her hand to open the door. *I'm on the second floor for Christ's sake.*

Cautiously, she peered around the edge of the vinyl slat nearest the frame and wondered if someone waited to gain her attention, gun in hand. She could only view a small section of the balcony.

All the excuses given to Royden and family for not leaving with them left a bitter taste in her mouth. After witnessing Charlee's determination in the bar, Abby was determined to give Royden time to think, to be sure of what and whom he wanted.

Intermittent cloud cover muffled nature's highlighting the small yard behind her unit. Several maple trees spread their bare branches, one of which ended within arm's reach of her balcony. A pinecone smothered in peanut butter and birdseed dangled from the thick limb.

She could make out patches of manicured lawn and the twenty-yard buffer of scrub grass lining the woods. A sturdy wrought iron fence divided the taller grass from the property line.

During summer, the large trees offered shade when she'd sat on her balcony and pondered the day's events over a drink or enjoyed an evening breeze as it swept away her stress.

In the next instant, oxygen came in breathy pants, her mind thrown back into an eight-by-twelve dirt-floored prison. She briefly closed her eyes against the visual assault. Her imagination picked up the slack and supplied the scratching noises she'd heard but never pinpointed in the deep darkness. Covering her ears didn't help.

Minutes passed as her eyes adjusted to the dark exterior environment. Instincts urged her to back away, yet an iron will planted her feet solidly on the hardwood. Her heart thumped louder, triple time to the diminishing but ominous metal against metal peal. She couldn't see anything that would make a metallic noise.

Wind whistled under the eaves yet didn't negate the intermittent crash of something she couldn't define. The apartment's window shutters were fixed, balcony furniture too heavy for less than gale winds, and the complex had no teenagers who'd pull mean pranks.

Perspiration moistened the skin between her shoulder blades and slicked her palms. Royden's advice concerning instincts springing from subconscious thoughts to offer a form of protection came to mind. To her, retreat equaled cowardice.

Just as she pulled her finger away from the blind and turned away, her peripheral vision picked up moving shadows. Was that a person climbing over the fence and into the obscurity beyond or moving shadows? Distance and low light prevented her from seeing more clearly. If she called Roy or her brothers, they'd cart her off, regardless of the late hour.

Safety trumped doubt.

Two steps back then into the kitchen added a small layer of security. Another glass of wine while calling Royden sounded like a reasonable buffer in contemplating what she'd say.

She'd checked the lock on the slider earlier and had made sure the security stick remained wedged in place. Since those measures wouldn't stop a bullet, she also pulled the outer sliding curtain closed.

Better to imagine an intruder returning than to see him on your doorstep.

"You're getting spooky girl. It's high time you got a dog." *Once I move to Royden's house...* Her brother Matt talked about a litter of shepherds bred by one of his friends. Though training a puppy would be difficult with her schedule, she had plenty of family to help.

Another clink outside convinced her the wine could wait. With her luck, the family would come in with guns drawn only to find the breeze had tangled the upper balcony's wind chimes and a piece had fallen off, tangling on her railing.

The cell phone slipped from her grasp and slid back to the quartz countertop with the first somber notes of classical music drifting into her space. The melody resonated with a dark memory she couldn't place. Turning her head to the side, she tried to pinpoint the source.

Walls separating the residences held a fair amount of insulation, yet a certain clarity indicated the music flowed from within her space as opposed to an adjoining unit. None of her neighbors listened to that genre, and the dark nature of the piece plucked at her nerves.

Like the cunning subtext of a document, muffled scratching underlay the notes with a discordance well remembered. *Oh god, scurrying rats.*

She'd been alone for two hours and already imagined all manner of scenarios ending in death. Picking up her cell, she started to call Royden, the same fear that prevented her from opening the slider kept her feet glued to the floor.

None in her family had ever suffered the challenges of mental illness. Abby wouldn't be the first. She, the only female child, closeted and protected all her life by testosterone-driven brothers.

No tangible evidence explained the increase in her heart rate or the perspiration dotting her upper lip other than the paranoia of a scared woman.

False bravado had molded into an invisible shield and served her well during the few months since her kidnapping. She'd done everything she could to ward off the terror hovering ever closer around her aura. A spirit inundated with fear accomplished nothing.

Before she could push the speed dial known to bring peace of mind, the doorbell rang.

The metallic tinkling had stopped.

The music stopped.

I'm losing my mind. Either that or my imagination has a bitchy sense of karma.

Hesitant steps shuffling across hardwood floors carried her to the front door. Peeking through the peephole, she saw Lexi's smile. Her friend gestured to the half-gallon of her favorite ice cream in her other hand.

At least part of the evening would be good. She opened the door, not expecting Hoover to bound inside. "C'mon on in. Um, but—"

"She's wearing her vest. Service dogs can go about anywhere." Lexi followed her dog to the kitchen. The established routine of visiting included treats of one kind or another. The small baggie pulled from her jacket pocket held homemade chewy biscuits. "How do you ask?"

Hoover dropped her shoulders and head to the ground and wiggled her butt at the same time. In the next instant, she sat and held one paw up. Lexi offered the expected reward then deposited her backpack on the kitchen table.

"How'd you know I needed this tonight?" Abby started to pull two bowls from the cupboard. "Just spoons, tonight?"

"Just spoons. And I didn't know, but *I* needed it. Katt was gonna come too but Matt's still pissed at her for dancing with a *potential* suspect." Lexi tilted her head side to side then smiled.

"She carries a stun gun... I know she had it Monday night—she wouldn't have come without it." Abby thought about the times in high school when she'd gone out with a new guy. Her brothers were present every time to see her off. Dates had never needed further warning. It made her wonder what Katt's teenage years had been like.

"Yeah, but you know how he is. A male version of a mother hen on steroids. I brought some movies if you're interested." Lexi took a spoon from Abby and headed for the sofa.

As soon as the girls settled, Hoover plunked her butt down between them and whined.

"Hoover, Abby has nice furniture. You don't need to be shedding all over it."

"It's okay. Didn't you tell me every hair is a magical fiber of love?" No sooner had Abby patted the seat once, the dog hopped up and settled between them, her head on Abby's thigh.

Two hours passed in comfort and good company with a furry companion by her side, cementing Abby's intention to get a puppy.

When movie credits scrolled down the screen and the ice cream carton was empty, Lexi stood and stretched. "Thanks for having me over. I needed a quiet evening."

"Thank you for the company. *I* needed it." She gave Hoover's head a final pat before standing. "Come again, any time."

Instead of heading to the kitchen to retrieve her backpack, Lexi moved to the door. "Hoover needs to go out. I'll be right back."

"Sure. The gate to the dog area is unlocked. And I'm sure at least Ethan is out there by now, right?"

Lexi grinned and shrugged a shoulder.

Abby smiled as the two left. Dog and hacker were as much a part of the other as Lexi was to Ethan.

If not for college and then law school, she'd have a dog, too. Now, with nothing holding her back, it was time.

When the duo returned, a small smile played about Lexi's mouth. "She's good for the night. I'll see you tomorrow."

"Wait, you forgot your backpack."

Lexi stood by the front door. No, I didn't. You'll need to give her a treat in the morning. There's a baggie of her raw food I stuck in the fridge. Make sure she doesn't get too many goodies, she's kind of a pig."

Abby's gasp filled the now-empty room, sans one mixed-breed shepherd. *Damn. I didn't see that coming.*

"Well, girl. It looks like it's you and me tonight."

She'd thought about the strange music but hadn't heard it since Lexi's arrival. When she'd turned off the television, all remained quiet.

Intuition dictated she should've recognized the piece, yet somehow its significance escaped her. A walk around the open area resulted in believing the music came from the unit above.

In preparing for bed, she realized the dog's presence lifted not only the pall of doom but lightened her spirit. No wonder all her brothers had at least one. She remembered Lexi's comment that Ethan could always find her if he knew Hoover's whereabouts. The two were inseparable.

After a single pat of the mattress, Hoover hopped on the bed and curled by her feet. Outside, the wind had eased, but Abby was still grateful for the dog's presence.

The curtain of sleep had just pulled her under its comforting mantle when the jarring notes of a piano sent the shepherd to barking. A push of a knob flooded the room with light, in time to see Hoover racing for the living room. The soft but discordant cacophony forced her to the nightstand in search of pepper spray.

Chapter Eighteen

The muffled music seemed to originate from the corner of her room by the door, yet no device marred the flat expanse.

An older couple occupied the apartment above and rarely made much noise, except when their grandchildren visited. Hoover returned, still barking.

A mental picture of hanging from the ceiling by her fingernails came to mind. Following the canine back to the living room, Abby gripped her canister of pepper spray tight. Still, she detected no tangible threat. The curtains in front of the slider didn't move, nor did any lingering shadows after switching on the living room light.

Her canine companion finally settled on a direction to focus her ire. Bouncing from one foot to the other in front of the sliding door didn't define the nature of the danger, but it seemed unlikely the dog sensed a deer or wild animal. Her keen sense of hearing or smell detected some type of menace.

Terror coated Abby's body with perspiration.

"What is it, girl?"

Abby had learned well the hard lessons concerning pride and danger. Snagging her cell from the table, she hit the speed dial.

Royden answered before the end of the first ring. "On my way. What's going on?"

"I-I'm not sure," Abby shouted to be heard over the dog barking. Now that she was in the kitchen, she heard a faint clinking noise outside the slider. Though she didn't have perfect pitch, she distinguished the sound as lighter, higher in tone.

Vomit rose to the back of her mouth. To experience terror when alone encompassed a different realm of reality than when Royden stood by her side holding a gun. If not for Hoover, she might have succumbed to her fear.

"I'm at your door, Abs. Coming in."

She hadn't heard the clicks of the knob, but in the next instant, Royden rushed inside, his gaze searching for a threat before coming to rest on Abby's face.

He secured the door and several heartbeats after securing the apartment, tugged her in his arms for a brief hug while listening to her explanation. "Ethan and Billy will be here shortly."

"If someone were to get inside, Hoover would have their neck between her jaws."

"I know. But I still want to have a look around outside."

Time fragmented into different scenarios where imaginary demons melted from the walls, taking shape and form to slaughter the occupants. Somewhere between the time Royden arrived and when he left to clear her rooms, the music had stopped.

If she hadn't been afraid of sounding insane, she would've told him about the soft laughter mocking her thoughts. When she'd pivoted to look behind her, no visible threat had appeared. It hadn't originated from her head after a couple glasses of wine with dinner.

Royden held her loosely as if afraid of spooking a defensive reaction. His expression equated to someone handling a wild animal on the verge of attack.

"I didn't imagine the music."

"I heard it when I first arrived."

"I didn't imagine the knocking outside the slider, either."

"What? Why didn't you tell me right away?" He took her by the elbow and led her to stand beside the refrigerator, a shield between her and the glass partition. "Stay."

If she hadn't been terrified, she would've barked. As it was, Hoover sat by her side and kept her calm. Intermittent growls depicted the dog's ongoing displeasure at something outside.

Royden pulled back the curtain and vertical slats, then peered out on the small balcony while talking on his cell. His tone held none of the reassuring warmth in dealing with her. Anger tinged the conversation even as he described the circumstances and directed her brothers to check the area surrounding her unit.

"Thanks, Billy. I assume you'll call—"

A slight pause.

"Thanks. I'll wait with Abby until backup arrives. I don't want to leave her alone."

The concern in his gaze melted her heart. He wasn't just her anchor in a whirling vortex of chaos. No, he existed as the solid base, as half of the foundation on which she stood.

Minutes later, she heard the squeal of tires and car doors slamming outside. Her brothers had arrived en masse.

Royden ushered them in, each McAllister angrier than the one before. They'd need to see her before searching the area.

"I'm fine, guys. Just a little spooked." It was going to be a sleepless night.

"Yeah, but you know we had to see for ourselves, half-pint." Matt ruffled her hair before heading out.

Their search didn't take long. Royden kept up a steady stream of dialogue while they waited. Matt was the last to return, his dog Damien by his side.

"I didn't find anything unusual out there tonight, but Damien and I will come back tomorrow and take another look." At hearing his name, the dog in question whined, as if eager for activity.

"Sorry to pull you guys out here so late. I feel like a fainting lily."

"You're anything but that, Abs." Royden's arm circled her waist and snugged her tighter to his side. "I heard the piano music when I first arrived."

"Music?" Matt and Caden asked simultaneously.

"Yeah, some kind of morbid, classical shit," Royden muttered. "We need to do a thorough sweep of the apartment. It had a weird muffled quality, but not like it was coming through walls. Source is probably near the bedroom."

"Ethan and Billy are checking with the neighbors on either side and the floor above and below this apartment." Matt turned at the sound of the front door opening, a question written in the arch of his brow.

Lucas shook his head en route to the kitchen, his frustration evident. "What'cha got to eat around here?"

"Not much, I'm afraid." Abby nudged him out of the way to start a pot of coffee. It was one thing she could make that everyone appreciated.

"Abby, you said it sounded like metal clinking against metal?" Royden shoved the window coverings back and opened the slider.

"Maybe some kids were chucking small stones, but I don't see anything other than the chairs you keep out there." Matt stepped out behind Royden.

"I didn't open the curtain but an inch or so." Abby retrieved mugs and set them on the countertop by the pot.

"I'm glad you're up on the second floor. Access to your balcony—" Matt's stream of conversation halted on a sudden inhale.

"What?" Abby pushed Lucas aside to see. The click of the light switch beside the door resounded in her head. She didn't need more fodder for nightmares.

Dangling from the balcony above and to the side, a shovel twirled in the breeze at the end of a thick piece of nylon rope. The length of the return disappeared in the branches of the nearby tree.

"Someone tied this to the handle, then managed to throw the end up and over the upper balcony before tying it off on a branch." Matt clicked his flashlight on and leaned over the balcony. "Which is why we didn't see anything from below."

The rounded blade of the tool bore evidence of its trade. Red clay clung to the edges. It appeared to be fresh.

Abby took an involuntary step to the side and stumbled over something near the wall. On closer examination, she picked up the object. "Oh, hell."

"What is it?" Royden turned her to the side. "Sonofabitch."

The shudder roaring up her spine carried a chill that reminded her of the underground prison. A voiceless plea screamed through her skull. "Royden?"

Matt pulled a nitrile glove from his pocket and took the stethoscope. "Billy, get this to the lab."

Dark crimson gleamed on the bell and covered the diaphragm. Grim expressions indicated the unanimous concern for a certain orthopedic doctor's well-being.

"I didn't—"

"We know, Abs. We know." Royden turned her into his arms, sliding a hand up her back and cupping her head against his chest.

"It's him. It's Zachery, Dr. Carrigan's brother. Has to be."

"A definite possibility." Royden brushed a kiss across the crown of her head as Lucas and Matt examined the shovel. "If it is, we'll get him. You're safe."

Tears brimmed her eyes at the hoarseness of his voice. If he continued to stand between her and danger, he'd die.

"He'll kill you to get to me."

"Nobody's going to die—at least not one of us." It was the closest he'd ever come to declaring intent to break any law to protect her.

Just like my brothers, he intends to kill the stalker.

Royden led her to the living room and sat with her on the sofa. The inane realization that she wore pajamas instead of a slinky nightgown registered as one of those facts reflected upon when avoiding a difficult situation.

He didn't speak, didn't urge her to open up, but merely sat with his arm around her shoulder. A patient man that knew how to make his quarry spill their guts without uttering a word. She'd teased him about it being a shrink thing, but detective work had honed the skill to a fine art.

"He's referencing the basement cell, isn't he? He wants me to remember." Tears streamed down her cheeks.

As if trying to provide their own form of comfort, Damien and Hoover padded to her side. Hoover laid her furry head in Abby's lap while Damien watched expectantly then whined. The shepherds' soft fur sifting through her fingers yielded a calming effect.

"It could well be but remember this. You escaped that hellhole and defeated him in the end."

"I know. I kept my wits about me and bided my time." Though she'd given the outline of what had happened after her kidnapping, she'd never revisited the horror, fear, and sheer panic that had comprised her every waking moment of captivity. Two days in complete darkness had left its stamp on her psyche and her heart.

"You made a plan and saw it through." Royden traced small circles between her shoulder blades.

"I've told you and everyone else what happened down there."

"Yes. Yes, you did. And you know that at the very least, he's going to be in prison for the rest of his life. He'll never get to you again."

Royden was great at reiterating facts she either knew or had surmised prior. It was his method of staying with the subject matter, in the moment, and drawing her out when he wanted her to talk specifics. She'd become equally adept at changing the subject.

"Someone is working on his behalf. Or, it's someone who's done his homework and wants to mimic what he did to me."

"And why do you think someone would copy his MO?" The brush of his mouth across the crown of her head reminded her how small she was, yet cherished.

The swirl of his fingertips along her neck grounded her in a way nothing else could, reminding her he remained by her side with every step she took.

"To bring me back to my worst fear? Yet how could he know I haven't suffered a bigger trauma in my life?"

"Maybe he has inside information."

"I've not spoken about that time with anyone else. I don't talk about personal information of that nature to anyone, not even to family."

"Which is why..." He waited for her to finish.

"Which is why it stays bottled up, and I compensate with daredevil activities." She'd known all along that the small power-packed revelation was something he'd been waiting to hear.

"I believe that's right." Again, he said next to nothing and waited.

"I thought I was going to die down there. That you nor my brothers would ever find my body." A small sob escaped, led to a choked cough, then stormed the floodgates holding her emotions in check.

"But you didn't give in to fear. You held it together, formulated a plan, and carried it through. You kept your head in the worst possible situation and survived hell. Not everyone can say that."

"I didn't crumble." It was the first time she'd realized and *felt* the truth of the matter. The knowledge cleared the path for other flashbacks to surface, things she'd forgotten or suppressed.

A shudder forced her entire body to twitch.

"What?"

"I remember spiders. I hate spiders."

"What else?"

"I heard rats, scratching and squeaking. It occurred to me that if I'd stayed down there long enough, I could've befriended them, something I read about in old-world prisons."

"You're not the only one with an aversion to them." He referenced Lexi's experience with a deranged psychopath.

Abby described the finer details of her captivity while Royden continued to offer support, both emotional and through his soft touch. So lost in thought, she hadn't noticed her siblings standing at the edge of the kitchen, listening to every word spoken.

The pain etched in their expressions mirrored that on Royden's face. "I didn't mean to make you feel bad, guys."

Royden helped her up, understanding her need to comfort the men who felt responsible for her kidnapping.

"Matt, Lucas, you know it was my own fault. I was the one who left the courthouse without an escort. I got myself into that mess." Anger forced the words out with more venom than intended.

"And you got yourself out of it, too," Royden reminded her.

"Jesus, half-pint. You're my baby sister." Matt held his arms wide, needing the affirmation as much he did.

"You have to stop feeling responsible for us all, especially me. It's time you set yourself free to live your own life, on your own terms."

"I look forward to the day Matt cuts loose," Royden murmured, a cocky grin tilting one side of his mouth.

She smiled when the rest of them made it a group hug.

"Does this mean you're going to stop doing all the crazy shit, now?" Lucas brushed the crown of her head with a kiss.

"I suppose so... but I'd really thought about going skydiving. It's one fear I haven't conquered. Mitzie says her brother's in this club—"

"No." From behind, Royden's emphatic tone set a limit he wouldn't cross. "I draw the line at jumping out of a perfectly functioning airplane."

"So, you'd rather I take up knitting? Perhaps become a card sharp?"

"I don't want to spend my spare time pulling you out of casinos, either. Thanks, but no." Matt ruffled her hair and stepped back.

"Then how about helping me find a dog. I want a puppy."

"That's the most sensible thing I've heard you say in months." Matt's smile reversed direction and forewarned of an unpleasant conversation ahead.

"I know. I know. I can't stay here, tonight. Believe me, after this, I don't want to." Her questioning glance to Royden elicited a sympathetic smile. "My things are packed."

Ethan and Billy returned, each shaking their head to the unasked question.

"It seems my stalker is trying to increase the fear factor before striking. He's playing with me."

"Which brings me back to the music. Did you recognize the piece, Abby? It sounded like someone took it and put it through a virtual blender." Royden searched the upper corners of the living room then headed toward her bedroom.

"No, but while held captive, the asswipe had a speaker in the upper corner of my cell. Several times, I thought I heard music, but I was drugged at the time and could have been hallucinating. It's hard to say."

"Damn." From the bedroom, Royden's exclamation morphed into a string of curses.

Lucas pulled Abby aside as Matt strode toward the source of Royden's anger. His epithets soon filled the apartment.

"No, Abby. Let Royden and Matt handle it," Luc murmured.

"I want to see, dammit."

Royden reappeared in the living room holding a small metal device covered with a thin layer of fabric. "Someone's been inside your apartment, Abs."

"That's how they piped music in my bedroom? Where was it hidden?"

"Behind the grate in the wall vent."

"Sonofabitch. The prick was in my home!"

Chapter Nineteen

As much as Royden wanted Abby in his home, this wasn't the scenario he'd foreseen. Lines bracketed her eyes and mouth, the strain of uprooting her entire existence weighing on her shoulders. The emotional toll of their discussion had deepened her furrowed brow.

She needed to get it out. Just because he understood the path of emotional healing didn't mean he could force her to walk it. Time was a fickle master, taking a victim back to relive their trauma one day, then rocketing them forward into the future on the next.

He'd noted the physical responses to stress in patients during his schooling and training days, which combined to flesh out and guide him through their horrors. Each case left scars on his psyche as they would have with any reasonably sane human. Abby's though, took pain to a whole new level.

"I know you and my brothers have taken extra security measures."

The stethoscope found on Abby's balcony surely belonged to Charlee, yet neither he nor Abby opened that tangled web. He hadn't heard from Ethan, who'd gone to check on the doctor. No news didn't equate to good news.

"Yes, and I'll explain them after we're settled."

"I don't think I'm gonna sleep tonight. That music... despite the obvious attempt to mangle the piece, there was something about it." She sighed as she set down the bag of perishables taken from her fridge and slid the backpack with Hoover's supplies off her shoulder. Mindless tasks of putting them away would sort her thoughts. "I can't put my finger on it."

"We could sit up for a while, watch a movie, play some cards, whatever." After setting her suitcase down, he took her jacket and hung it in the hall closet.

Hoover ambled to the kitchen as Abby opened the fridge "Actually, I think I'll finish this, get Hoover some water, and go to bed. I need to close my eyes even if I can't sleep." Putting thought to action, she filled the dog's water bowl and set it on the floor.

Royden felt her need for contact, to be held secure and know nothing would bring her harm. He'd go to any length to help her regain her former grip on life.

Once settled in bed and under the covers, she turned in his arms. "My thoughts keep circling back to that music, Roy."

The warmth of her fingers penetrated his thin t-shirt and brought about the normal physical response. His body was on board with her intention, but he recognized her methods of distraction, her approach to keeping darker memories from surfacing. If he couldn't persuade her to siphon off the recollections a bit at a time, they'd overflow the spillway and drown them both when she buckled under their stress.

"Sweetheart, is this what you really want, right now?" He cupped her cheeks in the dark and felt the first tears sliding over his thumbs.

"Damn it, cowboy. I don't want to remember any more of that shit."

"You're gonna keep it bottled up? Till when?"

"Till it blows my freaking head off."

Tugging her against him stimulated more of a response, his mind unable to quell the physical need. He ignored it.

"I know you want me."

"Abs, I will always want you. So much so that it hurts. I also want you to heal, which is why I'll only hold you tonight. Intimacy is not synonymous with sex."

"I don't think I've ever felt closer to you than I do now."

Relaxing in his arms, she pulled out more details from her dark experience. He'd waited months for her to expel the horrors of her past. As fate would dictate, it would take many times of delving through past horrors to truly defeat them. The catharsis proved a major step in her moving forward with their lives.

MORNING SUN filtering through bedroom blinds found Royden curled around Abby's smaller frame, her back tucked snug against his chest. As usual, her warmth heated him from the inside out and produced the typical morning reaction.

Their mutual need to connect on a deep emotional level transcended the craving for sex. They'd shared a spiritual joining, a bond formed that could withstand a nuclear blast.

During the night, he held her after depleting her reserves of remembered horrors. Then they talked about various things, many inconsequential. The normality of it all reinforced his determination to help her achieve and maintain an even keel.

"Hmm, I can't wait till this weekend when we go look at puppies. I've wanted a dog for a while. Are you sure you don't mind? Lexi said she'd keep him while I'm working."

"I think it's a great idea. I think every house should boast some extra hair on the floor, pup kisses on the windows, and dog toys to trip over going down the stairs." He nuzzled the back of her neck before adding. "Seriously, I do like the idea. I'll make a few calls and see about getting a fence installed."

He hadn't objected when she encouraged Hoover to sleep on the bed and figured his home would soon inherit a pup and all the trials and tribulations of a four-footed kid. Nurturing existed as an integral part of her spirit and he supported the endeavor, happy she decided on a large breed animal.

She didn't voice any objections when he took her to work and advised he'd pick her up at the end of her day. Thinning lips and tightened jaw provided the only visible signs of her frustration.

Without a scheduled court appearance, she had no need to leave the building, which gave him the entire day to work.

No sooner had he driven away from her office building than his partner's ring tone wiped away the warm comfort of Abby's kiss.

"Yeah, Billy. What's up?" The hair on his nape pricked as a shudder washed over him. The pause on the other end of the line didn't bode well.

"Matt and I are over at Abby's place. Meet us around back."

The connection clicked off before Royden could respond. *Damned cryptic McAllisters.*

No one ever accused him of having a lead foot, but enlightenment came with understanding how Matt must've felt for years. Keeping up with five siblings couldn't have been easy. He had trouble with one partner and one woman.

In the complex's lot, he noted the crime scene van taking up two slots. Beside it, the coroner's government vehicle took up another. McAllister work units occupied four more. Matt's overprotective streak didn't warrant the van plus the ME.

A cold chill passed over his body, his heartbeat sluggish.

The coffee from breakfast turned to sludge in his gut. He didn't have to see the approaching horror to know it existed, especially after finding the stethoscope on Abby's balcony. Whatever occurred, they were keeping it quiet over the radio, using phones instead. The media circus would find them soon enough.

Larrick, Ethan's partner, waited against a dark sedan. "Royden, that was quick." A slight southern draw colored his tone.

"What's up? What'd you find?" Royden scanned the quiet street as a matter of habit.

"Follow me. Matt returned with Damien at daybreak to extend his search." Larrick shoved off the vehicle and followed the trampled path hugging the side of the building. His subdued aura and rounded shoulders preempted further questions.

The complex employed a key card system to enter the main structure. Video surveillance at each corner of the six-apartment structure along with another camera center front and center back caught foot traffic coming and going.

If the stalker altered the system, why didn't Lexi pick that up? A subtle conversation in front of the family's hacker would determine if someone compromised surveillance before the department's techs could sift through evidence. Considering the attempts on Abby's life had yielded only one definitive clue proved the killer an intelligent and careful individual. *Everybody makes mistakes at some point.*

"Ethan said you were here when Abby called last night."

"I'd parked at the far edge of the lot. It gave me visual access to the front and along one side. A uniform parked on the other side. Since the back entails such rough terrain, it didn't seem plausible for anyone to come from that angle."

"Well, I doubt the remaining cameras picked up much either. Someone busted the one out back. We found glass on the ground around the pole, from the lens."

"Abby thought the apartment's fence offered a layer of protection." Rounded finials capping the pickets and posts of the wrought iron barrier made it easier for someone to climb over it. The five-foot decorative enclosure wasn't designed to keep out humans.

"She knows better," Larrick murmured. "She's in denial."

After circling to the rear, Royden's gaze fastened to the strip of grass bordering the woods. A large square of yellow crime scene tape cordoned off what was sure to become Royden's newest nightmare.

Opportunistic weeds and various grasses covered the area, lush with spring growth. The emerging vegetation contrasted the small pile of earth beside the hole. Damien sat quietly by the yellow and black barrier.

A tech dusted the handle of the short, metal ground stake that marked off a twelve-foot square area while another worked a grid pattern to cover the interior.

"We're finished with everything but the grave and its contents." The young tech shook her head. "I hate psychotic pricks."

Before stepping over the tape, Royden viewed a tragic scene that would haunt his sleep for months. "Dammit to hell." Further words were lost as he moved away and emptied his stomach.

"We didn't miss this last night. He dug this hole after we left." Matt looked up and gestured Royden to keep his distance. "We've got this one, but we will have more questions and we'll need a statement. Officially, you're off the case until ID is confirmed."

Royden didn't want to approach, knowing in his heart what he'd find. His ex-girlfriend, the woman he'd once thought of as his forever, didn't deserve this fate. Nausea churned his stomach. It took several deep breaths to find his voice. "So that's what the shovel dangling against the balcony indicated. I thought it stated his prediction for Abby, a warning." Royden closed his eyes. *Please no. Don't let this be Charlee.* Yet, he had to know. Neither McAllister tried to stop him.

When he crouched down to examine the grave's occupant, sunlight glittered off a ring sitting on the sternum of the skeleton. "The last time I saw her, she was going into the pub."

To the side, Lucas and his brothers stood in a semi-circle, deep in conversation while the ME examined the evidence.

Rage built inside him at the implication of what Abby could have faced during her terror. He didn't intend for her to find out. It would only shake her confidence. "Damn. He intended to bury her after what? What exactly did he do here? I can't wait to get hold of that dipshit!"

Caden jerked his attention away from his current conversation. "Yeah, this sonofabitch is asking for a piece of lead between his eyes."

Agreement from Ethan, Lucas, and Billy came in the form of nods and murmured confirmation. Matt briefly squeezed his eyes shut before murmuring. "That's not all. Take a look inside." He sidestepped as a photographer took pictures from a different angle.

Dizziness threatened Royden's composure, held by a tenuous grasp of reality. The closer he got, the more descriptive the scene became.

The killer had dug a two-by-six foot grave two feet deep, barely enough to cover a body, but would suffice even with the skull lying next to the victim's chest. A small baggie half-full of sallow yellow liquid sat in a skeletal hand.

Bleached white bones contrasted the soil on which they lay, which was intact except for the head. The killer left a small amount of skin on the skull. From it, a lock of wavy long black hair draped through the skeleton's ribcage.

Deep breaths staved off the round of dry heaves threatening to erupt. Royden kept his gaze on the distant horizon and concentrated on a mental flashback of holding Abby safe and secure in his arms.

When he obtained control over bodily functions, he studied the grave once more. It appeared the excavator had taken great care to make the hole uniform, the sides even and the interior level for the sole occupant.

"Soil's fresh dug." Caden stepped up beside Royden, gesturing to the pile beside the grave.

"Doc—" Matt hunkered down for a closer look. "Is that cinnamon I smell?"

"Yeah, there're a bunch of cinnamon sticks all around the skeleton. The killer took care to tuck them just under the bones, but I think some of the bones have been, well, saturated with cinnamon oil."

"For what reason? What affect?" Matt asked.

"Let me know when you find him. I've seen a lot of shit in the ME's office, but never anything like this."

Matt made it to the edge of the sectioned off area and took a deep breath while Billy and Ethan remained statue still, their faces tinged with green and dotted with sweat.

"Jesus. We have got to nail this asshole quick," Billy growled the words with closed eyes and a hand held to his forehead.

When Royden's sanity retuned, a coldness settled soul deep. He'd never contemplated murder before, but if the killer survived, eventually he'd get Abby, directly or through an intermediary.

"She's not been ravaged by the elements somewhere else then dumped here," the ME explained as he lifted a brow at the photographer.

"Yeah, I got enough. All yours."

"Considering the skull is detached, how do you know the victim is even a female and not a male body with a female head?" Matt tended to be thorough.

"Because of the pelvis, for one thing. I can't say the skull belongs to the body, but I'll tell you one way or another after examination in the lab."

"Front of the line." Matt's request sounded like an order.

"Yes. As an estimate, I'd say he removed all skin, muscle, and organs then boiled the bones, except for the skull."

"Why?" Royden looked to Matt for an answer, a plea to understand chaos.

"Maybe to give a preview of what he intended for Abby." Matt took a deep breath and scrubbed a rough hand over his face.

"If so, he didn't intend to take Abby last night. He knew the shovel would lead us to search the area and find this. He's toying with us." Royden mentally counted to ten, then twenty, then fifty.

Nothing could make sense of what he witnessed. "What does the note say?"

Between the skeleton's fingers, a folded sheet of thick paper fluttered in the breeze. A black fog hazed Royden's vision as the ME opened the message, a picture. The photo was of Abby from two weeks prior when Royden had taken her out to dinner. He remembered running his hands through her hair, left down and free-flowing in the breeze.

Macon sighed before he read the block writing across the top, "Abby's next. See what little sister has to look forward to? Can't wait to see her in the vat."

"Jesus. This can't be happening." Matt turned away with hands on his hips. "He boiled the body."

"What's with the cream soup looking stuff?" Larrick, mostly quiet until now, turned to the ME.

"Maybe the killer's pointing to specific details. Maybe he's bragging. I don't know. But when you boil bones versus letting them simmer, you get emulsified fat that gives it a creamy look." Macon pointed to the small baggie containing a thick liquid. "Like that."

"I'll know more once I've examined her." The ME shook his head. "She's only been here a few hours. There are a few blowflies present on the scalp remnants. No doubt, someone entering the dog park on the building's side would've noticed this if she were here yesterday. Either that or seen it from their second- or third-floor balcony."

"I interviewed a third-floor tenant last night."

"If the skull belongs to the rest of the skeleton," The older man bent to examine the victim's head, "that would fit, given the atmospheric conditions."

Caden frowned and tilted his head. "Macon, how do you know the skeleton is that of a female?"

Royden closed his eyes on a prayer. None of them wanted to admit the truth. The killer stalked Abby in the most brutal, horrific way, physically and mentally.

"Look at the pelvis. The bones are shorter, more rounded, wider subpubic angle. Males don't have a ventral arc. This is a female skeleton and skull, though I can't swear they belong together without microscopic examination."

"I see etch marks on the vertebra here." Macon pointed to the uppermost small bone. "I'll match it in the lab, and we'll give you a make on the weapon."

"Ethan?" A short, dark-haired man in a Tyvek jumpsuit signaled to the group. "I'm done here and will take the rope and shovel in for examination." The tech used large paper bags wrapped around the tool to best preserve DNA.

"Any prints?" Royden asked.

"No. But they'll take a closer look at the lab. Can't hazard a guess what they'll find in the way of DNA."

"Approximate age?" Billy asked, turning back to the ME.

"Once we x-ray, I'll check epiphyseal gaps. In other words, I'll see if the ends of the bone shafts are fused to short bone caps. Each fuses at different stages and helps to determine the victim's age."

Normal gallows humor failed to appear with the high stakes involved. No doubt, each McAllister envisioned Abby in the grave with some mocking memento clenched within a tight fist.

"Well?" Matt didn't need to explain his impatience for timing.

The ME's somber voice carried on the morning air. A sidelong glance and he continued, "I'll have something for you as soon as I can. I normally work to learn the how and the who but not the why. You want to explain how Abby is involved?"

"We don't know. At this point, we just don't know." Royden cringed with his words, realizing only time and a determined family separated Abby from a like fate. In the eleventh hour, he needed to delve into the mind of the monster and pray it didn't consume him.

Chapter Twenty

Successive deep breaths couldn't release the day's strain as Royden thumbed the lock on the kitchen door. The ride from Abby's office had been quiet. She'd quizzed him twice about what bothered him, then remained quiet, as if sensing his need for introspection

He had to tell her about Charlotte, yet couldn't bring himself to start the conversation. The love he'd felt for Charlee had long since transformed into the type of bond one shared by close friends and family. He should have seen tragedy coming.

"Have a seat and unwind. I've got a roast ready to stick in the oven, and I'll pour us a glass of wine." Royden watched the tension melt from her shoulders, something she probably didn't realize she carried.

"That sounds wonderful. Thanks." Hoover curled up on the sofa beside her. "It's amazing how someone's entire demeanor changes with the presence of a dog, isn't it?"

"I thought you could use a pick-me-up. And state law allows trained service dogs to accompany owners into public buildings. She certainly collected her due of oohs and aahs from your colleagues." The shaggy shepherd mix had drawn others close with doggy grins and loveable demeanor. Tension in the air had dropped and smiles multiplied.

"I thought I'd choke when she curled her lip at my supervisor. She's a damn good judge of character, as far as I'm concerned."

"Yeah, Mitzie said your popularity increased ten-fold after Brad stomped off." Royden closed the oven and set the time.

"Mind if I start a fire?"

It was still cool enough outside that the gas fireplace would add a certain coziness. Since the ensuing conversation would double the weight of her burden, he'd accept help from any angle. "Sure, go ahead."

Confirmation of Charlee's death came in the form of dental records and soon DNA would confirm it. If not for the previous attempts on Abby's life, she'd be a prime suspect in the doctor's murder. As it stood, his captain wasn't thrilled with the McAllisters banding around her instead of placing her in protective custody, not that he could stop them. He'd known the brothers long enough to understand how they operated and couldn't remand a potential victim to a safe house.

Abby would never forgive him if she found out from the evening news about the horror discovered behind her apartment. Though she had nothing to do with the doctor's death, she would carry the loss of life on her conscience.

With her kidnapper's trial approaching, months of tension built, layer by layer until she obviously felt the texture of fear ingrained in her soul. It accompanied the heavy sighs when she thought no one noticed and the slight drop in her shoulders. She thought him perceptive but didn't realize the depth of his understanding.

He'd been in situations where he thought he wouldn't see the next sunrise, hence was determined to ease her pain in whatever fashion necessary. Sex provided a quick if temporary release, but tonight he wanted her to experience the sweet release that depleted her energy and paved the way for a decent night's sleep.

Her come-hither smile on his approach clued him into her desire as much as the way she nibbled at her soft lips. Handing her a drink, he settled beside her and snuggled her close. "Long day?"

"Yeah, one of my colleagues is driving me crazy. Johen must consider me serious competition for the supervisor's spot. He gets sleazier every day. According to my assistant, he's starting rumors that I'm sleeping with potential clients."

Royden's eyebrows shot up and he set his drink down. "Sounds like he needs a little education."

"No, Royden. I didn't tell you so you'd intimidate him. I'm just explaining my day. All right?"

"Got it. Go ahead." There was more than one way to skin a cat. If he couldn't confront the man directly without upsetting her, maybe he'd make a note on his digital file. Katt and Lexi routinely raided their computers. The rest would prove hilarious.

"Lottie called. She's settled into a new place temporarily. She's thinking about relocating to Michigan where her brother lives."

"Sounds like a good idea. Has she heard any more from her ex or other gang members?"

"No. At least she said she hasn't. I don't think she'd withhold information after all that's happened. She'll come back for court but wants a fresh start. She can get that by relocating."

"Any flak from Brad—about anything?"

"No. He seems to be in some type of holding pattern. He watches me and monitors my work but doesn't say much. I'm thinking one of the partners advised him to back off. They don't want to malign an associate with one of the best track records in the firm."

"Maybe Lexi or Katt said something during their conversation about the firm's digital security. Both are very smart and know you're catching undue crap from both an associate and supervising attorney."

"It wouldn't surprise me." Abby set her now-empty wineglass on the table.

Though her habit entailed asking about his day, instead, she sifted her fingers through his hair. She'd avoided the elephant in the room, so he waited for a sign she was ready to hear about their progress in finding her stalker. For now, she was talking.

He didn't want the images from the morning in his own mind, much less hers. Instead, he'd give her something else to ponder while wiping thoughts of Charlee from his mind.

"I got a respectable estimate from a fence company. The representative from Lange fencing is coming out tomorrow to confirm the figures, and if all goes well, they'll be back next week to install a fence." Further details fleshed out the plan.

"We can go look at the shepherds this weekend?"

"That's the plan."

The playful glint in her eyes preceded the soft brush of her fingertips along his thigh.

"Abby..." She wouldn't miss the huskiness of his voice.

Her fingers stilled, the warmth seeping through his slacks.

"You—don't want to?"

"Seriously? It's not that I'm not aroused; it's just that you're so damn sexy. Plus, I'm a man. That desire is hard-wired into my DNA. Of course, I *want* to. Are you sure *you* want this? I don't mind holding you and just talking. You've had a hell of a rough evening yesterday and didn't get much sleep."

By letting her know he was good either way, he offered a choice despite his growing need making itself known. A slight squirm adjusted him but failed to ease the discomfort.

The tactile response arrived in the form of a light caress over his groin. He couldn't suppress the groan any more than tilting his hips into her touch. "Damn, you're persuasive."

She smiled as she leaned forward and met him halfway for a kiss. Her lips were always soft, but something different, lacking definition but profoundly substantial wiped his mind clear of the day's horrors. She always had an effect on him but tonight held a significance his mind couldn't grasp.

An ethereal bond held him fast, letting her explore his body with her fingers roving over his chest and across his shoulders.

"You always have too many clothes on." She feathered her lips down his neck, seducing, holding him prisoner for her sensual exploration.

He smoothed his hand across her flank and up to cup her breast, its weight the perfect handful. They were evenly matched in every way. He'd never imagined finding another soul who just *fit*. It was as if every nook and cranny of her spirit matched a corresponding niche in his own.

Clothes came off in a mutual tease, sensual, relaxed, and so contrary to what boiled inside him. The hunger gnawing at his chest and low in his groin made him impatient to show her, not with words, but through touch, what he felt and how much he needed her in his life.

The couch was comfortable to sit on but not intended for the heights he wanted to take her. Scooping her up, he managed one word, "Bedroom," between kisses.

The stairs presented no problem with her slight weight. Once in the bedroom, he laid her out on the mattress, his gaze drinking his fill but never getting enough. "My god, you're beautiful."

"I've been on the pill for a week..." Her smile encompassed one part seductress and two parts lust.

"Ah, I've been looking forward to this." He let his fingers drift over the softest skin, up her thighs, and across her flat abdomen, with stomach muscles bunching under his caress.

Her seductive smile lit the fuse on his diminishing restraint, yet he'd spend the rest of the evening showing her through soft caresses that she was his world and his future.

Her breath came in pants while her hips twisted side to side. Each gasping breath clawed at his diminishing control. "Your passion overwhelms me, sweetheart."

Soft pale skin equaled silk beneath his calloused fingers, the nonverbal pleas ignored in lieu of the anticipated storm leading to an explosive release. Grasping both hips, he held her still for the pleasurable torture. Whimpers and groans gave way to feminine growls with her hands grasping and tugging at his hair.

He kissed and teased until her thighs bunched and shook. The pressure building within her body would rock both their worlds.

Ensuring her pleasure before his own, he watched her world shatter twice before giving into his own need and settling into the cradle of her thighs. Anticipating what promised to be Heaven on Earth, he plumbed the depth of her gaze, telling her without words that he would always be by her side. Nothing of this world or the next would separate them. Where she led, he would follow.

It was the first time joining with a woman and not wearing protection. If he had his way, she wouldn't be on the pill either.

Though he wanted the complete picture and knew she did, too, the timing wasn't right. He was a patient man who knew the value of restraint. The gold at the end of the rainbow was well worth the wait.

This was the future flashback he wanted permanently etched in his mind. Abby, without fear, overcome with desire.

"Royden." The plea in her voice accompanied her legs using the leverage to try to complete them.

Every nerve ending roared to life. The heat and pressure forced a groan from his chest. Nothing had ever felt so good.

Despite their being together for over ten months, it felt better than the first time.

Nothing would ever compare, except when one day, they sought to expand the family.

A rush of excitement flooded his mind, her body quivering under his touch. He knew he could push her over the edge, but instead, stilled. When he pulled back, she clutched him with hands and legs, twisting her body to bring him back.

She gasped.

"Royden!"

He smiled at her desperation. Mutual need filled the breath between them.

Her impatience manifested in small cries and panted demands. He could feel her calves clenching his waist.

A deep breath, her back arching, and she slammed her eyes closed on a scream. Her next orgasm fired his own release.

With his energy depleted, his arms shook. Dropping to his elbows, he kept the bulk of his weight off her, but brushed side to side to feel her sensitized breasts rub his chest, knowing his soft smattering of hair would increase the sensation.

She pulled him tight, silencing anything he might say with a kiss. They'd surpassed the need for words.

Adjusting his position, he curled her body to rest against his chest, spooning.

"Hmm. That was incredible. No raincoat really makes a difference." The purred confession brushed his hand cradling her breast.

Her sudden stillness alerted him to her thoughts' change of direction.

"You know at least one of my brothers is keeping an eye on your house, right?" Humiliation colored her tone.

"Yep." He was glad she couldn't see his smirk.

"They probably just heard me."

"You are rather vocal." His chuckle brushed her hair.

"You did that on purpose."

"No, it was just a coincidental byproduct." Further words might get him in hot water. For all the hell each McAllister had put him through when learning their sister dated a cop, they deserved a little payback.

"Do you secretly hate my brothers?"

"Naw, but they've spent months declaring I wasn't good enough for their little sister. So, I'm not going to regret a little revenge."

"How am I supposed to face them?"

"With an ear-to-ear grin."

"Royden?"

"Hmm?"

"Yes." There was a smile in her tone.

"Yes?" Assuming anything around a McAllister invited trouble. "Yes to..."

"Yes, I want to get married. As soon as we can."

He squeezed her so tight she squealed and patted his arm to lighten the pressure.

There was no need to attempt closing his eyes that night. Sleep wouldn't come. Instead, a mental tally of what she might like in the way of a wedding populated his thoughts.

On the heels of bliss came the realization he had yet to explain the circumstances of Charlee's burial. The killer had stepped up his game. It was time for Royden to do the same, yet he couldn't bring himself to introduce horror into the perfect moment.

Abby woke to the heady aroma of coffee. If she had to wake up to an empty bed, the rich blend promising instant alertness proved the next best thing.

After a marathon session of Royden's lovemaking, it would be a miracle if she could formulate words much less walk. The beginnings of what felt like a permanent smile etched her lips.

The near-silent buzzing of Royden's phone drew her attention to the nightstand. Since it was common for them to answer each other's messages to family, she slid over and picked it up.

The text on the screen sent her bolting upright. A gasp followed the realization of the missive's significance. She knew danger lurked nearby, but the full impact didn't register until seeing Ethan's wording.

"Uh, Abs. What's up?" Royden leaned against the doorjamb with a cup of coffee in each hand.

Tears brimmed her eyes at the thought of her fiancé withholding information. They'd promised to not keep secrets. "What body is Ethan talking about?"

Royden approached on tentative steps. "I was going to tell you about it before breakfast. You needed a break last night, sweetheart. I'm not keeping things from you. We made a deal and you know I always keep mine."

"But this was yesterday!"

"I know, sweetheart. Let's go downstairs and hash this out."

"Why downstairs?"

"Because this room is an anger-free zone, sacred to me. Either we go downstairs or we both remove all our clothes before we talk." His smirk depicted his preference.

"I'm not taking my clothes off for a serious conversation." Knowing his body would distract her; she grabbed her robe lying over the chair and dropped the phone in his waiting hand after taking a coffee.

Anger and frustration carried her down on silent steps. Coffee was no longer necessary.

Once settled on the bar stool, she waited as Royden took a seat beside her. When he took her hand, she tried to snatch it back.

He held firm. "No, Abs. Please. I need the contact."

Enlightenment came with the sweat beading his brow and upper lip. The tension in his frame rivaled the strongest steel. Whatever happened yesterday had shaken him to his core. It was hard to remember sometimes that underneath all that solid strength beat a very human heart.

"I didn't tell you yesterday because *I* couldn't say the words and keep my shit together. I know it was selfish, but please understand.

We're in this together, and anything that affects you, affects me also. You have no idea how much."

With her other hand, she cupped his cheek. "That's all the more reason to keep me up to date. We help each other through the hard parts, too, cowboy."

He turned his head to kiss her palm, sighing when she cupped his face in both hands.

"Tell me."

"We don't have DNA confirmation yet, but it was Charlee." He retrieved his phone message and read it. "Okay, we'll have a little more information. They're tracing her movements."

"What aren't you telling me? Out with the rest of it."

Royden dropped chin to chest and closed his eyes as if in pain. "We found her in the field behind your apartment complex. That's all you need to know."

"Ohmygod, Royden. I'm so sorry." She frowned, already in attorney mode. "They don't think you're a suspect, do they?"

"No. My alibi is tight."

"I'm so sorry, Roy. I know what she meant to you. That you still cared."

"*You* are the one I'm in love with, Abs."

"Yes, I understand. I also know you're not the type to stop caring about someone just because you fell in love with someone else. I get that, Royden. You need to grieve, too. Allow yourself that much."

"Jesus, Abs. I'm gonna kill this guy. I just pray I find him before your brothers do."

Abby stood and wrapped her arms around his shoulders. "No, Royden. You're not. It would destroy a vital piece of who you are. A piece I happen to love very much."

The hopelessness in his gaze stemmed from the depths of his soul. When the time came for apprehension, he would remember this conversation. She'd make sure she stamped it into him on a cellular level.

"When you arrive at that pivotal point, think of me, our future, and our children. What kind of men and women do you want them to grow up to be?"

"I love you, Abs. I need you. Nobody's going to take you away."

"I love you, too. And I want us to have a long, guilt-free life ahead of us."

Depending on the circumstances and reaction times, her killer would die before Royden was even aware of his actions.

Chapter Twenty-One

Abby blew out a sigh as she let the curtain fall back over her office window. Nice weather brought employees out to the courtyard below to soak up the sun's rays while eating lunch.

Knowing Lexi and Katt were on their way to join her softened her ire toward Johen, occupying the seat in front of her desk. They were equals, but because he was a man, he assumed he should have the upper hand.

"I should've been the one to get the Credlin divorce. Our supervisor is more concerned about his hair than his work."

"Phyllis Rollison asked for me to represent her, Johen. It really is that simple. When Salsman pushed the point, she threatened to walk."

"Bradly said her big-shot husband contacted you about working for him."

The associate's whine droned on as Abby considered her predicament, fingering the chain and ring about her neck. She wanted nothing more than to marry Royden, but as long as her stalker remained free, it would put him in danger as well. Yet she was staying at his house. Was there much of a difference with a piece of paper? Her vacillation would drive them both crazy.

"Johen, I told him no. You know I can't, even though my client is no longer alive."

"Are you nuts? It's not so much a conflict if you leave the firm. You'd make three times the money, have less hours to work, and practically be your own boss without someone hovering over your shoulder every minute of the day." A resentful glare in the direction of the supervisor's office conveyed his meaning.

"I consider the Chinese wall extending to anything connected with the CEO. Besides, I know too much about him right off the bat. He's not somebody I'd *want* to work for." Arguing with colleagues accomplished nothing. Sitting in her chair, she opened the file on her desk, hoping he'd get the message.

"With no will to execute, there's no conflict."

Abby gritted her teeth with her colleague's lack of ethics and penchant for scheming. "With me gone, you'd be a shoo-in for the promotion." She wondered if she'd brought Hoover into the office today if the dog's sensitivity would end with a snarl at her colleague. If Lexi arrived before Johen left, they'd find out.

"See? Win-win situation."

"I've no intention of leaving the firm." Though she and Royden had discussed the situation and enough clients would follow her without encouragement, she wasn't ready. Employment with Salsman meant security. A priceless treasure.

"I hear the partners aren't real happy right now. Not only do we not have the wife's business, but you cost us the entire Credlin account. If you'd have dropped her, they'd be sitting pretty right now."

"First of all, *I* didn't cost this firm a dime. I served my client to the best of my ability and will continue to do so until the matter of the will is settled."

"What will?" The sly innuendo extended as a part of his natural personality. "I heard through the grapevine the original doesn't exist. And you know how tricky copies can be in a courtroom battle."

Her narrowed gaze didn't spark an instant response. "The one filed at the county courthouse." Her immediate boss was the only other attorney who'd known of the second original, besides her assistant Mitzie. "What?" That twitchy sensation on her nape magnified with the widening of his grin.

"Haven't you heard? It wasn't found. They're saying it might be a filing error or some type of computer glitch. Maybe it was never filed in the first place." The man's smirk said otherwise. "Now with your original gone, well, the partners are questioning your competence..."

"Sonofabitch." The fact her associate spewed details she hadn't known didn't surprise her. The rumor mill running rampant through their office thrived. Surely, Salsman had already interrogated Mitzie.

"Looks like I won't have much competition for the promotion after all."

He stood at the same time Abby shoved to her feet, her chair slamming against the back wall. *That was the purpose of his visit.* If she were a man, she'd consider breaking his jaw. With fists clenched and resting on her desk, she counted to ten.

"Hi, Abby." Lexi and Katt strode through the open door with a pizza box, a small plastic bag, and a six-pack of sodas in hand. Each did a double-take in assessing her posture.

Beside the girls and with leash tucked into her vest, Hoover growled. The deep rumble of the dog's warning forced Johen to take several steps back.

"That's sure as hell no service dog. He doesn't belong in here." The tremor in Johen's voice coincided with the slight shake of his fingers as he held them out in a defensive position.

"First of all, Hoover is a *she*. And *she* doesn't like it when someone, anyone, threatens one of her friends." Lexi set the pizza on Abby's desk and scratched behind the dog's ears. "Good girl, Hoover. You protect Abby in any fashion you see fit. But we may need to make sure some *two-footed animals* are up to date on *their* shots, 'cuz I don't want you catching anything." Turning to Johen, she added. "Did you know dogs have an incredible ability to ferret out trouble? It's as if they can read your mind, when, in fact, they're just reading your body language."

Katt nodded before picking up the thread of conversation. "For instance, when we first came in, it looked like Abby was going to have to physically defend herself. Hoover wouldn't stand for that. Nope, not at all." A cunning smile curved one corner of her mouth. "Lexi, maybe we should go have another chat with Salsman. He seems to be really taken with your help and would definitely listen to whatever you have to say."

"Hey. I didn't do a damn thing." The anger in Johen's tone faded with the dog's hard-eyed stare. As if circumventing the greatest threat of his life, he back-stepped then circled around the new arrivals in heading for the door. "You won't last long here now, Abby. The firm doesn't stand for incompetence. No matter how nice the piece of ass." The last words were spoken as he slammed the door behind him.

"What's going on? How can he call you incompetent?" Lexi flipped the lid on the pizza box.

Abby sighed and retrieved her seat, knowing that Johen, in one form or another, was due for a very difficult week from many unexpected angles. No one ever saw the girls' antics coming.

Katt rifled through the bag and extracted some plastic plates, handing them one at a time to Lexi.

"Not only does he know about the second will for the CEO's wife, he also told me the original at the courthouse has vanished. Hell, he knows more about my case than I do."

"Does that happen often?" Suspicion tainted Katt's question. "I don't know much about that kind of stuff."

"It's rare, but unfortunately it does happen."

"Matt said you might be striking out on your own. Is that true?" Katt's shoulders buckled forward as she unzipped her jacket. "Damn, Gila, You're impatient today." A quick look around and she settled the ferret climbing out of an inside pocket to perch around her shoulders.

Abby sighed. She loved her friends. They meant well. It reminded her of a sitcom she and Royden bonded over after they'd first met; a country family moving to the city and having difficulty adjusting. Actually, the difficulty occurred in the family's acquaintances.

"Royden and I talked about starting my own practice, but I'm not ready for that step. I need a little more time."

Abby accepted the offered plate of pizza and sat back in her chair. "There is one good piece of news though. Royden and I are going to look at puppies next weekend."

"Oh, really? Can we come too? I love puppies." Katt munched on her pizza, but her gaze danced with excitement.

"Me, too. I can help you assess their personalities," Lexi suggested.

"I was hoping you'd say that. To me, they'll all look like cuddly balls of fur, and I'll want to take each one home." It occurred to her that perhaps Lexi sported an ulterior motive for bringing her dog. "Lexi, why did you bring Hoover, today? I don't have a car here and promised Royden I wouldn't leave the building."

"Ah—"

"You wanted to see if she'd react to any of the employees, didn't you?" Abby sighed, knowing that whatever motive possessed her friends, her brothers would have thoroughly approved.

"You know she goes everywhere with me. Besides, she's a great judge of character. I trust her implicitly." Lexi shrugged a shoulder in nonchalance.

A tentative knock interrupted Abby's train of thought. Her assistant pushed the door open several inches.

"Abby? Sorry to interrupt, but this just arrived for you." Mitzie frowned as she held out a small cardboard box, about four inches square. The symbol of a nearby bakery decorated the top, a vector logo of a girl winking.

"Who delivered it?" Lexi asked, taking the box and setting it on Abby's desktop. "Was there a note with it?"

"I don't know who brought it, but there's no note, just your name written in block letters along the side. The receptionist called and said it was there when she got back from a restroom break."

"Why would someone stick a straw through the top of the box?" A chill slithered down Abby's spine as she reached for the delivery.

"No," Katt and Lexi blurted simultaneously.

"What's going on, Abby?" Mitzie pushed the door wide but didn't come farther into the room.

"I don't know... Girls?" Abby arched a brow and stood, one hand on her hip. "Care to fill me in on what you're hiding?"

"Let's see what's inside first." Katt untangled the discarded cellophane from the plastic plates and used it as a barrier to avoid leaving prints on the container.

"Wait," Lexi exclaimed.

Unhindered by her friend's advice, Katt lifted the lid enough to peek inside. "It's a piece of pie, but I wouldn't suggest eating it."

"Like I intended to? Why send it in the first place?" The straw filled the space intended as an eye on the logo. "What kind is it, Katt? Maybe that's a clue."

Royden was fond of sending gifts at times, flowers, baskets of goodies, etc. He'd never sent anything so dramatic.

"Mud pie." Katt's monotone voice forewarned of an unpleasant and illuminating conversation ahead.

"Okay, girls. Spill it. Now."

"Abby, um, the guys found something outside your apartment complex early yesterday morning."

Weakness in her knees forced Abby to sit. "I know they found Charlee, murdered and buried."

"Um, it wasn't just that." Katt's gaze drifted to the window coverings, her attention appearing miles away.

"Tell me."

"Yeah. It was a skeleton," Lexi murmured.

"Someone boiled her body, except for part of her scalp," Katt added. "Long black hair."

The dread she'd felt all morning slid over Abby's thoughts like an avalanche as new meaning of the straw took shape in her mind. "The bastard intends to bury me."

"Not gonna happen, Abby." Katt circled the desk and laid a comforting hand on her shoulder. "Not gonna happen. It's just a stupid scare tactic."

"One that involves my fiancé's ex-girlfriend." Abby glanced from Lexi to Katt. "What else. I know there's something else by the look on your face."

"Tell her, Lexi." Katt's face had turned pale.

"There was a note, referencing you." Lexi set her cup on the desk alongside her plate of half-eaten pizza.

Obvious thoughts flicked across each of their minds.

"Damn. I'd best call Royden about this pie." Abby reached for the phone then halted when Mitzie stuck her head back in.

"Abby? Salsman said he wants to see you in his office, ASAP. He sounded pissed off."

Chapter Twenty-Two

Royden couldn't wait for his partner to stop the vehicle before hopping out in front of Abby's office building. After receiving a call from Lexi, he was ready for a target on which to vent his anger. Anyone other than family would do.

If his partner's driving were any indication, anxiety swirled his emotions into a chaotic realm where nothing made sense.

Despite the trepidation roiling in his gut, Royden smoothed his expression so as not to scare the firm's receptionist. He nodded in passing, flipping his jacket back to reveal his badge and gun.

She said nothing, perhaps because the McAllister on his heels failed to disguise the anger radiating from him in waves. By now, the entire firm knew Abby had a deadly stalker and an overprotective family.

Two half-flights of stairs passed in several strides. Once Royden made it to the office and saw Abby was all right, he could take a deep breath. The killer struck before they could regain a handhold on sanity's coattails.

He found Lexi, Katt, and Mitzie in deep discussion. "Where is she?" He directed the demand at the assistant.

"Sh-she's in Salsman's office. He wanted to speak with her." Mitzie took two steps back toward the window when Billy entered the space.

"Why?" Billy's harsh voice filled the room.

"I-I don't know. He doesn't tell secretaries inner-office stuff." Mitzie's protective hand at her throat appeared an instinctual reflex in the face of a threat. "His office is on the other side, all the way on the end." She pointed to the opposite wing of the building. "His name's on the door."

Billy jogged out before Royden could root out the source that had made Lexi's voice shake over the phone. "That the special delivery?" He pointed to the cardboard box then hardened his jaw as the meaning became clear. "The killer intends to bury her in a coffin with a barbaric supply of oxygen."

Lexi and Katt stood mute, unable to express the fear written in their faces.

"Stay here and don't let anyone touch that. Okay? I'll be back after I've seen Abby." He didn't wait for a reply. As a private investigator and better half to his eldest brother, Katt understood procedure in dealing with evidence.

Billy's roar defined the destination before Royden turned the final corner on the south wing. Concern was expected, as was frustration. Absolute rage took him by surprise.

Royden entered in time to see Abby shove her big brother away from her boss's desk.

"Billy. I don't know how that footage was obtained or who sent it, or why. However, I do know this. If we don't keep our heads on straight, we won't find out."

Royden stepped between Abby and Billy but directed his attention to her boss. "Mr. Salsman, I'm Detective Patterson. Can you catch me up to speed, please?"

"Royden, you don't need to see it, too. I can explain." Abby put a hand on his chest.

He brushed it away and stepped closer to glance at the computer monitor, the picture a frozen moment in time. Abby stood beside her bed in her apartment, naked and smiling. The image burned a path south from his head. He stood speechless.

"This video arrived in my email this morning. Normally I delete incoming missives to my private account if I don't recognize the sender. However, this had Abby McAllister in the subject line."

"That was taken the night before last." Though he wasn't seen, Royden had stood on the other side of the bed, talking to his fiancée. It was as intimate a moment as if someone had filmed them during sex. Nevertheless, her brother didn't need the visual any more than her boss would.

Turning on Salsman, Billy thundered. "You can't hold this against Abby. She's a victim of this shit."

"Billy. Now's not the time. We have other concerns." Abby looked to Royden, her gaze begging him to end the standoff.

"Salsman, you can't fire her over this." Billy towered over the older man, his voice booming in the spacious office.

"We hold our staff to the highest moral standards. Until the source of this—this pornography is determined, I'm placing her on administrative leave. Word will get around, and I won't have the firm's name besmirched."

"It's legal, Billy. There's nothing we can do about it until we find the person who sent it."

"She quits." Though Royden spoke the words softly, they echoed in the quiet confines.

Salsman and Billy froze, each turning to stare at him.

Abby's glare promised retribution at a later date. "You can't quit for me."

"I just did. You're better than this, Abby. You're better than this entire place. I'd bet the farm that any client you've had contact with in the past will follow you into private practice."

"She can't do that. She can't coerce clients away from the firm. It's in her contract." Salsman's anger morphed into shock.

Billy smiled. "She won't need to. But you know how it is... as you said, word travels. And when others come here to see her and find she's gone—well—I won't feel sorry for you. Not one bit." His grin widened.

Royden knew that by the time the sun set, Lexi would've hacked records and made sure every client knew of Abby's departure. That occurring on the heels of discovering the video's sender.

As if realizing the same thing, Abby heaved a sigh, her shoulders sagging. "I won't ask if this day can get any worse, because I know better. It can *always* get worse."

Royden and Billy followed her down the hall and back to her office. Each echo of her heel on marble tile reinforced the fact he'd overstepped his bounds, undermined her confidence, and royally pissed her off. There were few things she couldn't forgive; manipulating her outside the bedroom topped the list.

Katt and Lexi remained by the door, blocking the entrance. Word of another incident had already spread, judging by the growing crowd and whispered murmurs. Tragedy, stalker, killer, among other gossip slithered on meager air currents.

Lexi and Katt stepped aside to let him pass.

"What happened, Abby?" Mitzie stood by the doorframe, petting Hoover.

"My family and Royden got me canned. Looks like I'm going into private practice sooner than expected."

Mitzie gasped and stepped forward. "Why? Because of the theft and the fact someone is stalking you? They can't do that."

"It's done." Abby scanned her office. "Well, if everybody grabs something, I won't have to search for a box. The files are company owned, so I can't take them with me... and I'll lose all my notes on my clients." A sidelong glance at Lexi and Katt assured they understood her loss.

To Royden's knowledge, Abby had never strayed from the letter of the law, which attested to her current emotional state and her fragile grip on reality.

Without hesitation, Lexi pulled out her laptop just as Katt did the same. Lexi smiled as she typed. "I guess you'll be looking for office space."

"I'm in," Katt grinned back at Lexi. "I hear Janis Street is a nice area. On the outskirts of town, it's closer to Royden's house *and* there's a dog park nearby. Great if you happen to have a puppy."

"Jeez. Word travels as fast in this family as it does in the office." Turning to Royden, she poked him in the chest. "Speaking of which, why didn't you tell me about all the evidence you found yesterday morning. I thought we weren't going to keep any secrets."

Royden met her glare with a sincere expression. "I was going to tell you tonight." A twist of his mouth and hard stare in Lexi's direction revealed his displeasure. "I didn't think it was appropriate to dump it on you all at once."

Abby got quiet. And still.

If not for the threat over her head, she would've stormed out. Royden knew her, knew that the helplessness roiling in her gut would find expression one way or another.

His high-handedness earned every bit of her ire.

* * * *

Abby stewed the entire way home, not daring to open her mouth due to the venom that would spill. As usual, Royden's heart was in the right place, but the Neanderthal streak comprising his ego forced him to act on her behalf.

"You know you overstepped your bounds." Despite not being able to imagine her life without him in it, she needed him to respect certain limits.

His quiet capitulation, "I know," spoke volumes.

On the rare occasions they'd argued, they always came to an understanding. Regardless of what he said now or promised, his instincts would always force him to protect in any way he thought appropriate.

The question remained, could she live within that mindset.

"Abby, I can change, grow, adapt."

He also knew how her mind worked.

In fiddling with the ring about her neck, she knew she'd made him nervous. Manipulation was not a part of her arsenal. In relationships, as in court, she faced issues head-on. "I know. And so can I. I love you."

"You're my world, Abby. My reason for getting up in the morning."

"And you're one of the reasons I follow the letter of the law, but like you, I've crossed a line today that I can never redraw. It's a slippery slope." She covered his hand resting on his thigh, letting him know through touch that they would survive the storm.

"And I thought you did it so you could bail your brothers out of trouble. Don't worry, we'll have each other for a guide."

She twisted her lips in a pout. "I'm still pissed off at you."

"I know. I deserve it."

"They're never going to take me back."

"Which is why we're going to start looking at rental space for your new office."

"I don't know if I have enough—" She didn't want to finish the sentence, didn't want to depend on Royden financially. It would be another mark against her struggle for independence.

"We're in this together, Abby. I don't have the specific education to help with the type of work you do, but I can help you get started. It's the least I can do." A shrewd grin matched the look in his eye before he gazed out the driver's window. "On the other hand, if you wanted to make it *legal*, you could always put the ring on. What's mine is yours."

She'd never been a waffler. "I will. However, I don't want to spend my honeymoon looking over my shoulder. Do you?"

"No. I do understand and respect your reasoning. So, let's work with what we have and need right now. That includes a space for you to work."

"But I'm not bringing anything to the table. I still have student loans and will for at least three more years."

"Abby. Do you think me so shallow that I see dollar signs when I look at you? I know it's not how *you* see *me*."

"No. I see the man who makes me complete."

"Good. Then you understand how I feel. If we were the same in every way, we wouldn't be compatible. You've spent your entire life proving to your brothers that you can handle yourself. Well, you've succeeded. It's time to set that aside and move forward."

By the time Royden pulled into his driveway, they'd settled their differences, which still left Abby without a job and the threat of a stalker. It didn't mean she wasn't mad; she was pissed, but mutual respect and understanding shaved the edge off her need to lash out.

"Royden, if the killer was good enough to track me to New Zealand, then he's good enough to know I'd move in with you after leaving my apartment."

"Probably, which is why Caden and Lucas were here earlier sweeping the house for audio/video eavesdropping. Lexi and Katt are working on electronic security."

"As much as my family interferes in my life, they're always there when I need them, even without my having to ask."

"They're family."

"As far as work, I can think of several clients that will leave the firm. I'm going to have to find space, and supplies, and an assistant."

"Are you thinking about Mitzie? You two work well together, right?" Hesitation tempered his voice.

"We've talked about it before. She said if I ever left, she wanted to come with me. Now, I'm not sure that's a good idea. At least until we know more."

"So, how do you feel about lunch and a quiet afternoon? Meanwhile, we can look online and find some potential office space to check out."

"Lexi and Katt have already been looking." Abby shook her head. "My family seems to stay one step ahead of me."

"They love you."

"I know. Can Lexi find out who put that video on the net?"

"If anyone can, she's the one. If not, I'm sure she can figure a way to destroy whatever sites—"

"Don't say it, cowboy. If it's not legal, I don't want to know." It was a coward's way out. At this point, Abby wanted to protect Royden, too. "At least they didn't catch us in anything—physical."

"Whoever it is, recorded a very private part of your life." Royden's hands clenched around the steering wheel before he cut the engine. "Let's get inside and relax for a bit, talk, and map out a game plan."

Royden's home paralleled the man himself. It didn't fit any one particular style, more of an eclectic mix of architectures that welcomed and relaxed the observer. Inside, subdued patterns and colors added to the soothing nature of a lived-in home.

The few belongings she'd kept in her office required two trips to the house, deposited in the small study downstairs.

When they'd settled on the sofa with a cup of coffee, Abby thought about her next step. "Even my laptop belonged to the firm."

"Just as well. This way you'll build your practice from the ground up, complete with electronic security, good proximity to your ideal location, and if you set up on the outskirts of town, you'll have a great view."

"You've been thinking about this for a while."

"Guilty as charged."

"What about him?" Whereas she'd accustomed herself to controlling a situation, she recognized Royden's sideways approach. Effective, but lacking the confrontational aspects she employed. The end result remained the same.

"I'll keep you in the loop every step of the way from now on."

"As it occurs?"

"Yes. As events happen, you'll know where the investigation is going. But—I expect the same in return. I want to know where you are at all times, who you're with, and what you're doing."

"Well, thank you for not hiding a tracking device in my briefcase, though I'm sure its crossed your mind. As independent as Katt is, I'm surprised she hasn't strangled my eldest brother."

"That's because as a private investigator, she goes looking for trouble and it saved her life not long ago. You don't."

"She saved herself by bashing the prick with a shovel. As far as me, trouble finds me anyway. I guess Katt's keeping an eye on Credlin."

"Yes."

"The man's worth millions. He's not going to do his own dirty work."

"Which is why we're keeping a very *close* eye on him."

"Meaning Lexi is hacking his life to pieces." Abby covered her eyes with her hand as if that could disperse the image of her friend going to any length to achieve her goal. "She's got her own hands full now. It makes me wonder, why she and Ethan haven't set a date for their wedding, yet."

"I think they want to coordinate with Caden and Kaylee, and Billy and Remie." Royden set his empty mug on the side table and nudged her closer. "I'm surprised Megan and Lucas don't tie the knot at the same time."

"Let's talk about us..."

Chapter Twenty-Three

"Come now, Brad. Surely, you can do better than this. Your supervisory skills seem to be slipping." The slow glide of Havoc's fingertips down his flank toward his swelling flesh took the sting out of her words. "First, she wouldn't go out to dinner with you, then she gets fired instead of put on temporary leave."

"Hey. When I talked with Salsman first thing in the morning, I told him she had a jealous ex stalking her. The timing was perfect. He was furious, like his star pupil got caught smoking in the bathroom." Brad urged her to her back before leaning over to suckle her breast. "Damn, Havoc. You sure live up to your nickname."

"Then why did he fire her? That wasn't supposed to happen. You obviously oversold the information."

A soft plop released his prize. "No. One of her brothers along with her boyfriend showed up. Detective Patterson told Salsman Abby quit. It took her by surprise as much as my boss. He was going to suspend her until we sorted it out. He loves little power plays." Doubt crossed his features, the kind of look one got after stepping in a pile of manure. "How did you get that video anyway?"

"I was nicknamed Havoc for a reason. I snagged it digitally. The bitch shouldn't be so full of herself to send porn through the mail. Interception happens to be a particular talent of mine." *And when Lexi finally traces that email back to you, the cops will knock on your door.* Because Brad had been such a good sport, she'd scramble the evidence before PPD could file formal charges.

"O—kay. I just don't want to be implicated in something illegal."

"Damn. I knew the McAllisters would be persistent, but I figured the shrink would see her as too much work."

"He's a psychologist, not a psychiatrist." Brad frowned as his hand stroked downward over her tight stomach. "What's the scar from?"

The last thing she needed was for her target to be distracted. "Childhood accident." In fact, her stepbrother had decided to test her pain tolerance with a knife. One of his many *tests* she'd survived to prove her worthiness. She remembered the agony which accompanied the crimson beading along the line drawn with the sharp blade.

"You said you'd see Credlin's account swing my way, but he tried to hire Abby away from the firm. Now that she's quit, what's to stop her from taking up with him?"

"Let me worry about Abby. Credlin won't employ her. That was just a red herring for her boss' sake. I wanted him desperate enough to keep her yet torn with the need to protect his firm's reputation." She shrugged a shoulder. "Just messing with your boss' head."

"Can't say that I mind that. He makes me sick sometimes."

"Yeah? You should cook him longer."

Since she'd worn a wig when seducing the other attorney, she hadn't needed to dye her hair again. The fact her current mark would never work for Credlin wasn't something he would discover until it was too late. At that point, he wouldn't talk due to his part in harassing Abby.

"You're the one trying to kill her?" His hand stilled on her mound.

"Of course not. Do I look like a sharpshooter and explosive expert?" She took a deep breath and arched her back, pressing her breast into his hand. "I just sent the pie to take advantage of the situation. If she weren't such a slut, she wouldn't have a string of jealous ex-boyfriends on her heels. My best friend loved her in law school, but her career path took precedence. She used him." Tired of waiting, she straddled his body and took him within her grasp. "Are we going to talk or are you going to give me something good?"

Once sated, she curled against his side, running limp fingers through the light furring on his chest. It seemed he'd accepted her part in scaring the bitch, but now she had a bigger problem.

The detective's home employed security she couldn't circumvent. To navigate her new strategy, she needed information. The McAllisters were so paranoid, Havoc couldn't get close enough to observe the bitch's comings and goings. Nailing her at the detective's house would've been fun but wasn't an option. Success depended on Abby being alone and following sequential steps in a timely manner.

"You're right, you know." She lowered her voice to a sultry whisper, wanting to distract as well as inform. Threats wouldn't gain his cooperation as well as positive incentives. This mark's buttons included greed and ego.

"About?"

"Abby. I shouldn't have sent the pie. It was mean and I regret it. I'd make amends but she'd probably hang up if I called. If I went to her house, she'd probably have her boyfriend arrest me."

"Hmm. You may be right. He's wound pretty tight." Brad rolled his hips forward to encourage further play.

"I admit it when I'm wrong, but I should apologize face to face, when Patterson isn't looming over her."

"First you'd have to find out where she's staying."

"No doubt, she's shacking up with her latest joystick, that detective." She let just the right amount of petulance color her tone.

"He should be easy enough to locate."

"But I don't want to show up when he's there," she whined.

She wouldn't set one foot near the property until devastating the entire family, knowing how they joined forces. "Do you think you could call her? Maybe apologize for not backing her up. You could tell her you'll get her job back. Find out if she's by herself so that I could go and grovel."

"I suppose I could do that." His gaze focused inward as he reached for her.

"It's going to take me a few days to get up my nerve and put together an appropriate speech, but for now, I think there's something more important on your mind." With her goal achieved, she decided to enjoy the fruits of her labor. The putz wouldn't know she'd used him until Abby was dead, too late to go to the police.

Her brother had laughed at her bungled efforts against the McAllisters but gave his stamp of approval on the doctor she'd used as an experiment. He'd warned her taking a life up close and personal entailed a different mindset and required practice before claiming the ultimate prize.

The result had proved more satisfying than she could've imagined and fueled her desire to hear Abby beg in the same fashion. Not that she'd pleaded when in the basement prison.

That's what separates an artist from a nerd. Daryl had so much to learn and for once, she would be the teacher.

Havoc never dreamed of becoming an assassin as a small child. She'd spent her formative years ducking the swing of her father's belt or fist. More to the point, she'd avoided following in her sibling's steps in going to college. She smiled at the thought of sending Daryl a postcard from Europe, gloating on her success.

From an earlier recorded conversation, she had the name and address of her next victim, but not the phone number. That detail had required a bit of research.

A simple phone call had secured the first part of her plan. The next would satisfy her need to maim along with testing her manipulative skills.

Lottie hadn't known about Abby's resignation, but agreed to meet at the remote diner where there was little chance of a familiar face spotting them. Knowing enough about the firm allowed for a seamless conversation to set up the ruse.

On arrival, the gullible twit had crumbled with the gun pointed at her gut. Securing her in the back seat had taken seconds on the far corner of the lot.

Now, the rearview mirror revealed nothing but dust, trees, and an old café that had seen better days. Final success would occur near a remote cabin she'd prepped earlier. This victim was weak and deserved death for sniveling and drooling on her back seat. *It takes the fun out of playing.*

"Did Emilio send you?" A choked sob interrupted Lottie's trembling words. Whimpers escaped as she shifted to adjust her position, hog-tied with her hands and feet secured in a knot behind her.

Havoc regretted leaving her face down. Now she'd have to clean the stolen car. "Someplace secure, just like I promised. I always keep my promises."

"Are you going to kill me?"

"Depends on how well you play your part." A shame she hadn't thought of this to begin with, but if she had, she would've missed the pleasure of the CEO's body. He'd been the most delicious specimen of male she'd ever enjoyed.

Besides, this way I can ruin three attorneys and one rich executive with one blow. Even Daryl couldn't accomplish that.

She hated attorneys. They'd told her brother he might not serve time, yet she knew he'd be lucky to ever see the light of day again as a free man. She'd spent long enough pumping staff for information while just pumping staff.

The possibility of knocking Detective Patterson down a few pegs made her smile. Shrinks were so much more fun to play with. With Abby's impending death, many people would suffer. Cataloguing their declines as collateral damage provided wonderful side benefits.

As far as Lottie's death, the gang's meddling already provided the stage for her brutal murder. It gave no pleasure to frame them, but too many loose ends would raise suspicion.

The shack she'd secured lacked easy access or neighbors for miles. No one to hear the screams or stumble upon body parts. The sum total equaled the perfect backdrop to terrify McAllister when the time came—without threat of discovery.

Once she cut the engine, she took a deep breath. Victory was so close, so sweet. From the back seat, little whimpers were just the beginning of a beautiful memory.

Fresh air, filled with the scent of pine and earth along with the sounds of songbirds, set the scene for her next act. Pride filled her chest. She'd defeat her personal demons *and* forge a new life for herself. She'd be every bit as good at this as her brother.

"Okay, honey. Let's move it." The rope around Lottie's ankles cut with a slip of the knife. Grabbing her victim by the wrist bonds, Havoc yanked her back and out of the vehicle, banging the girl's shins en route.

"I-I'm coming. I'm going to cooperate." Tears smudged the dried tracks on her face. "What are we doing here?"

It was time to enjoy life a little, which would make the coming betrayal all the sweeter. "We're going to play a little game. I'm going to record your voice as you read a script. In return, I'll make all your problems with Emilio disappear."

"Wh-what do you mean?"

"Just what I said. Neither he nor his cronies will ever bother you again. And the police will never suspect you. I'll swear on a stack of bibles." *Because corpses don't commit murder or get irritated by an ex.*

"What do you get in return?" The girl's step lightened. Despite glancing around the deep forest in apparent expectation of some trick, her gaze lit with interest.

"Just for you to read a paragraph. Once I have it, I'll set you free." To further secure her prey's cooperation, she added, "I need to make amends to someone I've wronged. She'll never talk to me without your help. So—in return for this favor, I'll make sure Emilio never rapes you again."

"How did you know about that?"

"Friends in all the right places, my dear." In the spirit of mutual collaboration, she smoothed her hand down Lottie's back then circled her shoulders as they climbed the steps to the porch. Creating confusion in a victim was her superpower.

Her extended family had abandoned the shack long ago when their dysfunctional unit split for the last time. Memories of the police forcing her cuffed father into a patrol car twisted her lips in a sneer. She'd been sixteen. Her pathetic excuse for a mother had just left, telling her good luck. If not for Daryl, she would've fallen into the hands of social services. A shudder circled her spine.

Havoc wanted to do something spectacular with this girl's body. She had a nice shape, pretty face, and subservient spirit. The latter could be overlooked in lieu of the mark's value. Timing proved the only possible hitch.

Inside, musty air made them both cough. She guided her prey to a rickety stool by the kitchen table which wobbled with the slightest touch.

"Here, sit. I've got to get my backpack out of the car."

"Could you... loosen these bonds? Just a little." Hope filled eyes that would soon show terror.

Anticipation made her mouth water. "I can do you one better. Sit quietly, and as soon as we're done, I'll remove them."

Meek and mild, not how Havoc liked her victims. She preferred spitting mad, the way Abby would soon be. The question remained, would Abby attempt to subvert her anger in hopes of discovering a way to escape?

After retrieving the necessary items, she stepped back inside to find the girl hadn't moved an inch. It paid to be a convincing liar.

Spending hours watching yourself on video to detect all those nasty little tells, a tapping finger, a gaze that slid away, or a change in your voice's pitch that signaled deception, certainly paid off.

"Okay. Here's the deal." Havoc placed her double-edged knife on the counter in front of Lottie. "I'm going to hold a tape recorder up for you to recite your lines. Once done—you're free." By the time the recorded message lured Abby to the designated spot, Lottie would have drawn her last breath. So much fun, but the timing needed to be perfect.

Chapter Twenty-Four

Since finding Charlee buried in Abby's backyard, cold rage consumed both Royden and his partner. Focus and clipped words defined their current exchange. Every minute equaled more time slipping through their fingers, time Abby might not have.

"Credlin is involved somehow, but I can't imagine him being in league with the psycho, Carrigan." Royden had proven himself a decent puzzle solver, but this embroiled multiples he couldn't separate.

"Once we figure that out, we'll see how all this fits, and end this madness." Billy tugged his jacket over the bulge at his waist after exiting the car. "I'll hit the professional vein, you go for the jugular, the personal stuff."

The reversal from normal procedure gave Royden pause. His partner held a particular card close to his vest. *Dammit, not now.* Only time would unlock its secret.

"Your assumption we can play head games with this CEO might be premature. Information gleaned from digital resources doesn't equal time face to face." In order for that ploy to work, one had to know a good bit about their target *and* spend time with them. Credlin proved to be a very private individual with funds for a team of lawyers. "If he knows the extent of our knowledge concerning his private life, he'll clam up faster than a witch's ass."

"So, we make it look like a fishing expedition," Billy's crooked grin reflected both disdain and amusement. Figurative smoke rolled from his ears.

"Remember. Once he brings in his legal watchdogs, progress halts." They'd kept their previous questions general in an effort to get a bead on the suspect's overall behavior while they dug into his background.

"Now that we've poked around inside his world, let's give him a little taste of what we know. It'll keep him off balance while you delve through his mind." Billy murmured while scanning the grounds.

Royden nodded then tilted his head toward the upper front corner of the mansion. The CEO made no effort to hide his security cameras, which didn't mean there weren't others concealed among the ornamental trees or elaborate landscaping.

Billy smiled and nodded in return.

"As long as you don't lose your temper." Royden flashed a smile and received the bird in return. His neat-nick partner kept a cool head until a family member came under fire. As the only female sibling, Abby had endured lots of situations fending off their over-zealous protective instincts during her teenage years.

Unlike employees at the CEO's hi-tech company who wore uniforms of a sort, several grounds keepers dressed in jeans and casual shirts. One trimmed yew bushes into works of art while another collected the clippings.

Two men, one at the front door and the other walking the perimeter fence wore black tactical gear. At the gate's guardhouse, security had worn the same style black pants and boots.

"I never lose my temper." A muscle in his jaw ticked as they started to climb the steps.

At the top of the elaborate entranceway, the guard held his hand up. "Mr. Credlin is around back. He said you can meet him in his greenhouse. Just follow the brick walkway around the side."

"Thanks." Royden considered the suspect's possible ploys. Once out of security's earshot, he pointed out to his partner. "He thinks—"

"Yeah, he's going to flaunt the fact he grows orchids. How could he get access to forensic results so soon?"

"Money. Either he has a tech in his pocket or a hacker." Royden's gaze scanned the vast immaculate yard. An ornate fountain took center stage to intricately carved benches where one could sit and enjoy the soft burble of water. Waist-high hedges formed a maze as a backdrop, which opened to a back yard full of various flowerbeds surrounding a glass and metal structure.

The greenhouse covered a small portion of the massive yard but maintained a large footprint, just the same. Royden estimated it about sixty by two hundred feet. The unit consisted of several sections, portioned off according to the plants inside. Two women and an older man tended to the orchids and hybrids grown.

"We can sort our leaky situation later. At least he's not going to be as ahead of us as he figures." Billy grinned, anticipatory glee furrowing his brow.

Royden had seen that particular look before, when the psycho Abby nicknamed whisper imprisoned her in an underground cell. She'd explained the moniker as her way of making the monster less scary. At that time, the whole family went rogue.

"Okay, let's assume and verify he knows the dirt from Abby's office is a match, pointing to an advanced gardener. He wants to appear transparent and cooperative."

"I'll see through him without a problem." Billy opened the door to the greenhouse.

Royden bit the inside of his cheek to keep his retort silent. McAllisters had a way of changing horses in mid-stream without advance warning.

Credlin met them near the entrance. "Hello, detectives. What brings you here today?" That same shrewdness about the eyes took in the officers' appearance.

"We have a few more questions, if you don't mind." Royden worked to keep his voice calm while ferreting Billy's change in approach.

"It's in my best interest to help in any way I can. I want the prick who targeted my family." Rage simmered in Credlin's voice.

"Nice place you got here." Billy thumbed the six-inch leaves of a young orchid. In flicking the tender root, he broke a piece off. "Oh, sorry. I didn't know they were so delicate."

Credlin gritted his teeth then smiled, the tightness belying anger underneath the façade. "The aerial root draws in moisture and carbon dioxide in order for the plant to thrive."

Royden sighed inwardly. To be honest, he supposed this was Billy's attempt at *playing nice*. After all, the suspect was still vertical and didn't have a gun stuck in his face. "Thank you for seeing us on such short notice." Royden held out his hand to shake, not liking the forced role of good cop.

"Not a problem, but please understand I am a busy man and have very little free time." Gesturing to the rows and rows of plants, he added, "This is my source of inner Zen, where I go to get centered." Slight contempt infused the last words spoken while the homeowner's gaze narrowed on Billy.

"I see you don't use regular soil here. What is this stuff?" Billy bent to have a closer look.

"Of course not. It's a special blend made specifically for my hybrids. You can't buy it on the open market and since I employ the man who developed it, I own the patent."

"Figures you wouldn't use off-the-shelf stuff." Billy wiped a smudge of dirt on the metal rack and held it to his nose. "It doesn't smell like anything to me. I thought you fertilized flowers with chicken dung."

Royden sighed, realizing Billy wouldn't stick to their plan, forcing an adjustment in his own approach. Billy did bad cop very well. "Excuse my partner, Mr. Credlin. He's not a gardener."

"No, he's not. I hear he's an explosive expert with um... *vast* and *varied* experiences." If the man referenced one of Billy's impromptu detonations, his source of information proved better than expected.

Billy made a *tsking* sound in the back of his throat. "Very uncool."

"By the way, if you want a sample of the soilless mix, all you have to do is ask." Credlin pulled an empty baggie from his jeans pocket and held it out to Billy. "I would offer you a small bag of it, but I figured you'd want to collect it yourself. Feel free to look around, but *please* don't touch the plants."

Royden accepted the bag but put it in his jacket as Billy pulled out an evidence bag. Royden sighed.

Billy grinned.

"I hear you now have complete control over the company since your wife and child have passed." Billy picked up a nearby orchid and turned it upside down before Royden could stop him. Pieces of the bark mixture fell into the bag he held.

"What? I didn't touch the plant."

"They didn't pass. They're dead!" Credlin took a half-step forward then stopped, closed his eyes briefly, and fisted his hands at his sides. "The rest remains to be seen, probate and all that." One of the nearby workers moved toward the opposite end of the structure.

"But your wife was close to her family. Isn't that so? Don't you think they're gonna raise hell?" Billy countered.

"Obviously, you know the details. However, I did not kill them." The last words gritted out as the suspect took a stiff step forward. "I loved my daughter and would gladly give half of my company in trust to her, even if it was controlled by my ex-wife."

Billy stood toe to toe with Credlin. "But she wasn't your ex. Which means you get everything." Billy's diving for the suspect's most vulnerable organ provided a ruse, throwing the man off kilter.

Royden nudged Billy aside. His partner had succeeded in his attempt to throw the interviewee off balance. As usual, McAllister had a second agenda, apparently trying to incite the executive to violence.

"Someone has targeted your wife's attorney on several occasions. Any idea who might do that?" Royden blocked Credlin's view of Billy, a vain attempt to calm the homeowner.

"No. I don't. If you'll look at the timing, it doesn't fit. My... wife's accident occurred before the doctor was taken."

"You appear to be up to date on current events." Royden held the man's stare, observing for the smallest sign of increased anxiety. The exec didn't flinch. Either someone had tutored him extensively in the art of deception, or he was innocent. Either scenario was possible.

"Wouldn't you be if the roles were reversed?"

"As I understand it, you've hired two investigative firms, one in Oregon and one in Ohio." Billy stepped around the end of one table under the pretense of admiring the vast expanse of flowers.

Royden tried to keep his face impassive. He shouldn't have been surprised his partner stayed one-step ahead of him, considering the hackers in his family. Keeping up with the McAllisters equaled a full-time job in itself.

"Then you realize I want to find out who killed my family as much as you do, preferably *before* you do. They meant everything to me, as yours does to you, considering the *lengths* you've gone to in the past to protect them." The fact Credlin pulled off the gloves lent an old-world feel to his desire to settle things, physically.

Royden blocked Billy's approach, a warning frown telling his partner to back off.

"Mr. Credlin, how many people are in your employ?" Billy's feral grin equaled acceptance of the unvoiced challenge.

"Here or abroad? How is Abby, by the way, Detective McAllister?" A short recovery time followed by a returning salvo. "I heard someone made an attempt on her life, what... two times." The sneer in his words matched that of his lips.

"She's fine. And—we're closing in on the prick who's marked her."

"Good, then you probably shouldn't be wasting time here. Rumor has it that the evidence recovered from her office will match my own special blend of growing medium. I assure you; I, nor any employee of mine has had anything to do with your sister's problems. I don't know who wants to set me up, but I can prove my whereabouts on each occasion. Furthermore, I am now making certain my time is accounted for, one hundred percent of each day." Confidence in the fact no one could catch him accounted for the aggressive stance, the husband's true colors. By doing so, he apparently hoped to show he'd laid all his cards on the table.

Unexpected.

The fact Credlin had known the specific reason for the visit wasn't surprising. Despite the anger he radiated, the widower maintained eye contact and didn't reveal any nonverbal signs of deception with subsequent questions.

When they'd concluded the interview, Royden contemplated the answers en route back to their unmarked car. "He already knew his wife's death wasn't an accident. Why didn't you tell me about the investigators he's hired?"

Billy opened the driver's door then hesitated. "Yeah, Lexi called me this morning. Said that he's hired two firms, one from southern Oregon and one close to the town where his family died. I don't think it's a ruse. He wants to find the killer before we do."

"Which means we need to stay one step ahead. And you couldn't have given me the information before we went in there?" As with Abby, Royden played catch up with the rest of the McAllisters. Considering the threat and attempts on Abby's life, Royden didn't voice further complaints.

"I wanted you to go in there with a clean conscience."

"There's no such thing around a McAllister. No wonder Abby's headed to ulcer land." Royden dropped down into the passenger seat and shut his door. "Shall we revisit Johen, the associate attorney who was competing for a promotion?"

"Might as well." The chattering squeak and hissing of Billy's cell startled them both. "Damn it, having one hacker in the family was bad enough, now Katt is catching up. She keeps changing the ringtone on my phone to that damn ferret's babble."

"Don't feel bad, she does it to everybody. The girls want us to know who's calling." Royden listened as his partner nodded and remarked on the incoming information.

The phone snapping shut coincided with Billy's frown. "Katt says Johen recently started making purchases from Cleman's garden center."

"I do *not* want to know how she came by that knowledge." Royden turned his thoughts and gaze out the window.

"Which is why she called me."

"If Matt finds out what she's doing..."

"He won't from me." Billy grinned, knowing his partner wouldn't out one of their best sources of information when it concerned Abby's welfare.

Royden contemplated the slippery slope to hell during the quiet drive. Walking a figurative tightrope between Abby and his partner provided a constant source of friction. Information obtained through illegal means would never make it into court, yet ignoring it could cost someone her life, someone he loved. No risk was too great.

Green pastures and thick woods rolled into small developments, then to the suburban area where the associate attorney owned a small rancher in an up-and-coming neighborhood.

"Seems odd for him to take several vacation days and not go anywhere." Royden appraised the home's neat appearance. The cookie-cutter structure boasted neutral colors, steep-sloping rooflines, and a small front porch. One holly tree and several flowering specimen trees dotted the front yard. A long root buckled the brick walkway leading to the front entrance, lending a quaint appearance.

"Abby use to do the same thing until she met you." Billy paused before tugging the screen door open. "Has she come around to the idea of private practice?"

"Yes, thank god. Now all I have to do is convince her to marry me."

Billy's shrug belied the frustration within. "That would be nice since you are living together."

"Like every other McAllister isn't doing the same thing? Goose, gander, etc." Each of Abby's brothers lived with the other half of their soul, and Royden wondered at what point they'd take the plunge. It wasn't difficult to see they'd all made good matches. It seemed the hesitancy lay at the women's feet, as if they waited for some invisible affirmation to proceed.

"Remie is still settling into the ME's office. I've given her about as much slack as I can handle. *And,* she's determined we're going to live on the farm she inherited. Can you see me in coveralls holding a pitchfork?" After his own near-death experience, he'd stopped wearing suits, but still shied away from jeans and t-shirts.

Chapter Twenty-Five

The doorknob turned on Billy's second round of knocking. Inch by inch, it opened to reveal Johen Claver's wide eyes and hesitant smile. "What can I do for you—Detective Patterson is it?" The associate attorney kept his gaze on the less angry appearing cop.

"Yes. We'd like to come in and ask you a few more questions. Do you mind?" Royden smoothed his expression to one of friendliness. Billy's usual scowl tended to discourage open-mindedness.

"Or you can come down to the station and sit in an interrogation room." Billy set his foot over the threshold to prevent Johen from slamming the door in their faces.

The homeowner sighed. "I have nothing to hide. Come in."

The defensive scratch in his voice caught both detectives' attention. A second's glint in Billy's eyes declared intent to dig deep into extracurricular activities.

"Let's have a seat in here, gentlemen." Johen gestured to a small den off to his left.

Royden surveyed the neat interior. Relatively new furniture held brightly colored cushions while hardwood floors gleamed with the skylights' rectangular patches of light flooding the living room. An open floor plan revealed the kitchen and eating area beyond, leading to a Florida room. He noted the plants there but decided to wait to spring the trap.

Once seated, Johen looked expectantly from one detective to the other. "If you're here about the threats to Abby McAllister, I'd think that would be a conflict for both of you. Your reputations precede you when it comes to protecting her."

Leave it to a lawyer to go on the offensive.

"Which is why we're investigating the death of a young woman whose remains were found not far from here." Royden cleared his throat, wishing he could wipe his guilt away. He'd had nightmares of Charlee's death. Someone so vibrant and full of life didn't deserve that ending.

"I didn't have anything to do with that. I heard you found a body in an open grave behind an apartment complex. It was in the papers."

Suspicion came naturally to some professions, attorneys one of them. The fact his gaze bounced between the two detectives could come as a matter of habit.

"You stay well-informed," Billy replied.

"Who was it? Since the news reports stated it was an open grave, I imagine lots of local critters went at the body, but considering the location, there couldn't have been too much damage before someone found it. They haven't posted a picture of the victim yet. Haven't you identified her?"

Royden covered his eyes, unable to remove the picture of his ex-girlfriend in an open grave. From preliminary reports, the killer tortured Charlee before death gave her release from agonizing pain. His remaining bagel and coffee burned up his chest. He swallowed hard before facing Johen.

Billy's measured look pointed out the obvious. The attorney didn't know the killer had boiled the bones clean. A detail they'd held back. Johen probably knew nothing about the doctor's death.

"I hear you're competing with several others for a promotion at work." Billy's change of subject coincided with Johen's heel bouncing on the carpeted floor.

"There're five of us, though Abby was the only other that had a shot at it." As if just realizing his poor word choice, Johen scrubbed a hand down his face.

"Do you mind if I use your rest room?" For once, Billy's expression held nothing but innocence.

"Help yourself. Down the hall, first door on the left."

Royden wasn't sure what his partner hoped to find yet knew he was out of the loop.

Johen held his hand up to punctuate his point. "Look, we're competitive, but it's not worth killing over. If I don't get promoted this time, I'll get it in another year or so. I'm not a killer and I don't wish Abby harm. Hell, I've asked her to dinner several times." His apologetic glance slid to Royden.

"How'd your wife feel about that?" Royden couldn't keep the edge from his tone.

"A *working* dinner. Some may consider her a ballbuster, but she's sharp as hell. She has an edge I don't."

Minutes later, Billy retuned, a slight grin tugging one side of his mouth.

He's holding a mental hatchet.

"Where were you Sunday night?" Billy's fingers thrummed his thigh in time with the bluesy music piped over an intercom.

"At home, in bed with my wife. She's gone to the store now."

"Does your wife take a sleep aid at night?" Billy cocked his head to the side, waiting.

"What? How'd you know that? Did you go snooping through our med cabinet?"

"Please answer the question," Mr. Claver.

"Yes, she does." The tic at his left eye increased while his right cheek bulged from tongue pressure.

"Before you ask, I was with my family all weekend when you and Abby were at the caverns. I have no intention of hurting her." Johen enunciated his response, directed toward Billy.

"You seem to know a lot about Detective Patterson and Abby's whereabouts." Billy's glare added a nonverbal threat.

"Seriously? She's the talk of the office. There're more stories and conjectures circulating about her than anyone I know."

"I guess the fact someone broke into her office caused quite a stir." Royden watched the attorney carefully.

Johen's gaze slid to the outside window as he paused to rub his hands down his pant legs. Tightness about his eyes narrowed his gaze. "Yes, detective. Her very presence distracts us all these days. We never know what's going to happen next."

After a few more questions, Billy nodded to Royden and stood. "I assume you don't have any plans on going anywhere?"

"Of course not. Why would I? My entire life is here."

Royden gestured to the sunroom. "Mind if we have a look around? Since you don't have anything to hide, I can't imagine that being a problem."

"Go ahead. I don't care." Lack of trust and uncertainty coincided with the sheen on his face. Johen wiped the beaded moisture from his brow. "Let me give you a tour so you don't get lost."

Confusion knitted the attorney's brow, but the only question eliciting an *off* response had centered around Abby's office. If he worked in tandem with a killer but didn't know of specific plans, only a sideways approach would elicit the answers they sought.

Royden stepped inside the sunny room with white wicker furniture and a small TV despite the homeowner's attempt to lead them elsewhere.

"Ah, I see you grow orchids. They're beautiful. I wanted to start growing some but not sure they'd survive. Billy pointed to the small leaf of one plant. "Don't they require special soil?"

"You don't grow them in soil. It's a special mix of bark and whatever... that allows you to see the roots. When they turn gray, they need water. See all the tiny holes in the container? That lets it drain *and* allows me to better see the health of the plant's bottom half." Johen picked up the nearest pot to demonstrate his meaning.

"So where do you get the mix?" Royden closed the distance and inspected the plant close up. "This is nice."

"My, ah, friend started me on them. She's really into that stuff. Says it's all in the mix." Johen licked his lips and cocked his head down, a prey's instincts of wariness.

"Huh, that sounds great. Could you put me in touch with her so I might ask her about it? I think I'd like to try it before I kill everything in the kitchen window." Royden picked up a piece of the bark. Looks pretty unique. She some type of genius?"

"Yeah, probably is." Johen's lip curled as he dry-washed his hands. "She seems to know a lot about dirt. Really does her research. If you want, you can take a bit with you. They don't need much." His enthusiasm for plants matched his aversion for the person instigating the hobby. The contradiction was a red flag.

Royden pulled out an evidence bag. "Sorry, this is all I have to carry it with, but thanks." As an afterthought, he added, "Hey, you mind if I share it with a friend?"

"I don't care what you do with it." Hesitancy mixed with mistrust slowed his words.

Billy shoved his hand in his pocket. "Sorry... phone's vibrating. I'll step outside and take this call. Probably my girlfriend wanting me to bring her lunch."

"Why don't you take this and stick it in the car?" Royden handed him the sample of soilless mix.

Billy grinned before heading toward the front door. Several minutes passed before he returned. "Are we set, partner?"

"Yep." As if on cue, Royden turned to Johen, his demeanor changing from friendly to businesslike. Not surprising, his partner took the lead.

"Johen, where did you go the night someone broke into Abby's office?" Billy's tone deepened, taking on the threat in his stance.

"I was home, like every other night. What's going on?"

"You're saying if we took that sample of your potting mix, it won't match the evidence found in Abby's office?" Royden knew he'd thrown the dice, but the stakes were high, and he wanted a lead.

If Johen knew of the mix's rarity, he also knew he was in a catch-22 position. Not handing over a sample would've made him look guilty.

"What? I never heard about any evidence." Johen glanced from Billy to Royden. I asked Abby... As if in pain, he closed his eyes. "I want that sample back. That's an illegal seizure, fourth amendment violation."

"No... *that* was evidence given, freely and without restrictions." Billy's grin widened.

"I don't have anything to do with this. Someone's trying to frame me."

"Who would do a thing like that to an upstanding young attorney? You saying that someone's trying to mess with you, too? That you're a victim?" Derision colored Royden's tone. "Seems we have an epidemic, partner."

"You've got nothing. Any number of people could have that mix."

"Hmm. Um, no. It is not sold commercially. It's made for a special customer, only one in fact." Billy edged closer to the suspect.

"Abby grows orchids? She has trouble with one African violet on her desk." Johen backed away from Billy and into the shelf of plants behind him.

"No. Not Abby," Royden confirmed. "Why would you think she'd break into her own office?" Billy asked.

"I... I don't know. I want you out of my home. My girlfriend gave me the soil. She's been teaching me how to grow these damn things."

"Name and address?" Billy asked.

"Sophia Garrison. I... I don't know where she lives."

"So, you're claiming you have a girlfriend but don't know where she lives?" Royden arched a brow and waited.

"We haven't gotten that far."

"What—you haven't gotten into her pants, yet?" Royden shook his head. Abby's assessment of her colleague proved spot on.

No wonder it'd taken so long to build their relationship. She had every reason to be suspicious considering the men she'd met.

"Do you at least have a picture of your accomplice?"

"Um, no. And I'm not complicit in anything." Crimson spread up the attorney's neck. "She's short, has a slight southern accent, and wears her hair in a black bob."

"What do you say, partner? Should we put out a bolo for a short girl with black hair?"

"Oh, god. It never occurred to me she was setting me up." Johen paled, shaking his head. "Please don't tell my wife."

"We can't make any promises she won't find out. You know how these investigations go." Billy's confidence declared it a certain outcome under specific circumstances.

"I want you to leave. Now."

"Okay." Billy smiled. "We'll just run the evidence to the lab and ask for a rush. When it comes back a match, we'll meet you at your office to put you in cuffs in front of your boss."

"Or... we could wait until late in the evening and take him from home, in front of his family." Royden sealed the deal to get the suspect's cooperation.

"I'm not trying to hurt Abby! And I didn't kill anyone."

"Then you can either help us or wait for us to come get you." Billy smiled in the face of the attorney's rage.

"I am not the one who's messing with her." A voice that was too loud, eyes impossibly wide and showing the whites all around, along the suspect's feet shifting to face the door depicted three tells, a cluster of deception.

With the sample obtained from the CEO, along with his testimony concerning the mix's origins, they stood an excellent chance of the DA liking the case. It was time to narrow the list of suspects and starting with small fish proved the path of least resistance. Johen seemed a viable suspect for the break-in but not the attempts on Abby's life. His alibi over the weekend and during the New Zealand vacation had previously checked out.

"Now the question you have to ask yourself is this. Do you want to cooperate and make this easy? Or would you like to wait until we have the warrant and come take you away in cuffs." Billy made a move to retrieve his metal bracelets from a back pocket.

"Dammit. I didn't do anything, but I'll work with your sketch artist to get a composite drawing." A bleak outcome surfaced in the attorney's gaze, knowing his girlfriend had used him for her own ends. "The sex wasn't that good. Hell, I don't even remember it."

"Well, that's gotta be disappointing." Billy shook his head. "The DA's gonna love this one."

Johen hung his head. "I just wanted the promotion. I haven't killed anyone."

"You didn't *arrange* for the wife and daughter's accident?"

"What? No, no, no. This can't be happening. I didn't do that! I wanted to handle the case, yes, but I had no reason to hurt them."

Royden's hand on the man's shoulder took the starch out of the suspect's spine. Sagging shoulders in defeat, he followed Billy to the door.

The theme song to a popular crime show on TV halted Royden's step as he snagged his cell. "Hold on a sec, Billy. Abby's calling." His gut told him trouble approached with the momentum of a freight train.

"Hey, sweetheart. What's up? Everything okay?"

"I think so. I just got a call from Lottie, but she hung up before I could question her. She said her ex called and that he knows where she's staying. She went out to Mt. Hood Forest to hide. I'm changing my clothes and going over to calm her down so I can get her out of there."

"What? Hell no. You wait until I get home. I'm going to drop Billy off at the station and we'll go together. It'll only take a few minutes."

"No need. I've learned my lesson, cowboy. I called and explained the situation, asked for a police escort. The barrack has a unit en route."

"Damn it, Abby. Wait. I'll go with you."

"No, Roy. I've got backup. I'll be safe. I need to go now."

"Damn. Leave your phone on." He waited, wondering if she'd come back with a smartass remark.

"It's not fully charged, so I'll turn it on when I get there." In her typical *go mode,* she disconnected the call.

By the time Royden pocketed his phone, sweat dripped down his temple, not cooled by the morning breeze. "Let's go. I got a bad feeling about this."

Billy settled their prisoner in the back seat as Royden waited impatiently. Once behind the wheel, his partner spoke. "I agree. Something doesn't feel right. I've felt all morning like I'm being watched."

No sound emerged from under the hood when the key turned in the ignition. "C'mon dammit." Billy tried again. "This thing never fails."

"Let me take a look," Royden murmured on exiting. Fate often threw bad timing at him, but this didn't feel coincidental.

He didn't know a lot about cars, but sabotage could be easy enough to spot if wires or hoses lay disconnected. They'd been in the house for twenty minutes, the car out of their sight. Someone could have managed to tamper with it then walked down the street, but he hadn't informed anyone about the day's agenda.

Under the hood, nothing seemed out of place, the distributor cap wires remained attached, as were the battery wires. Since he'd heard no *clicking* noises, he couldn't immediately point to a faulty starter. He scanned the quiet street in either direction, finding nothing alerting him as *off*.

"Turn on the headlights, Billy." Dual beams declared the battery charged. "Maybe it's the ignition switch."

Beside him, his partner grumbled obscenities. "I'll call it in. It shouldn't take long to get someone out here."

The only thing more frustrating than waiting was listening to Billy growl threats against fate. "Royden, call Abby. Tell her I said to wait up."

"I can't; she turned her phone off due to low battery. I can, however, call the station and get hold of the officer escorting her." Royden retrieved his cell and punched in the numbers. After making his request, he waited for the officer to return the call instead of announcing the issue over the radio.

When his cell finally rang, he'd run out of patience. "Patterson."

"Hi. This is trooper Fadden. What do you need?"

"Is Abby in the car with you?"

"No, sir. She insisted on driving her own vehicle so she could take the subject to another location."

"Where are you headed?"

"We just turned off Route 26 onto a spider road in Mt. Hood National Forest. She's pretty determined to get there quick. She said it wasn't far."

"Final destination?" He should have gotten the exact location and directions from Abby when she'd called.

"Not quite sure."

"Do *not* let her out of your sight."

"Understood, Detective."

"As soon as I have a vehicle, I'll call you back." Royden disconnected the call.

Billy had closed his eyes, breathing deep in an apparent attempt to contain his temper. "I'll call Lexi and ask her to track Abby's phone as soon as it's active."

Royden twisted to face Johen. "If anything happens to her, don't worry. We won't bother with handcuffs. *I* will come for you, not during working hours and not during daylight. You'll know before you draw your last breath who you're facing."

Johen paled in the back seat.

Chapter Twenty-Six

Abby turned onto the bumpy road resembling a well-traveled deer path. Had the turnoff not been marked, she would've stopped and waited for Royden. *What I wouldn't give to have Hoover or Damien with me now.* Both dogs were protective and possessed an uncanny ability to sense danger, but she didn't want to risk Lottie's fear of animals or risk Hoover getting lost after chasing a deer.

The fact Oregon had more National Forest Roads than any other state gave little comfort when the trees cocooned her in a solemn and darkened world.

As a kid hiking trails with her brothers, she remembered the vast expanse that held such fascination. Now, a sense of finality blossomed in her mind. Lottie said she'd fled her apartment the moment her ex called. The forest was the last place anyone would think to search for a self-declared city girl. The reasoning had made sense at the time.

Now, Abby wasn't so sure when her body vibrated from an overload of vivid imagination and hyped up on excessive caffeine. She'd needed the early morning boost after a restless night.

The officer escorting her was vaguely familiar and had presented a professional front. No doubt, her brothers had been the one he called when he'd picked up his phone as seen in her rearview mirror.

It doesn't explain why my mind is conjuring images of death and destruction.

The road narrowed and twisted until she had to slow to a crawl, her body jolted left and right from the deep ruts and potholes of the convoluted path. If she needed to turn around, she'd have to go a ways to find the space to do so.

A red cloth tied around a tree trunk marked the next turn onto a dirt road. Deep tracks marked the path of a previous vehicle leading to an unmarked drive. No mailbox, overgrown weeds, and her twitchy imagination deemed her current mission foolhardy.

Looking at her directions again, it seemed she should've reached her destination. To take her mind off the dire situation, she flipped through her mental catalogue of favorite times with Royden, bungee jumping, rollerblading, or just sitting in front of the fire and cuddling on the couch.

Flashbacks of huddling in the corner on a dirt-floored underground cell filtered through her mind despite her determination to wipe them away. The vacillation gave her a headache.

In the early part of the previous century, the U.S. Forest Service had developed a program. The intention of Cabin in the Woods allowed citizens to establish homes in the National Forest, paying a yearly rent for the use of the land. The twenty-year permits came with restrictions for the property's use. She'd seen a few homes dotting the land here and there. Most appeared well kept, even inviting.

A small sign ahead signaled the end of her journey. She didn't hesitate to pull onto the dirt driveway. The cabin looked a little worse for wear with a sagging porch and some missing wooden shakes on the roof. No one sat on the rickety chair. *Lottie has a right to be cautious, but where's her vehicle?*

The narrow path used for an entrance came to a T in front of the cabin. Abby stopped a short distance away. Behind her, the trooper turned on his flashing lights, the blue strobing the surrounding forest.

Her escort was out and moving forward before she'd unbuckled her seatbelt. While rolling down the window, she turned on her cell.

"Stay in the car, Ms. McAllister. I'll check out the cabin and bring your witness out."

Chivalry was far from dead. In this instance, his taking the lead allowed her to inhale a deep breath.

The trooper's hard gaze scanned the surrounding woods before advancing the thirty yards toward the door. Apparently, his intuition warned him of danger, too.

Abby started to open her door, prepared to tell her escort to wait and let Lottie come out on her own.

The cabin door opened when he was halfway to the steps with his hand on the butt of his pistol. He stopped. "Ma'am, are you Lottie Davidson?"

The petite brunette wore a loose gauze shirt and long flowing skirt that swayed with the slight breeze. Her hands were in her pockets.

Abby opened her door to warn the officer. "No. That's not Lottie. That's... that's Jenna. She's Mitzie's friend who met us at the bar." *Lottie didn't say she was with anyone.* Before Abby could finish, the woman repositioned her hand, clearly showing the outline of something long and narrow covered by the flowing cloth of her skirt. She'd fired her gun before the trooper could clear his weapon.

Abby ducked behind her door, her thoughts unable to disentangle the horrific events, throwing her mind back in the past.

The officer spun sideways and stumbled while clutching his neck. Blood leaked from between his fingers and down his arm. Shock in his gaze proclaimed the impossible happening.

His body arched back, and his knees buckled with the force of the second shot. One hand clutched his side and the other gripped his neck. He dropped face down in the leaf litter.

A scream died in Abby's throat as her gaze found the shooter's calm façade, grinning like she'd won the lottery. Her hair was different but those eyes, the eyes held a coldness few people could match.

How had she missed the signs? Pieces of the macabre puzzle came together in a twisted joining of unlikely events yet failed to unveil the overall portrait of death and destruction. The girl seemed too young to contain the evil emanating from her gaze.

Abby was too close to the cabin to run, hence wouldn't make it into the woods before bullets brought her down.

A feral smile lifted the corners of Jenna's mouth. "You can come out now, bitch. There's nowhere to go."

Abby nodded and raised her hands in a show of surrender. A thousand different possibilities flitted across her catalogue of possible outcomes. None existed where she survived.

She'd wanted to wait to start her marriage until her future held no threat. Now, she wouldn't get the chance. She was in the middle of nowhere, facing a psycho with a gun, with no support and no weapon. In leaning over and dropping her hands to push open the door farther, she slipped her phone from her pocket and into her sock. It seemed the best impromptu plan available.

"Where's Lottie?" Standing, she looked around. She might be able to outrun Jenna, but not the gunfire.

Inane thoughts filtered through her mind. The top contender included running in a crouch and using her car door as a barrier until she reached the rear of the police cruiser. Any distance would help before crossing open ground into the surrounding brush.

If Jenna had remained on the porch instead of advancing, it might have made a half-baked plan. Despite not knowing the area, Abby did know how to navigate in a particular direction from a static position.

"Come on now, Abby. Not only will I let Lottie free, I swear no further harm will come to her."

"How do I know you'll keep your word?" The sound of scurrying footsteps stopped her from retreating. The killer had anticipated the move.

Abby sidestepped with her hands up. She'd run out of options. Though cabins were arranged in tracts, wide expanses spaced them far apart. The current dwelling either existed outside the authorities' parameters, or simply didn't have close neighbors. Even if she could get away, it wouldn't do to lead chaos to someone else's door.

"I'm coming." She stepped forward, not surprised the killer stood just beyond the front of her car, able to duck and take cover should Abby have had a weapon. "Who are you?"

"I'm the author of all your nightmares to come, even if they don't last long."

"I thought Carrigan's brother orchestrated all this, but I know he doesn't have any sisters. Are you his girlfriend? One we didn't know about?"

"You mean your hacker family hasn't nailed my identity?" A *tsk tsk* coincided with her pouting lips. "I'm Carrigan's half-sister. I don't share the last name because *my* parents never married. I'm also the one who's going to finish the job he began... You McAllisters think your shit doesn't stink, but I assure you, they'll all get their comeuppance. I'll be sure to spread it out over time, so they won't see me coming." With her gun, she motioned Abby sideways. "Where's your cell?"

"In my purse, on the front passenger seat."

"It can stay there. They'll trace the cruiser anyway. Clever girl. Good thing I planned for such eventualities."

"Where's Lottie?"

"In the cabin, of course." The killer spared a glance at the cop in passing. He hadn't moved or made a sound since falling. "No need to waste a bullet."

"You said you'd let Lottie go."

"I did. Not that it matters, I don't think she'll go far—as a corpse."

"You said you wouldn't hurt her!"

"I said I wouldn't cause her *further* harm. And I won't. I can't." The tinkling laughter mimicked that of a madman.

"Why the charade?'

"You have no idea to what lengths I've gone or the fun I've had. I'll tell you about it on our journey. This way." She motioned Abby forward with the gun. "By the way, you can call me Helena. I liked the name Jenna, hence used it in cultivating a friendship with Mitzie."

"You've been pumping my assistant for information."

"I tried, but it didn't work. So, I gave her a friendship necklace with a small mic in it. Had to trade it out for a fresh battery during our girls' night out, but that wasn't any problem."

"Did you arrange the accident that killed Phyllis Rollison and her daughter?"

"Sure did. That was the easiest part of the puzzle. The genius part is what followed."

"You arranged for someone to break into my office. Why?"

"I wanted to create chaos, my penultimate goal. I've succeeded in leading your brothers and cop boyfriend on a merry chase. For the coup de grâce, I'll have a fall guy, the CEO himself."

"You got Credlin to break into my office?"

"No, you're not paying attention. That was the work of your associate, Johen, and *I arranged* that. I promised he'd get the promotion if he did. Well, plus I blackmailed him. With what he's done to get it plus the wig, makeup, and contacts I wore when around him, he can't give me up to the cops. Then I *also* slept with your boss, Brad. He's so damned greedy, wanting Credlin's account so bad he jumped at the chance to influence the partners."

A deep sigh of satisfaction conveyed things Abby didn't want to contemplate. "You whored yourself to get what you wanted."

"I wouldn't put it like that. Hell, I've never had so much fun orchestrating this elaborate of a plan. You see, I've always been competitive with Daryl, my half-brother. He thinks his nerdy brain makes him superior. Ha." Jenna shoved Abby in the back to move her forward into the woods. I'll show him how an artistic talent using mayhem can outperform a nerd."

"You're insane."

"On the contrary. I'm brilliant. Your idiot brothers will never disentangle it all. I slept with Credlin because I wanted the final laugh and bragging rights when I looked back at my labyrinthine success. I also want to gloat to my sibling with how close I came to all of my pawns, changing my looks so they can't point to one woman, then manipulating them however I saw fit."

After a few minutes, another piece fit into place. "You went all the way to New Zealand to shoot me? Why'd you wait till I was in the water?"

"It was the closest I could come to mimicking your prison on short notice. But that's not all." Jenna followed Abby but kept enough distance to prevent any offensive maneuvers. "I've led your PPD on a merry chase."

"How so?"

"I might as well tell you, as you'll have at least a bit of time to contemplate my elaborate victory."

The chuckle reaching Abby's ears numbed her muscles. Her killer no longer intended a quick death by bullet. No, something more sinister awaited. She thought of the time Lexi and Caden faced a horde of crazed, engineered rats. They'd recovered with time, something Abby didn't have.

"Why kill Charlee?" To think the doctor had died for this woman's entertainment pierced Abby's soul.

"A woman dumb enough to accept my assurance I could help. However, I did give her a decent last meal. I even super-sized it."

"Why did you... boil her down to the bone?"

"I was curious how long it would take. I've always wanted a skeleton ashtray, you know, for keys and stuff. The damn thing is, once I got her almost clean, I realized the skull just wasn't going to work. What a waste of time. But innovation saved the day. I left her long black hair as a funny anecdote to Royden and your brothers. I figured the police might suspect you or your boyfriend."

Acid churned in Abby's stomach. "What are you planning to do to me?" Visions of stepping into a boiling vat of acid made her stumble, her hand catching on a tangle of thorns.

"Oh, nothing near so painful. You should be grateful." The sinister laugh declared otherwise. "I think you'll figure it out pretty quick once we get to our destination. It's not too much farther. Once I deposit you, I'll be on my way."

"You knew I'd come if Lottie called."

"Yeah, you bleeding hearts always do. She was born trash and died the same way." Jenna snorted. "Look at the bright side. They'll track the police cruiser and find both the cop and Lottie. They both get a decent burial. Win-win situation."

"What about me?"

"You'll already be in the ground... Remember the pie I sent you?"

"Oh, god." Abby fell to her knees, her hands landing on budding briars. "Not again."

"Oh, but this time is different. It's better. You'll have time to contemplate your pathetic life and the loser cop you didn't marry. I bet you regret that now." Jenna chuckled. "I do hope you're not pregnant though. I shudder at the thought of killing babies."

Abby tuned out the drone of Jenna's words. Her mind couldn't face another underground prison without shattering.

"You're competing with Carrigan, your stepbrother? This is all just an elaborate game." In her heart, she knew, but needed to hear it. Nothing would make sense except to the mind of a sociopath.

"Of course. Daryl Carrigan is my stepbrother. You've experienced advanced sibling rivalry 101."

"You talked about Daryl when we were at the bar. I didn't make the connection."

"I didn't give you a reason to make the connection. It was his nickname growing up. It' what I've always called him, kinda like when you call someone named Robert, Bob."

One name said it all. Abby had indeed come full circle.

Chapter Twenty-Seven

The lunatic referring to herself as Havoc guided Abby through the forest while avoiding people and bragging about her ingenious plan. Descriptions of sexual exploits confirmed the assassin's twisted psyche.

Royden and her brothers would locate the trooper's cruiser yet not know where she'd gone. Two more deaths weighed on her conscience.

Anger burned through her soul. "My brothers won't stop until they find you. And handcuffs won't be the first thing they reach for." Her kidnapper, despite derangement, seemed to have no sense of self-preservation.

The thought of suffocating in an unmarked grave weakened her legs. Again, she fell. Thorns tore at her skin and clothes, but this time when she stumbled, she grabbed them, hardening her jaw against the pain. The small amount of blood left would be plenty for a well-trained S&R dog.

Matt would bring Damien, one of the best tracking canines in the department. No doubt, the timing wouldn't spare her death, but her family would find her and have closure.

"On a bad day, I'd shoot you for leaving a trail. Honestly, it's insulting. However, just to show you I do have a heart; I'll let it slide... Because you see, they won't be in time. This way, they'll have hope before failure crushes them all." A vicious chuckle, as well as her actions, reserved her a special place in hell. "If I weren't sure the eldest prick would bring his dog, I'd hang around to get some real candids of Royden holding your dead body."

With all Lexi and Katt's hacking, they'd never uncovered Carrigan's extended family. Then again, the twisted doctor who'd nearly killed her brother was as devious as he was brilliant.

"Are you going after my brothers next?"

"Hmm, eventually, yes. Before that though, I think I'll get some snapshots of them grieving. Their guard will be down, and I'll be able to get some decent close-ups with a good camera. They'll make nice additions to my scrapbook."

"You keep a scrapbook?"

"Sure, haven't you heard? It's one of the most satisfying hobbies a woman can have. Anyway, after I've collected enough pictures, I'm thinking of breaking my idiot half-brother out of jail. I might need his help when it comes to taking on your entire clan. Plus, I'll also have a fall guy in the end. Carrigan can go back to jail. Isn't that clever?" Her tittering laugh startled nearby squirrels, forcing them to scamper up a tree.

Abby's heart wept for the lost opportunity of sharing Royden's life and love. If she could do one more thing, it would be to give him closure and pray he found peace.

Thick woods opened to a small natural clearing where overgrown grass and weeds took advantage of available sunlight. It appeared workers had removed larger trees from an area in preparation for a home then abandoned the site before construction began.

Twin furrows led from the SUV parked in the meadow's center to disappear into the woods. Beside the black vehicle, Abby spotted a shovel sticking in a pile of dirt—and the hole. The intended purpose forced her stomach to empty.

She hit the ground hard, her braid snagging on a tangle of briars. A minute passed before she could breathe again without more acid erupting. Positioned on all fours wasn't how she'd planned to face her killer.

"Come now, Abby. I know you're tired and not feeling your best but look at it this way. You can rest for eternity.

"No!" Before she could twist around and gain her feet, pain exploded in her head.

The blackness quickly devoured her thoughts, her fear, and her hope.

PAIN. UTTER DARKNESS.

Abby strained to find the faintest glimmer that would illuminate her tomb. The air was musty, and she lay on something hard. Lack of familiar sounds terrified her as much as the unknown. The unforgiving material underneath was painful against her lower back.

Think. What would Royden do?

Assess the situation. Matt had taught her that much. She took a slow breath and concentrated, closing her eyes and pretending it was a test. The odor of damp earth declared otherwise.

Hysterics would serve no purpose, so she squashed the thought of her body growing roots below and sending up shoots of beautiful flowers. When she figured her way out, and she would, she'd never plant another vegetable without thinking of the roots surging under the soil.

Cold. Despite the above average air temperature, her space was cold. Which told her Jenna had dug a deep enough hole to account for a lower temp. Without a reference, there was no way to tell how long she'd been unconscious.

Her questing touch encountered rough wood above and to her sides with only inches of spare room in either direction. Splinters broke off and embedded in her fingers. A random slide and thump above declared someone or something near her grave. *She's filling it in with dirt.*

Abby shifted her body side to side. The wooden box left little room to move. Pure blind terror refused to give name to the compartment in which she lay. Her macabre thoughts served up a picture of mud pie with a straw in the center.

It took a bit of contortion in the limited space to check her scalp. Pain radiated from the side of her head where a lump rose, along with crusted material. *Blood.* She'd been there long enough for the bleeding to stop.

In moving her hand, her fingers brushed against something small and round. *Vinyl tubing?* The top of the box was less than six inches from her nose.

Random thumps continued, reverberating in her chest like the bass beat of a band.

Havoc started humming a tune, which might be the last thing Abby heard. She wouldn't give the satisfaction of screaming epithets.

Panic encroached from all sides, filling her mind with terror and stealing the ability to think. Royden said every puzzle had an answer. One just needed to quiet their mind to discover it.

Above her face, she again encountered the small flexible tubing. *Fresh air.* Any connection to open air was welcome. Lifting her head, she closed her lips around the tubing and sucked in a breath.

During a class in law school, she'd studied a case of a woman buried alive. Signs of low oxygen content included confusion, euphoria, headache, shortness of breath, and dizziness. Considering her probable concussion, she had no how idea to separate the symptoms. The one thing she did know—terror and panic would see her dead quicker than if she kept a cool head. She'd done so once in an underground prison. She could do it again.

If she could finagle a way to reach her phone stuffed in her sock, she might be able to send a text. The fact she could hear Jenna meant she wasn't buried too deep.

Royden's words after the cave-in kept her from having a panic attack. She let them flow through her mind now, as if he lay beside her. If she passed out, she might not wake up.

Bending her right knee and twisting her body as much as the space allowed, she reached her jeans at calf level but couldn't stretch to grip her phone. Panic rose in waves, beaten back by the memory of Royden's calming instructions.

Again, she lifted her head to breathe from the tubing. She could do this.

The next attempt to reach the electronic lifeline gained her access to her sock after using her left foot to hike her right jean's hem upward then slide the device forward.

With her cell in hand, she smiled and took another breath from the tubing. Instead of life-giving oxygen, a sticky sweet goo that tasted oddly of cinnamon and honey flowed into her mouth. She gagged and sputtered to clear her throat.

"Ha! I knew you'd wake up soon, bitch. I wanted you alert to contemplate the rest of your short life. However, I was nice enough to leave you a sweet reminder of me. Bye, Abby. I'll tell my stepbrother you'll wait in hell for him."

Further muffled words confused as much as frustrated. Seconds later, the sound of a car door slamming and an engine roar signaled Abby was indeed, alone.

She gripped her phone then felt for the button to backlight the keys. The screensaver, a picture of Royden on the end of a bungee cord, reminded her of all the good times they'd shared.

In the upper right-hand corner, she saw one bar. *Good enough to send a text.* In the opposite corner, the battery icon flashed. *No!*

She didn't know specifically where Jenna had buried her. It wasn't as if she could send coordinates. Her life came down to a few bars on her cell and probably less than an hour of oxygen.

What she *could* do entailed sending a text... To Matt, who always felt responsible for his siblings? To Royden, apologizing for not marrying him? To her parents, for providing all the love and nurturing needed to follow her dreams?

Time and a desperate heart tapped out a message to Royden, praying he'd receive it and forgive her for not waiting.

Royden, I wish we'd married. I will always love you.

Self-defense classes had strengthened and toughened her body. If she had a little room, she might've been able to weaken the old wood by pounding on it. *Letting in dirt would suffocate me that much sooner.*

Her last act included removing the diamond ring from its chain and slipping it onto her finger. Royden would understand.

Chapter Twenty-Eight

Billy gripped the steering wheel until his knuckles turned white. "Call Lexi first. I don't buy the coincidence of Lottie calling Abby the same time our car won't start." Peeling out of Johen's driveway in the borrowed officer's vehicle slammed them both sideways.

Royden didn't need an explanation. His thoughts revolved around Abby and holding her again. "We're about twenty minutes out. Where're your brothers?"

"I'll get them on conference call." Billy punched his cell to activate voice commands, cursing with each stab. "Where did Abby say she was headed?"

"Mt. Hood National Forest. It's a damn big area to cover... impossible without help." An incoming message alert with the first bars of their favorite legal sitcom offered a reprieve from the figurative boa constricting Royden's chest. "It's from Abby."

"What's it say?"

The hope in Billy's voice died a quick death when Royden dry-heaved.

"Oh god. No, Abby. No!" Royden opened the passenger window and gulped huge volumes of air.

A sharp turn taken faster than the car could handle lifted two wheels from the asphalt.

"Damn it, Royden. Talk!"

"She says she loves me and wishes she'd married me." Tears blurred Royden's vision.

Billy's roar filled the car.

All at once, the McAllisters' voices over speakerphone demanded an update. Matt was the closest to the area.

"Hold on, guys, Royden's gonna get Lexi on board so we can all keep up."

The familiar beeps and buzzes of a computer startup signaled Lexi's incoming call. Royden swiped right then put it on speaker.

"Royden?" Lexi's cautious optimism filled the car.

"Trace Abby's phone. Now."

"On it. Tell me why."

"She said she went to meet a client and would turn on her phone." Family connections ensured they'd understand verbal shortcuts. "A Trooper Fadden is providing escort. She just sent me a text saying she wished she *could've* married me."

"Damn!" Lexi's expletive overrode the background noise of her keyboard search.

Over the open line, silence from four siblings.

"I got nothing, Royden. Her phone's gone dead."

"What? You're a freaking genius on the keyboard. Find her!" Royden roared.

"Calm down. We won't do it by losing our heads. I can tap into the system and find the police car. Give me Fadden's number, it'll save time."

"Can you track him?" Billy asked before Royden repeated the number of the last call received.

"Yeah, give me just a sec to pull it up. Reception is going to be spotty. Matt, do you have Damien?"

"Yes," Matt's words came through cold and calm. Royden had seen the eldest McAllister's dog at work before and prayed his talent wouldn't be needed.

"Abby's smart. She'll buy us time." Billy's assurance offered much-needed hope. "I'm surprised she let her phone run down. That's not normal considering how attached she is to it."

"Nothing has felt familiar to her since the bastard shot her in New Zealand. She hasn't been able to get her feet on the ground. It's why she wouldn't marry me."

Houses passed in an endless blur, each street less familiar than the previous in their race toward the highway.

While Billy updated his brothers, large yards yielded to small farms and thick woods with miles yet to travel.

Royden and Abby had hiked in the National Forest several times, but the area contained thousands of miles of ever-changing conditions.

"Okay, Royden. I'm sending coordinates to Billy's phone along with updated road conditions. Recent rains along with problems incurred over the winter have shut down a few of them. I'm rerouting you all to the most direct path."

"Thanks, Lexi. We're just skirting the outer edges now." Billy tamped his breaks to make a turn. "The map shows we're about ten minutes out." Cutting the connection to Lexi cleared their heads to focus.

"Billy, I've passed a visitor's center. I'm ahead of you guys." Matt informed over Damien's barking in the background. "Lucas, Ethan, Caden, locations?"

Clipped conversation placed each brother compared to the others. One by one, their voices declared a united front and approach.

"Larrick is going to oversee the associate attorney's interrogation at the station. We left him with the uni when we borrowed his car." Royden filled in the last puzzle piece. "Matt—"

"Almost there. Katt and I have hiked through here, but I'm not familiar with this specific location. It's a vast region."

Royden swallowed hard, afraid of what he might find. Over the radio, Forest Services' request for an ambulance declared Lexi worked in the background to keep the rangers in the loop. At the entrance, one of their line officers waited to direct EMS to the site.

Royden couldn't look at his partner for fear of witnessing an untenable emotion. The guttural roar in his mind restricted rational thought. "She's smart. She's capable. She's a survivor."

Billy remained mute except for a groan. McAllister's flushed skin, corded neck, and nostrils flaring spoke volumes.

The ensuing silence spilled into an eternity where Royden couldn't think, couldn't function, and didn't care.

Flashing blue lights on the truck behind them signaled more backup. Ahead, Matt's truck parked behind the state police cruiser partially blocked the view of Abby's car. Both doors stood open.

Billy was out and racing toward the cabin before the engine quieted. The set of Matt's shoulders as he hunched over the downed officer magnified the panic filling the atmosphere.

Royden rushed toward the cabin to find Abby but halted with Matt's sharp command.

"She's not inside. I cleared the cabin, and her phone isn't in her purse," Matt reiterated the dog's command to stay while one hand pressed a jacket sleeve against the trooper's neck and the other pressed the bulk of material over a gut wound. The downed officer's eyes remained closed, but his chest rose and fell in a steady rhythm. "Billy, give me a hand. You'll stay and oversee the scene until we have backup."

Behind them, a Forest Ranger's truck skidded to a stop. Two men raced from the vehicle, hands on the butts of their guns.

Matt made abbreviated introductions. "I need you to help this man and keep all personnel away from the cabin. It's a crime scene." Matt yielded care of the downed officer to the rangers. "I found him face down, trying to hold pressure to his wounds."

Damien's excitement stemmed from his owner's anxiety and broadcast as short chuffs and weight bouncing foot to foot. When Matt stood, the shepherd danced around him.

"Get me something of Abby's from her car," Matt commanded. "Damien needs something for scenting."

Royden was a step ahead and shoved a pair of mittens from the glove box into the eldest brother's hands. "C'mon. Let's go."

The shepherd took a sniff of the offering and barked his signal for readiness.

"Your consultant identified you as brothers to the missing woman," the closest ranger offered as he crouched to assess the trooper's condition. His partner retrieved a first-aid kit.

"Yes." Matt stood after the ranger assumed care of the trooper. "Make sure no one enters until CSI arrives. There's an unidentified female victim inside." Barked orders received no opposition.

The other ranger nodded as he scanned the area. These circumstances weren't in their wheelhouse of experiences.

"Is it Lottie Davidson?" Royden choked out, nodding toward the structure, his mind racing ahead to consider various possibilities. "Abby's got to be here somewhere, but underground. It's what the killer meant by sending the pie and straw."

Matt nodded to the ranger holding a blowout patch from his kit against the officer's neck. Blood was soaking the pressure bandage. A quick assessment formed a probable timeline and events. "He's alive, but barely. If he hadn't regained consciousness and shoved all the dead leaves and small rock against his neck before passing out, he probably wouldn't have stood a chance. She can't have been gone long."

"I'll pop the trunk and see if there's a blanket," Billy murmured, heading toward their borrowed car.

"I got it already. Let's go." Royden surveyed the area after handing the blanket to the ranger to prop up the officer's lower legs.

He wanted nothing more than to rush forward and search for his soulmate, but the woods were thick and small animal paths were everywhere. Trampled grasses and weeds combined with briars to thwart all but the most determined. Abby didn't have time for them to take a false trail.

Matt bent to place his forehead against the dog's head. "Please, boy, find her. Find Abby."

"Her battery went dead after she sent me a text." Royden coughed to disguise the break in his voice.

Without hesitation, the dog pulled Matt toward the edge of the clearing heading east. When he stopped and sniffed a small thicket of briars, Matt loosened the lead. "Blood."

Royden and Billy followed with gun in hand. "She's left us a trail to follow." Hope had begun as a seed when they knew Abby wasn't in the cabin. "The killer has a special hatred for her, wants her to suffer before dying. He won't kill her right away."

"Why bring her out here?" Matt skidded down a small ravine and hopped across the narrow stream at the bottom. Damien strained at his leash to move faster.

"This has to be related to Carrigan. He'd kept her in an underground prison, yet she escaped. That alone is a significant punch to his ego." Royden slipped on the steep gradient uphill but grabbed a thickened branch nearby for support.

"But the first attempt in New Zealand had nothing to do with being buried. None of the MOs match," Matt continued, trying to piece together parts that wouldn't fit.

"She can't be too far ahead. The timeline doesn't allow for anything different." Billy focused on navigating fallen obstacles and low-lying branches.

"Maybe he considered New Zealand an easy opportunity, an early trial." Matt paused at the sound of voices, giving Damien a quiet signal.

In the southern distance, several teenagers and a middle-aged woman hiked along a worn path. Matt glanced back and shook his head before signaling his dog to continue the search.

Damien had no interest in the hikers, instead pulling forward. Every few yards, he stopped and sniffed at branches or forest debris.

When they came to a clearing, Matt held the shepherd back and crouched behind the underbrush.

Royden knelt beside him, mindless of the thorns. "No." His heart hammered in his chest. He couldn't swallow around the knot forming in his throat. "Those are tire tracks beside the—" He couldn't think, much less say the word. A strong hand yanked him back when he bolted up.

"It doesn't mean there's nobody lying in wait to ambush us. We can't do her any good if we're wearing lead." Matt sent his dog forward to search. "Let Damien clear the area first."

Royden shook him off and bolted forward, unable to wait. If Abby lay breathless beneath the pile of dirt, he had no use for air. His world would end with her. "Abby!" Years of training and experience dissipated in thin air.

Semi-cleared ground appeared to be the abandoned site of a planned cabin. Parallel channels defined the tire tracks leading away from the fresh grave.

"There's something sticking out at the top—some kind of... hose?" Royden held a vague awareness of the shepherd barking at the site and digging beside him. His enthusiastic rumbles marked the occupant's presence.

Matt and Billy each took position on the other side of the oblong patch of freshly dug earth.

"Abby." With no shovel, they cupped their hands to push mounds of freshly turned soil aside. "Oh, shit. The killer put a hose in there to supply oxygen, then filled it with something and clamped the top shut." Royden's bellow startled the shepherd, who paused before continuing to dig. "Here, start here. This tube is probably just above her face." Royden took precious seconds to unclamp the tubing and force the obstruction clear. "She'll get a little bit of air."

Matt joined him, his harsh breath filling the atmosphere. "Jesus, no. Please, no."

Eternity passed with each scoop in removing the barrier. Three men continued to yell Abby's name, pausing occasionally to listen for a response.

"Carrigan wouldn't kill her then give her air. He'd want her to suffer. She's still alive." Royden's desperation blocked all other thought.

"Agreed, but how long has she been in there? How big is the space? Is she injured?"

Unadulterated rage filled Royden's mind. "I will kill the prick. I will hunt down whoever he sent and kill him."

Matt remained silent, using his effort to move dirt.

Something solid scraped Royden's fingers with the next handful of soil removed. "Here. We've got it. It's not very deep."

"Abby!" Matt's wild excavating matched the panic in his voice. "Remove the rest to the edge so we can get the top off."

Frantic scraping led to bloody hands but finally cleared the top of the coffin. "Help me pry it off. It doesn't look attached that I can see... Abby!"

A squeak of wood on wood and the top opened.

The site greeting his eyes scalded Royden's thoughts. Abby lay inside, dirt smudging her closed eyelids and cheeks. Blood crusted her hair behind her ear. Her fingers held the phone which sent the last message.

Slight breath caressed the fingers he placed above her nose. "She's breathing. There's blood, but not a lot of it."

Matt checked her pulse. "Fast but regular."

"Help me get her out." With Matt's help, Royden lifted his precious bundle into his arms but couldn't relinquish her.

Sitting back on his haunches, he settled her in his lap. With a light touch, he caressed her cheek, her lips, then her throat. "Sweetheart? It's over now. You're safe. Please, open your eyes."

A low groan let him know she swam from the depth of her latest nightmare. "Cowboy? That bitch hit me in the head."

Royden gently probed Abby's skull. "Yeah, you have a lump back here. Looks like it clotted up pretty much before..." He couldn't force himself to say more.

"Cowboy?"

"Yes, sweetheart."

"Let's get married."

"Tomorrow is good for me. How about you?"

"How about a real wedding?"

"I'll settle for a ceremony, any kind you want. But a minister is going to marry us tomorrow, in our home."

"We'll argue about that tonight."

"Looking forward to it."

As if just realizing the full reality of her dilemma, she met his gaze with moisture spilling out the corners of her eyes. "Trooper Fadden—"

"Was still breathing when we arrived." Matt, quiet until now, had knelt beside them. With awe in his voice, he continued, "You left us a trail."

"You were the one who taught us as kids, remember?"

"Yeah. Who was it, Abby?"

"Carrigan's half-sister."

"Hell. How the hell did we miss that connection?" Royden continued to pet her hair and nuzzle her temple.

"Because her parents never married, and Oregon doesn't acknowledge common-law marriage."

"Son of a bitch. We'll get her now."

"Lottie?" Confusion knitted Abby's brow.

Royden shook his head, his heart heavy for Abby's loss. "We're gonna get you out of here and to the hospital." Royden stood with Matt's assistance.

Carrying his heart's owner entailed little effort while Matt coordinated efforts over the phone. Thick brush and rough terrain slowed their progress.

Though they now put a face to the enemy, they still had to find her. "We can keep Abby's survival a secret for a while if we avoid the ER." Billy helped clear their path.

"Remie will be at your house, ostensibly to help you calm down. She can examine Abby," Matt added.

"Remie is a medical examiner." Royden didn't want to remind Abby how close she came to being on a cold steel slab."

"She's family and a doctor, who won't draw suspicion over being in your house," Matt replied.

"Abby's gonna need an x-ray of her skull." Royden objected to taking any chances. Unfortunately, there wasn't a good way to turn.

"We can manage that through Megan's veterinary clinic." Matt pulled back a branch to let them pass.

"Why not Remie? The ME's office has human equipment," Royden protested.

"Just a good precaution. The killer's less likely to watch a vet's office than the ME's office if she's following news reports." Matt kept a steadying hand on Royden's shoulder as they navigated the steep ravine and over the stream.

"I'll watch over Abby while you guys find the bitch." Royden had no intention of letting Abby out of his sight again, regardless of the measures required.

* * * *

A WHIRLWIND of X-rays in a veterinarian's office the prior afternoon, followed by Remie's exam and endless questions kept Abby's mind busy. Billy's better half had pronounced her fit and prescribed bed rest until morning. No one cracked a joke about the ME examining a live patient.

Now, the quiet proved overwhelming until Abby shut out the myriad thoughts and images flooding her mind. She'd asked for a few minutes to herself before the ceremony, despite the outpouring of love from her family gathered below.

Downstairs, a door opened and closed, followed by soft murmurs drifting up to her room.

A soft knock preceded Lexi and Katt padding to where she sat on the end of the bed.

"Hi, guys. I'm almost ready."

"Good, because you have one very nervous looking groom down there." Lexi smiled as she picked up the brush from the dresser and knelt behind her. "I didn't believe shrinks got nervous, but he's been shaking all morning."

"I still think we should've slipped the cowboy something to loosen him up. Ya know... it's not too late." Katt held out her hand and offered a scarf to Abby. "Something blue. I read it denotes fidelity and love, not that you two need it."

"Thank you, Katt, and please don't roofie my fiancé. He'll be fine." Abby accepted the scarf and arranged it around her neck. "My mom let me borrow her embroidered handkerchief. It's been handed down from mother to son for generations." A nod toward the dresser indicated the delicate lace cloth.

"It seems like it's happening so fast." Yesterday evening, her brothers' hovering and waiting on her hand and foot had left her no choice but to startle them out of their predictable pattern.

The food fight, something one of her brothers had done months ago, fit the bill. It had proven to be the greatest stress reliever in dealing with overbearing family. Noise levels kept to a minimum didn't diminish the return of their precious comradery.

To maintain outward appearances of a grieving family, each had brought assorted dishes to the point Royden had no place to keep them.

The unanimous decision to keep her survival a secret offered a degree of comfort despite knowing Jenna roamed free. Sooner or later, lack of news would spur curiosity, then anger, and then rash action.

Not until her brothers left the prior night did Royden sit calmly by her side, holding her close and waiting. Absent was the raised eyebrow, pursed lips, and pinching the bridge of his nose.

Patience and expectant silence urged her to babble while experience had taught her the benefit of opening up. For the first time in her life, she hadn't felt weak about crying.

"We've seen this wedding coming for months. Why do you think the rest of us have held our men in check?" Lexi smiled as she stood.

"Wait. What? You've been waiting for me?"

"Yup. We didn't apply for the licenses because you have too many friends in the courthouse and didn't want you to hear about it from any other than us."

"But... if we wait, then we could all do this together!"

Katt looked uncomfortable before murmuring. "We will—when the time's right."

"Yeah, after we catch Jenna. Carrigan's half-sister has proven to have vast and accurate resources in tracking me."

"Then, we'll plan a huge ceremony, for all of us." Lexi held her hand out, grinning from ear to ear. "It's time."

"Wait. Just a few more minutes. Let's set some tentative plans, if not a date." Abby brushed nonexistent lint from her jeans, needing another minute to compose herself. It wasn't the wedding she'd always dreamed of, but it was better than she could ever have imagined.

"I have to admit, I am surprised you didn't want to wear your mother's dress today." Katt leaned back on the bed with her hands supporting her weight.

"I do want to wear it for the public ceremony, but it needs to be altered and Royden and I figured having anyone else know I'm alive didn't seem worth the risk. What's important is that we *get* married, not *how* we do it. At least for now."

"Ah, I get it. Matt and I talked about a backyard ceremony." Katt looked sheepishly at Lexi. "We'd still do the dresses and all that, but then, afterward... we could have the reception, well, McAllister style."

Lexi gasped then let out a belly-shaking laugh. "Oh my god. I told Ethan the same thing. We've all been waiting for you, Abby, but we didn't talk about particulars."

Another knock on the door and Megan sidled in. "Hey, you girls okay? Lucas sent me up to check. Says if you don't come down soon, Royden is gonna pass out."

"Then let's get this show on the road." Abby couldn't have been happier than to see her family together.

"I'm sorry we have to do this indoors with no proper music and all the shades pulled." Megan led the party downstairs where Royden and the McAllisters waited.

Abby smiled at Father Waters, someone she'd known for years. In front of him, Royden stood, dressed in jeans as they'd agreed, but with the addition of a tie.

Flower deliveries after a loved one's death kept up the pretense of Royden grieving, with the McAllisters gathered around him for support. Vases covered every available surface.

Her parents had understood she didn't want to walk down an aisle this time. She wanted to meet Royden halfway, on her own two feet. Her father had smiled but remained silent.

Her brothers lined Royden's great room with moisture brimming their eyes. Their better halves took places by their sides and held hands, smiling as Abby walked by.

Abby placed her hand in Royden's and let him tug her tight against his chest. The slight tremor in his arms matched the tremble in her legs.

"I love you." He cupped her face and tilted her chin up for a kiss.

He'd said it many times during the past several months, but the warmth in his eyes melted her heart.

"Ah, guys?" Lucas cleared his throat as Megan elbowed him in the ribs. "Well, that's supposed to be *after* he says, 'I do.'"

Royden pulled back and faced the minister while Kaylee handed Abby a bouquet of flowers. It couldn't have been more perfect.

Chapter Twenty-Nine

The evening turned cooler than expected as Havoc huddled behind the trunk of a gnarled cedar tree. It felt good to be back in normal sized footwear without wads of cloth cramping her toes.

She'd arrived at dusk, wanting to snap a few shots of the mourning family for her album. It made sense they'd gather here to comfort the grieving fiancé.

An odd sensation pricking her thoughts created as much discomfort as the new boots on her feet. Something felt off. None of the earlier news reports described the deaths of Lottie, the trooper, or a missing McAllister.

No public notice of an upcoming funeral, yet Lottie had taken her last breath with a knife in her belly. She'd shot the trooper in the neck and the gut. No way could he have survived that.

Patterson was a shrink, known for playing head games just as much as the McAllisters. Maybe they were eavesdropping on her marks, waiting for her to contact one and confirm the attorney's death. Since the detective had planned to marry the bitch, he must be devastated. Maybe that was why news stations remained silent.

Yesterday, she'd opted to flee instead of watching Royden and the McAllisters lose control with their devastation. Cleaning collateral damage entailed a tedious process when necessary. One she could handle later, after things cooled down.

Her gut gurgled with her insistence to sneak back and gloat, but she wanted a lasting memento of their grief. At least a few snapshots. Another delivery truck brought flower arrangements. Condolences for the fiancé.

Other than that, the McAllisters and their women remained sequestered in Patterson's house with curtains drawn. No sound penetrated the walls. Damn, she wanted to see them cry. The two brothers observed arriving kept their faces down. Redemption came with the arrival of an older couple, whom she assumed were the parents. The woman cried on her husband's chest.

The convoluted trail left behind, even if each of her marks talked, would lead the cops on a chaotic chase for years. Searching for a brunette, a redhead, and a smartass with a black bob would leave them thinking conspiracy. They'd never know who took their baby sister away, not until she returned to finish the job.

From the camera she'd hidden in a pine tree on the northern side of the property, she'd seen a minister or priest, they all looked the same, arrive earlier. If he'd come to comfort the family, why wasn't there public news?

Carrigan would receive the coded letter routed through Zachery and hit the roof. The bragging missive ordered him to call her burner phone. In the end, he'd understand her need to brag about completing a mission he couldn't accomplish. Chaos was her best friend and she'd mastered him well.

Her breath froze as another McAllister exited the front door. His expression remained somber as he looked around, en route to his car. The only vehicle left belonged to Patterson.

The one mark she hadn't hurt was Mitzie, Abby's assistant. The thought of the cops arresting her for conspiracy in divulging specific information encouraged a smile.

Stealthy steps carried her through the woods parallel to the back porch. As with the front and sides, the detective had drawn the shades with little light leaking around the sides.

Patience was not one of her virtues. In her current endeavor, she'd maintained a sense of timing and control unrivaled by her stepbrother. Unlike him, no one could catch her.

The reminder of Carrigan's confinement shed new light and engendered caution. The family of cops would be on the hunt soon with no holds barred. In lieu of that, she decided to retreat, check the hospital admission records for anyone with a head injury and gunshot wound, then return later for a sneak peek. Instead of sitting at ground level, she'd made a perch for herself in a maple tree.

With all the excitement, she'd forgotten to get a trophy from the lawyer. No doubt, she'd find a picture of the attorney and the detective inside when she snuck into the house to leave a final taunt after Royden left. A piece of tubing she'd cut off from Abby's temporary air supply would serve the purpose. A picture sent to Carrigan would get two birds with one stone.

* * * *

"C'mere, cowboy, and show me how you'd tame a wild horse." Abby smiled and leaned back against the pillows. Cool air brushing her nipples contrasted the heat emanating from Royden's body.

"Well, *Mrs.* Patterson, the doctor said to take it easy... How about I show you how I make love to my wife, gentle and mind-bendingly slow." Royden set one knee on the bed and leaned forward. The brush of his fingers up the inside of her leg stopped at the crease of her thigh. "All this—is finally mine."

"I can't believe I was such a fool, wanting to wait."

"A technicality we've corrected, my love."

"My brothers didn't seem at all surprised. I'm glad your house is big enough to accommodate everybody." She recognized the breathlessness of her voice, a common occurrence when her man stood ready to take them to new heights of ecstasy.

"It's time to talk about wedding details." The huskiness of his tone declared it the last thing on his mind.

"Now? You want to talk specifics now?" A deep breath didn't steady her heart with his little nips along her sensitized flesh.

His soft yet energizing touch feathered over her hips and up her flanks until cupping her breasts. He had no intention of relieving her stress anytime soon. The conversation alone, meant to distract, resembled the nuisance buzzing of a fly.

"Sure. I was thinking of something different, as in unusual. It would have to be in order to fit a McAllister, the first of the siblings to fall into matrimony." Royden plucked one nipple as his other hand sifted through her southern curls.

She gasped and arched her back, urging him to find her center. "Okay, whatever you want. Now. Please?"

"Not so soon. I don't want you exerting yourself." Royden knelt back on his heels. "So, a nontraditional wedding it is."

His words sounded sincere until she recognized the devilment in his gaze. "Royden. Please. Now." Teasing worked both ways. His self-restraint proved quite impressive.

His eyes widened then narrowed. She had his attention.

"You've been mine from the start. You just weren't ready to admit it." A small groan escaped as he brushed her belly with the backs of his fingers.

"Sustained, counselor. Move it along." Twisting her hips side to side, Abby nibbled on her lip, wondering how long she could hold out.

"You've delayed the inevitable. There's a penalty involved here." The grin declared it would be enjoyable. He moved her hand sliding toward her center away, pinning it against the bed.

When he leaned in to blow lightly on the black curls, she knew he'd keep her on the edge as long as he could stand it. Releasing her wrist allowed him to focus his attention where she wanted.

"I'll pay the fine later." The feel of his hair sifting through her fingers didn't satisfy the hunger burning low in her belly. "You know, when I was in the—underground—I fantasized about running my fingers through your hair. It kept me focused."

Royden sucked in a breath. "Not the direction I want your thoughts to travel."

In the next instant, he'd settled his body over hers, keeping the bulk of his weight on his elbows. The small circles he sketched over her forehead and cheeks preceded him leaning in to brush his lips over hers before skimming over her jaw and neck. The taste of him, so achingly familiar yet new, fueled the desperate hunger that set her body to flame with each brush of his lips and each nip of her tender flesh.

Gentle at first, the kisses became urgent, filled with all the fire of their combined souls. She gripped his head and pulled him tight, twining her legs around his waist. He tasted like champagne and heat, all male with a twist of urgency.

Transformation from slow and gentle to needy and raw sent her thoughts spiraling out of control. "Make me yours forever, Royden."

"You've always been mine."

She'd wasted so much time, not understanding the outside world could never break their bond. Their union would endure through pleasure and pain, hardship and success. It provided the base on which they'd make their stand for all time.

His hunger matched her own desire to join them body and soul, one unit for eternity.

"Ahh, I can feel all of you." She'd never felt so full.

"Open your eyes, sweetheart. Look at me." Single beads of moisture leaked from the corners of his eyes, yet he didn't speak.

In his gaze, she saw their future, destined but not yet written. The kiss of his unspoken vow warmed her heart, surrounding her in a cocoon of love and protection. He would give his last breath for her.

Powerful slabs of muscle defined the angles of his body, honed by years of exercise and self-discipline. He used every skill in his sensual arsenal to bring her pleasure.

The brush of his warm breath caressed her neck, his silent determination to go slow driving her to new heights of sexual awareness. To have all that power aimed at bringing her pleasure fueled her need to return it ten-fold. Every touch, every breath, every glide was the sweetest agony ever experienced.

"I love you, Royden. I always will." Murmured words lingered between them, his like confession so erotically charged that her spine arched as pleasure fogged her mind and blocked all thought. Her body spiraled up so fast and wound so tight, the orgasm took her by surprise.

He took her scream with a kiss and subsequent low groan, her name on his lips.

He belonged to her for all time.

Cuddled tight during the aftermath, Abby let her thoughts drift. "You went slow to drive me nuts. The talk was to keep me on track."

"I went slow because I wanted to commit every inch of your body to mind and soul. I want us joined so tight that nothing can ever separate us."

It was a bad time to bring it up, but now that her body was sated, her mind wouldn't stop. "Do you think she's out there, now?"

"Don't know, but we'll find her. According to your brothers, Jenna hasn't contacted either of your colleagues or Credlin."

"She wouldn't dare contact Mitzie. Hell, I bet both Lexi and Katt are digitally monitoring every move they all make." Abby smiled at the thought of her hacking friends on the prowl. With even the smallest shred of evidence, they'd be relentless.

"We'll find her."

"I don't want her killed. With all the charges we can bring, she'll get either a lethal injection or life without parole. I want her to live a long life—behind bars."

"I'd vote for the needle. But right now, I'd like to talk about our formal ceremony."

"Ah, yes." She couldn't hold in the sigh as he brushed his fingers over her shoulder and across her collarbone

"I'm game for whatever my bride would like."

"I'd love to have it here, in your backyard. We could invite family and close friends, make it a celebration no one will forget."

"I hear the *and* in there."

"Well..."

Chapter Thirty

"Abby. I don't like leaving the house, not for a second." Royden briefly closed his eyes, searching inward for the calm to prevent him from crushing her to his chest. *Stubborn woman wouldn't see sense if it bit her in the ass.*

"Royden, we discussed this. We both want this to end. I don't want to start our new life with a death threat hanging over my head." Abby gently scraped the dinner plates and put them in the dishwasher. "You've spent two days at home. You need to go to work to keep up appearances."

"I'd rather start back on day shift."

They'd spent the morning in bed, planning on him working the evening shift. "I should have taken another day off. It's customary to get three, you know."

"Yes, for immediate family. But according to public knowledge, we're not married. Actually, we still aren't. Not legally. The paperwork hasn't been filed. Two days is all you get."

"She may have fled the state."

"Without knowing she'd succeeded? No funerals, no news release, and Ethan said the floor nurse taking care of the trooper answered a call from his sister."

"Yeah, I know. He doesn't have any siblings. His security is tight. *He* is safe."

"So am I. You know I'm a good shot. I have your backup gun. I know who I'm looking for now. The shades are down, and I won't answer the door. We have video surveillance on all corners of the house. *No one* is getting to me."

"Abby, it's not that I don't trust you... I'd feel better if you had a dog here, too." Royden wrapped his arms around her and nudged her closer. "I don't trust that devious, conniving, bitch."

"You know at least two of my brothers are out there, somewhere." A vague motion indicated the woods. "And having either Matt or Lexi's dog here would raise all kinds of red flags. Besides, dogs have to go out occasionally.

"Caden and Lucas are out there this evening. Matt had to practically tie Kathryn down to keep her from joining them."

"As a private investigator, she's seen her share of adventure, but I don't want her involved here. If Jenna is out there and you don't go to work, she'll know this is a trap."

Royden sighed. "I've got jeans and a shirt in the car. As soon as I get down the road, I'll park at the abandoned mill, change, and work my way back through the woods. You keep your phone with you every second. If you don't answer, I'll call in every cop within a thirty-mile radius."

"Got it. Now put on your solemn face before you go."

He filled her request without difficulty. Adapting a long expression wasn't an issue.

The McAllisters had insisted on one of the brothers staying in the house, but Abby vetoed the idea from the beginning.

Once in the car, he took a deep breath. He didn't have to fake the dread in his heart or the worry that levered his shoulders down. His cell rang as soon as he turned out of his driveway. "Matt?"

"Yeah. Caden's on the south side on the hill. Vantage point is good."

"Where's Lucas?"

"Skimming up the east side. When you get set up on the west, tap your com."

In discussing the terrain with his partners, they'd determined the north yielded the highest likelihood for an intruder's approach. He wanted to be the one who strangled Carrigan's sibling. He finally saw how protecting family trumped upholding the law. He'd never contemplated murder before, but it now stood forefront in his mind.

"Got it." Royden no sooner finished than the line disconnected. "Huh. Typical McAllister."

It seemed eternity passed quicker than it took for him to change and sneak back through the woods. Each little snapping branch or rustling leaf stilled his progress. Though he hadn't experienced survival training like the McAllisters, he was every bit as motivated.

The full moon would hamper their progress if they needed to cross open ground to the house, but in the woods, sparse natural beams highlighted his journey.

When finally in place, he tapped his com, relieved to hear the response. No one would break radio silence unless necessary.

He was no stranger to stakeouts yet had never been on one so personal. The consequences for failure were untenable.

Inside, Abby would be straightening the house, doing anything that didn't make noise. In the back of her mind, she'd probably drawn up a list of requirements for her new practice, decided on a general location, and staffed it with appropriate help.

Several hours passed with unseasonably pleasant weather offering small biting insects an opportunity for a warm meal. He'd forgotten to bring bug spray and wouldn't risk the noise of smacking them. Instead, he brushed them away with as little movement as possible. The McAllisters would laugh.

The occasional update from Matt, located down the road in his truck, kept them up to date. When his voice broke the silence just before midnight, the news didn't surprise him.

"Guys, listen up. Lexi texted me. Carrigan just made a call about two hours ago to a burner phone. She got the number and triangulated the signal to a derelict motel on the outskirts of town. Jenna's still in the area."

Royden's thoughts centered on Abby and pulling remnants of the puzzle together. The whole charade boiled down to a bizarre sibling rivalry. He couldn't imagine the twisted upbringing that spit out such gnarled minds.

A branch snapped in the distance off to the north. The single sound could come from a passing deer or smaller animal.

Breath froze in his chest. Lightning hummed along his nerves, bringing his thoughts to hyper-alertness. He'd set up deep enough in the woods to allow for movement when spotting his quarry, yet close enough he could get to Abby should their prey slip through their fingers.

It didn't take long before another small snap focused his attention on a small movement. Minutes passed as the form took shape. Small, wearing dark jacket and pants with a matching balaclava. The size suggested a woman's presence.

From the distance, he took note of the outline and the way she moved. Cautious yet confident.

He tapped his mic three times to indicate a presence in his location. Since Abby was safe inside and either Lucas or Caden would signal Matt to call her, he waited and gave the intruder time to approach his house.

Blood roared in his ears, the pulse a drumbeat in his head. He had a chance to end the threat, once and for all. Recognition of the freedom stretching ahead of them sharpened his focus and determination to end Carrigan's sibling.

As he prepared to stand and maneuver at an angle to intercept, he noticed more activity twenty yards behind her. The second intruder was large, moved in a quieter fashion as if well trained.

If they were together, their spacing made no sense.

Royden tapped his mic again, leery of moving and spooking the second uninvited guest. Emerging briars and thorns were too thick in his section to determine which, if either, carried a weapon, so he assumed they were both armed.

He kept his motions small and quiet, maintaining line of sight with the second trespasser. It galled the hell out of him to lose track of the woman in favor of tailing the one assumed to be a man, judging by the size.

A flurry of motion.

A woman's muffled shriek.

They're not working together. Who was the second outsider?

The sound of a woman's low verbal abuse quickened his step. Lucas and Caden were closing in but couldn't have intercepted her so soon.

The voices grew louder, allowing him to piecemeal the conversation together. The name Phyllis Rollison rang a bell. *Credlin?*

The CEO didn't strike him as the type to do his own wet-work, yet grief forged new paths of expression in each person. The urge to kill both Carrigan and his sister edged out rational thought.

Royden drew his gun and closed the distance.

His path, created by either deer or something larger, permitted him to step within shooting distance, each target well within sight. Still, he waited to see how the scene played out.

"You picked the wrong woman and child to kill." The male stood behind her, towering over her smaller frame, and pulling her hands behind her back. A light clink resembled the snapping of handcuffs.

"You're not a cop."

"You're right about that. And frankly, with what I'm getting paid and what you've done, I don't give a damn what he does with you. Anyone who kills a kid deserves whatever happens. Hell, I intend to help and still have a clear conscience."

"Credlin hired you? I can pay you double to walk away."

"Crazy harridan. There's not enough money in the universe to make me look the other way. I have something that's alien to your nature. It's called a conscience."

"Freeze. Both of you." Royden strode forward with his gun trained on the male. "Who are you?"

The man's shoulders tightened, and he slowly turned his head. "Doesn't matter, Patterson. This *thing* was going to kill your woman."

"Which is why we've been awaiting her arrival." Royden stepped forward but kept five feet between them.

"We?" The male intruder looked around.

"Yeah. We." Caden maneuvered from behind a tight grouping of trees. "What'cha got, Royden. Two for one?"

"No. I suspect this is one of Credlin's hires. Isn't that so?" Royden faced the dark-haired male wearing a brown baseball cap.

The larger man remained silent.

"Sonofabitch. All this and someone else snatches her right under our noses? That's embarrassing." Caden shouldered his gun. "Should we give him the same treatment we planned for her?"

"I'm a licensed private investigator. You can search me and find that much."

"You're also trespassing." Lucas joined them, stepping closer to the female. "So, you're the bitch who tried to kill my sister." Over his shoulder he asked the larger man, "What's your name?"

"You can call me—just Jake."

"Well, Just Jake. This is your lucky day. I think it's a good night to take a walk. Don't you? As much as I'd like to know what your boss intends for this one," Caden nodded toward Jenna, "I'd rather *see* her behind bars than to wonder if she made it to the bottom of the river. And by the way, you have totally screwed my plans for the night."

"I say, let him have her." Luc shrugged a shoulder.

Royden recognized Luc's controlled rage. "Not now, Lucas. We have other issues to deal with." Jake's presence equaled a dash of cold water.

"What issues. I don't see any problem." Gently, Caden edged the investigator back and smiled. "Excuse me, I need to take a look at these." Pointing to the cuffs, he continued, "Hey, Luc, Royden, take a look at these. They're different." His smile coincided with a nod at the investigator, then toward the faint trail back to the road.

Royden stepped forward but didn't fully turn his back on Jake. "What?"

Lucas smiled and urged Royden closer, positioning himself between Royden and the PI. "Royden, have you ever seen anything like them before?" A slight chuckle gave up the ruse.

"Guys, you can't let the man go. We're cops." Royden rolled his shoulders and pivoted to chastise the elder McAllister. From his peripheral vision, he noticed Jake had disappeared. "Great, guys. Just great."

"Hey, we have what we need." Feigning surprise, Caden added. "Oh damn. The second one got away."

"It's not like you weren't planning to put a bullet in her brain, Lucas." Caden nodded to Royden. "For that matter, I know damn well what you were planning. Now, you can't."

"Dammit, Caden. If she ever gets out..." Royden began.

"Then we'll deal with her our way and without witnesses. We know who she is, we can track her." Lucas turned to the woman and pulled off her mask. "As for you, I'd say you're getting off easy."

"You guys have such a *McAllister* way of doing things." Royden grumbled.

"We're not cops. That's why it's us out here and not Matt and Billy." Caden smirked and held his hand up for his brother's reluctant high five.

"I still think we should've let *Just Jake* take her back to Credlin. Might've been interesting to know exactly how it ended," Luc grumbled.

"So, it didn't dawn on you to let the world know we caught her until we had a witness." Royden sighed. If he'd have had his choice, Jenna would be dead. *And Abby would never forgive me.*

"It *will end* with this one getting a lethal injection, and I intend to be among the people behind the glass wall watching as she takes her last breath." Caden's feral grin encompassed what they'd all felt. "Furthermore, in letting Jake go, we ensured *you* will have a clean conscience, for our sister's sake."

Chapter Thirty-One

"I still can't believe this is happening." Abby squirmed in her chair as one of the hairdressers finished pinning her locks in a fancy updo and secured the veil in place with its comb.

Five other chairs to her side held McAllister soon-to-be brides. Royden's home office equated a cramped preparation area but none complained since they were together.

"Stop looking at me, you all. It makes me cry." Kaylee, the quieter and more empathetic of the women, sniffed and dabbed at her nose with the tissue in her hand.

"Please don't cry, Kaylee. Caden will stomp in here and scold us all," Katt chastised. "Then I'll have to resort to something drastic...Actually, I think I have just the thing—"

"No!" Remie and Megan choked out simultaneously.

"No practical jokes today. We've done enough to the men already with the games we've designed." Remie, a medical examiner recently returned to Portland, provided a strong moral compass, and curtailed the more adventurous aspects of Lexi and Katt's penchant for mischief.

"I can't wait to see them bust open the piñatas." Lexi quieted with Katt's hand on her knee. A conspiratorial wink promised laughter and embarrassment in spades.

"What'd you girls do?" Abby's nerves couldn't take much more. After all she'd been through, a multi-wedding of McAllisters promised to unravel her composure.

"Nothing that'll hurt anyone," Katt's venture at innocence fell short of intent.

"It's a good thing the party is after the wedding, because I can think of at least two brothers who are probably gonna want to tan hides." Abby directed her meaningful stare at Lexi and Katt.

Behind them, the three hairdressers chuckled at the girls' antics.

"All right, Megan, you're ready. What do you think?" The stylist held a large mirror for the veterinarian to see.

"Oh, Megan. You look great." Remie smiled as she too accepted a mirror to survey the result.

"This is the most memorable day of my life. I wish my mom were alive to see me now." Megan held her hand up to her eye, careful not to smudge her makeup.

"She's seeing this. You have to believe that." Kaylee, sitting next to her, patted her back. "I think it's wonderful that we're doing this together."

Let's get your dresses on, ladies." Mitzie smiled at Abby. You all look incredible. Damn, you're a lucky family."

"Hey, your time will come. Just wait and see." Abby stood and hugged her assistant, trying to relieve her friend's guilt. "Don't say it, Mitzie. It wasn't your fault. You couldn't have known the locket she gave you contained a transmitter." Abby shook her head. "Hell, we all went out together. Jenna, Havoc, whatever she calls herself, she fooled us all."

"But never again, right?" Mitzie shook her head when she caught herself chewing on a fingernail. "Trial won't be for another four months."

"Never again. Even if she doesn't get a lethal injection, she won't see the light of day. She killed at least two people and tried to kill a cop." Abby didn't want to think of court, the law, or anything to do with Carrigan. She was finally free.

A young woman dressed in a white shirt and navy skirt knocked on the doorframe and entered. "Abby? Everything's set. The men are restless and threatening to come in if you don't get moving." Laughter infused the wedding planner's tone.

"Is Rachel ready?" Abby asked.

"Yes. She insisted they didn't place the piano in the right spot, but we've got it all sorted out. I have to say this is the most unusual backyard wedding, er, *weddings* I've ever planned. Not to mention the quickest."

"Plus, you incorporated *all* of our family. Even our furbabies." Lexi smiled then grimaced when looking at Katt. "I'm sorry we couldn't fit Gila in there, too."

"It's okay. He'll have his part to play during the reception, I'm sure." Katt grinned and hiked her eyebrows up several times.

The rest of the women groaned, because every wedding needed a ferret.

"Thanks, Kimmie, we'll be right down." Abby nodded to her new family.

"Our men are an impatient lot. And we've been waiting on Abby for months. I think Billy was starting to lose hope until he figured out why we all held them at bay." Remie smoothed the fabric of her dress and surveyed the group. "Ready, ladies?"

Abby took a deep breath. "This time, it'll be legal." Outside, the piano music changed to a more traditional tempo, their signal to get moving. Though she'd spoken her vows, she wanted this, not only for herself, but also for her family and friends.

Once in the kitchen, she took another deep breath and checked her gown's train. Her father stood by the slider, his arm out, waiting for her nod.

Though Lexi and Remie didn't have fathers to walk them down the aisle, each had close friends to perform the honor.

The air smelled of spring flowers and budding leaves, fresh and clean from the previous night's sprinkle. During the weddings' planning stages, each bride-to-be conveyed the same desire. To have a natural and memorable affair.

Abby was the first to walk the red carpet situated between rows of occupied chairs. Her father's forearm shook slightly beneath her hand, but his resolve remained solid.

Ahead, Royden stood between Matt and Billy, with enough room for her in between. The grooms waited several feet apart under the massive trellis festooned with white wisteria and red roses along with smaller flowers tucked in sporadically.

The guest list consisted of close friends and family, less than two hundred in all. The hush falling with the start of the wedding march had demonstrated their anticipation as much as the small gasps and wide smiles.

Each McAllister waited, Ethan and Matt shifting their weight foot to foot. Billy and Caden stood still, but their gazes roamed the crowd, ever returning to the home's back door in search of their brides. Lucas grinned like a Cheshire cat, his stance open and relaxed.

Beside each man and in keeping with the women's requests, their four-footed furballs sat waiting. Abby's new pup, a long-coat shepherd, remained on leash but sitting quietly by Royden.

Royden's focused intensity reminded her that she was his world from beginning to end. When close, he held out his hand, accepting her from the eldest McAllister with a gracious nod.

Kaylee came next, her father's grin proclaiming him proud and secure with his daughter's choice.

One by one, each woman glided down the aisle to stand by her man. The line of grooms dressed in dark navy suits added a spectacular contrast. Several photographers took pictures from various angles, capturing the mood on film.

Six weddings for six McAllisters went faster than Abby could focus on. With the last "I do," came a roar from the crowd.

Time for the festivities.

ABBY LEANED BACK against Royden's chest, relishing the heat and strength surrounding her. "I think Kaylee's mom might have a heart attack if she witnesses too many of the events. I don't believe she understands why we all changed into jeans and casual clothes."

"Hmm, I wouldn't be so sure. She's been a cop's wife for forty years. But I'll give her dad a heads up *before* the balloon pop race."

"Better tell them now. Kimmie just signaled for the toasts." She couldn't contain her happiness. The fact all her brothers married on the same day, combining the reception into one gigantic party overwhelmed her.

On the other hand, she and the other brides had secretly added their own amusements to the mix, wanting to keep their men off guard and see them loosen up. Matt proved to be the universal target.

The DJ set up near the house and now tapped his mic for all to settle. The men had chosen the songs and arranged for the yard's center to become the dance floor once the chairs were cleared away.

With the announcement of the father-daughter's first dance came the initial strains of the song Abby had chosen. Her father, so tall and strong, escorted her to the middle of the dance area among the other brides.

"I've waited so long for this day, baby girl." Moisture brimmed the gaze of the man Abby had always tried to emulate.

"I love you, Daddy." She rested her head against his shoulder, listening to him praise her strength and character. The music was soft, the temperature mild, and the air full of sounds and scents of spring. Their family had not just survived each catastrophe but thrived and found their mates.

All too soon, the dance ended, and another song began. Royden was there, tucking her against his chest and holding her gently.

"You're overthinking again, sweetheart. Tell me what's warping through your mind." Concern deepened his voice.

"Just thinking about all we've been through. Everything has led us to this day, this moment."

One by one, each McAllister took his bride in hand and led them to circle her and Royden. She looked around, feeling unworthy of such luck and love. Guests watched from a short distance, waiting to join them.

Matt stopped and held his hands up. The music screeched to a halt as the DJ waited for direction. Everyone quieted.

Matt's grin held a secret. The prearranged departure from the expected routine so unlike him.

"Royden? What's going on?" The realization that her eldest brother was breaking character accelerated her heartbeat.

"Ha. You girls aren't the only ones who modified the plans." His smile held equal parts mischief and excitement.

"Okay, folks. This is a celebration!" Matt chortled in anticipatory glee, contentment in his gaze when taking his wife's hand. "Let's celebrate!"

The starch ever present in Matt's spine melted with the first loud beats of a footloose melody. Game for adventure, Katt grabbed her man and swung into the fast rhythm, followed by the rest of the McAllister couples who stepped back and circled their eldest brother and his bride.

Except for the music, an odd hush fell over the crowd as Matt and Kathryn showed off their dance moves in the circle's center. Bystanders took up the rhythm, clapping in time as the couples cut loose.

After a bit, Matt and Kathryn melted back to the perimeter as Billy and Remie took center stage, once again proving how little Abby knew her brothers.

When her turn came, Royden twirled her to the center, matching her moves then flipping her over his arm. Breathless with excitement and laughter, they ended the dance and held each other tight as the next song began with a slow soft melody.

The crowd roared.

Abby gasped at having seen her eldest brother dance. "Damn, he's got moves! When the hell did that happen?" She, nor anyone else, had ever seen him let off steam as he did now. Laughter bubbled up as she shook her head. "Now I realize you haven't been distracting me with your own moves. You were practicing."

"Yep."

Abby studied her husband's expression as he swayed her to the softer pace. "You knew all along what he was going to do?"

"Of course. I encouraged it, too."

The next dance ended with brides and grooms still out of breath and laughing. A glance at Megan, Kaylee, and Remie declared them equally surprised. Not much got past Lexi and Katt.

This time when the DJ tapped his mic for attention, Kimmie, the ceremony's planner, waited until all quieted before speaking. "Okay, ladies and gentlemen, let the games begin. For those willing to play, it's time for truth or dare." An apologetic grin toward the men preceded her continuing.

"For those who'd rather sit back and observe, enjoy the good food, music, and entertainment." Kimmie gestured to the more mature folks gathered near the back of the house. "We have life-size checkerboards for those that would like to partake. Also, there's a jar in the center of the food buffet table. Feel free to add your best idea of what a good date-night might be."

Billy groaned when his gaze met Remie's. "That had to be your idea. You probably filled guests' heads with all kinds of wild suggestions."

Remie smiled up at her husband. "Most of which I think you'll enjoy."

Kimmie motioned the bridal party to one side where special tables were set with twelve shot glasses. Bottles of liquor surrounded the ornate floral centerpiece.

The McAllisters gathered around, each man with his arm about his bride's waist or shoulders. Abby smiled at Royden, wondering what secret he could've hidden.

"Since Matt is the oldest, we should start." Katt turned to her spouse expectantly, the devilment in her eye earned a plastic smile and groan from her new husband. He obviously regretted his part in this particular activity.

Selecting a folded slip of paper from the bowl on the table, he read, "What is the worst thing you've done to your partner." Matt scrubbed a hand over his eyes, ignoring the rest of the McAllister's guffaws. "She has so much to choose from."

Katt paled a little then shrugged a shoulder. "Well, last week when you gave me a hard time about Gila," she patted the ferret draped over her shoulders, "I put a used tampon in your sock that you'd set out for the next day. *And*—I made sure to tuck in the string so you wouldn't see it till you tried to put it on. Lucky for me, you set your clothes on the bathroom sink while taking a shower."

The table, along with nearby guests, erupted in fits of laughter. Matt dropped his chin to chest and sighed. "This is gonna be a long marriage, but at least I'll never get bored."

Royden squeezed Abby's shoulder before murmuring. "Your turn, sweetheart. And thank god you don't have that type of ornery streak."

He paled with her confession of, "You sure about that, cowboy?"

Her thoughts turned maudlin, having wanted to address the issue for two weeks but unable to figure a way to bring it up. Regret filled her heart as tears brimmed her eyes. He would never know how much she regretted hurting him. "The worst thing I've done to you—I'm sorry I didn't marry you the first time you asked. I should've said yes in the caverns. I'm so sorry."

A hush blanketed the crowd as Royden gathered her in his arms. "Sweetheart, I understood. Really, I did. In addition, I respect your need for independence. It's one of your strengths I admire most."

The soft brush of his lips across her own accompanied the *oohs* and *ahs* from the crowd. He didn't stop with a simple kiss. The depth of his emotions crowded all thoughts from her mind. If not for others present, she would've let him undress her on the spot.

His hands brushed down her spine as he backed her up, gently, until a tree trunk prevented further movement. He had no such reservations about stopping if the tongue in her mouth twisting her desire into an uncontrollable inferno was any indication.

A vague awareness of guffaws and backslaps combined with Royden's sudden stiffening focused her thoughts on the present and their surroundings.

"Damn it, guys." He stepped aside and held his hand out, shaking his head and trying to brush something off his back. "What is that crap, anyway?"

All gazes fell to Katt, holding a super-sized water gun. Royden's advance on her ended with them nose to chest, with the plastic gun between.

"It's Gila's special blend of flavored water, honey, and a little booze." Her eyes widened as Royden snatched the toy away.

When he turned to set it on the ground, the ferret jumped from her shoulders to his back, now covered with the mixture. Frantic clawing ensued as the animal tried to gather his favorite treat.

"Hell! Get the damn thing off me. No wonder Matt calls it a monster."

Taking mercy on them all, Matt lifted the ferret off and held him close to his chest. "Ow! Damn thing bit me—again. Time out in your cage, buddy." Swift strides took him into the house for a quiet time.

The games proceeded without further incident. Abby's gaze traveled over the crowd. Calmer folks danced to the sedate music or enjoyed some of the tamer games. Corn hole, horseshoes played with toilet seats, musical chairs, or a scavenger hunt. Some even ventured into playing volleyball.

Matt and Billy balked at the balloon popping relay game, claiming discrepancy in height, but the women soon coerced them into participating. Each bride tied a balloon to her husband's back waistband and stood behind them. They formed two lines, Matt, Ethan, and Lucas with their brides on one side, Royden, Billy, and Caden with their respective brides on the other.

Twenty yards ahead, two wooden-back chairs sat facing away. The men at the front of the line ran to the chairs and held onto the wooden slats while the women came up behind them, grabbed their hips, and pulled back while jerking their own bodies forward in an effort to pop the balloon in between.

The grooms had to stoop to correct for differences in height. All in all, each had the time of their life, until the next game commenced.

Six porcelain bowls sat on top of a large, round waist-high table. Each piece of ceramic consisted of a round upper half that tapered to a smaller bottom attached to an oblong base. The crowd watched as Kimmie's assistants poured several gallons of clear carbonated soda and alcohol in each one. "Okay, folks. It's time to bob for donuts. This is a team effort. I'm placing specially covered donuts that will take cooperation between partners to retrieve and consume."

"Staples for any cop," Kaylee shouted.

"They won't dissolve unless you drop them *after* taking a bite, and even then, it will take time. Now, each of you must keep your hands behind your back. Pair off, husband and wife each to a bowl. Bobbing for donuts will now begin, ending with the first to finish their dessert. Remember and consider the size of the donut. Each couple will have to work together so as not to drop their treat back in the bowl. Don't worry, they won't dissolve quickly."

A roar from the crowd signaled their approval, much to the dismay of the McAllister men.

"These *bowls* look suspiciously like toilets..." Ethan grumbled as he scanned the spectators.

Matt turned to his bride. "You thought of this one, didn't you?"

"Actually, it was Larrick's idea," Lexi spoke up.

From the sidelines, Ethan's partner held up a beer. "That's for all the redneck jokes over the years... *partner.*"

Darkness fell but the laughter and dancing continued well into the night, each couple moving through the list of activities toward the final game.

Last man standing.

Abby elbowed Royden in the ribs. "This should be interesting, but let's go first."

Abby took her place on the level tree stump and accepted the pole with pillows wrapped around the end.

"You know what to do, guys. Have at it." Kimmie motioned for them to begin. "The reason we left this game for near last was to increase the women's advantage. They don't have the upper body strength, but we've made sure to even the odds throughout the night by ensuring the men drank sufficient alcohol. Enjoy the decreased coordination, gentlemen." Her words diminished under the round of applause and laughter.

Abby didn't wait, taking a swing at her spouse. Prepared for her antics, Royden ducked but lost his balance. Her second swing knocked him from his perch.

Never in her life could Abby have pictured such an evening. When Remie and Billy joined them at a quiet table and Billy gloated over winning the sack race, Remie leaned close to Abby and whispered. "Don't worry. He'll get a shock tomorrow morning."

"What'd you do?" Abby hadn't been surprised to see Remie fully join in the family's antics but wondered what she'd planned.

"Let's just say, having a medical degree helps. He's going to pee red for a day or so."

Abby made a mental note to call her brother in the morning to gloat.

To top off the festivities, bride and groom stood shoulder to shoulder for the family portrait. In each hand, a colored smoke bomb issued its hue into the night, caught on film for a memory of how each separate soul joined and mingled to form part of a whole. In front of them sat the dogs, dressed in their own wedding finery, except for Gila, who draped around Katt's shoulders after release from his cage.

Later, Abby sat on Royden's lap, enjoying the family's banter long after the last guest had said goodbye. Glancing at her brothers and their wives, she mused, "We've each seen the worst of what life can throw at us, yet here we sit, united and happy."

"It's because we're family." Royden feathered his touch through her hair.

"I wouldn't have survived if not for all of you." Tears brimmed her eyes, the gratitude in her heart swelling until she thought it would burst.

"Hey, no tears," Matt cajoled.

"No, silly. They're tears of happiness and appreciation. For so long, I thought I needed to be completely independent to be strong, but it's the family connections that make us each strong."

"Yep, we knew you'd get there eventually, half-pint. After all, you married a man who made you the center of his world." Billy smirked until Remie swatted him on the shoulder.

"God willing, we'll have many years of family get-togethers and one day, we'll be the older couples watching our kids get married, shocked breathless and embarrassed as all get out." Abby held her glass up for each to toast.

* * * *

I hope you've loved reading The McAllister Series. If you've caught up from the beginning and are looking for more exciting adventure and romance, fall in love with Keiki Tallerman, a kick-ass young prodigy searching for her parents' killer. Read the excerpt for A Critical Tangent, first in the Moonlight and Murder Series.

A Critical Tangent

"Aw, Keiki, if I could find the fun button in your brain, I'd switch it to permanent on. You're always working. You should've come hiking with me. Fresh air would do you good." Shelly tisked then smiled. "Not that there's anything wrong with loving your work, but you have an old man psyche trapped in a young woman's body."

"Thanks, Shelly, but no." Keiki manipulated her latest drone to perform the simple but intricate task of picking a flower. The outing did sound nice, but Shelly needed private time to mourn the loss of her sister.

"The next time you fall asleep working, I'm going to town with my entire set of permanent markers." Shelly held her hand out to accept the offered blossom pinched from its low-growing stem and giggled. "You'd look good with cat whiskers and exotic pink eyes."

"Test that theory, and I'll replace your scented shampoo with baby oil." The threat of laying waste to makeup or hair products usually ended any debate. "I'm about out of battery life. Can you bring it in?"

"Sure. Turn off the motors."

Damn. The soft whirr from the small rotors altered in pitch as they shut down one by one.

Malevolent shadows crawled along the edges of the surrounding woods, receding with the rising sun. Even from miles away, Keiki's skin crawled.

"I hear something." Shelly rested a palm beside her woodland flower plot to lean forward.

Through remote viewing, Keiki watched her doppelganger freeze then tilt her head to the side, wrinkles of concern marring her forehead.

"What?" Thanks to the hilly terrain, two-way communication crackled off and on.

"Huh, must be a rabbit or squirrel. Anyway, as I was saying. Become a spinster with hundreds of drones instead of cats. I'll keep you in contact with the outside world." Again, Shelly paused and tilted her head as if listening to something off in the distance.

"Hey, why don't you come back now and we'll have breakfast?"

"Yeah, okay. I'm coming. Can you extend the range on this thing's transmission ability? The video feed isn't so great." Lips nibbled between her teeth marked Shelly's worry when she leaned forward to whisper.

"I'm working on it. What's wrong?"

"I'm kinda spooked. Something doesn't feel right." Her fingers' wobble shook the drone's body. It listed sideways with a squeak.

"Shelly?"

"I'm fine. It's just my clumsiness in challenging gravity... Oh, about the frat party tonight, wanna go?"

The viewing angle changed again as Shelly stood.

"No. And before you start, I do have fun. I just don't have time to party with you and Gabby. *Some* people stay focused on their future," Keiki grumbled as she monitored her prototype's efficiency on her laptop and sipped a caramel latte.

A distinctive metallic snap coincided with her device's struggle to function.

"Oops. Sorry, Keeks. An arm broke off above your tracker thingy. I'll stick it in my pocket, and you can glue it back on, or whatever. Do we still have audio and visual feed?"

"Yeah, just bring the rest of it back in one piece, okay?" Keiki groaned, predicting the hour it would take to fix. "Careful. That thing is one of two prototypes, but that one gets the best reception." Keiki set her coffee down, the cup tilting when settling on her friend's access card. "Oops, your work ID now has a brown ring on it. You really should be more careful with it."

"How rude of me to leave it where you'd drink your coffee."

"That's why we get along so well. We think alike. I'll stick it on my dresser. It'll be safer there."

"If you'd stop losing yours, you wouldn't have to borrow mine... shit. Something is coming." Fear coiled through Shelly's voice. "Sounded like a branch snapping down the trail. Something big and heavy."

"Is it a black bear? You know what to do."

A silent moment passed.

On screen, the image shook.

"Uh... who are you? What do you want?" Shelly's wrist rotated, tilting the angle of the drone's camera to the trampled weeds.

Through the odd angle, booted feet shuffled backward to leave two furrowed tracks. No one had ever intruded on her friend's private sanctuary.

"I'm a messenger, here to show your boss what happens when he refuses to work with us. We tried being nice. Now it's my way."

Miles downgrading the audio quality to mediocre didn't soften the cruel bite of a temper coming unhinged.

Metal clinking preceded the thud of her drone landing in the meadow's weeds. Its lens picked up nothing but decaying fall foliage.

There was a slight pause, as if warring factions sized up the competition before a fight. Keiki's imagination conjured worst possible scenarios. "What's going on, Shelly?"

Reily's Books

Romantic Thrillers
McAllister Justice Series
Tender Echoes
Digital Velocity
Bound By Shadows
Inconclusive Evidence
Carbon Replacements
Shattered Reflections
Remnants of Evil
Moonlight and Murder Series
Shifting Targets
A Critical Tangent
Pivotal Decisions
Seeds of Murder
An Unlikely Grave
Deadly Interception
Love You To Death
Psychic Thrillers
Mind Stalkers Series
Bending Fate
Silent Depths
Shadow Guard
Whispers After Death
Mind Hunters
Guardian Series
Shadowed Horizons
Shadowed Origins
Shadowed Passages
Shadowed Spirits

REILY GARRETT

Paranormal Romance
Immortal Lovers Series
Unholy Alliance
Blood Union
Standalone paranormal romance
Tiago

About Reily

Reily Garrett is a writer, mother, and companion to three long coat German shepherds. When not working with her dogs, she's sitting at her desk with her fur kids by her side.

Author of chilling suspense and snarky romance, her stories span the distance of romantic thrillers, paranormal romance, and erotic romance. Regardless of genre, each book delves into a dark and twisted imagination yet is tempered with romance and a touch of humor.

Reviews by Kirkus Reviews, San Francisco Bay Review, and BestThrillers.com best describe her work:

"This could be James Patterson, Lee Child, and Tess Gerritsen rolled into one, but the dark, twisted methods used by the serial killer could surprise even those readers..." - San Francisco Bay Review

"...steamy, seductive police procedural..." - BestThrillers.com

"...well-researched thriller that remains romantically genuine throughout." - Kirkus Review

Prior experience in the Military Police, private investigations, and as an ICU nurse gives her fiction a real-world flavor.